By Andi Lee

ANIMAL LARK
Mischief Maker
Risky Business

Published by Dreamspinner Press
www.dreamspinnerpress.com

# Risky
# BUSINESS

## ANDI LEE

DREAMSPINNER PRESS

Published by
DREAMSPINNER PRESS

5032 Capital Circle SW, Suite 2, PMB# 279, Tallahassee, FL 32305-7886 USA
www.dreamspinnerpress.com

This is a work of fiction. Names, characters, places, and incidents either are the product of author imagination or are used fictitiously, and any resemblance to actual persons, living or dead, business establishments, events, or locales is entirely coincidental.

Risky Business
© 2021 Andi Lee

Cover Art
© 2021 Tammy Moore
Cover content is for illustrative purposes only and any person depicted on the cover is a model.

Trade Paperback ISBN: 978-1-64108-271-6
Digital ISBN: 978-1-64108-270-9
Trade Paperback published December 2021
v. 1.0

Printed in the United States of America
∞
This paper meets the requirements of
ANSI/NISO Z39.48-1992 (Permanence of Paper).

*For Dad.*

# Acknowledgements

To The Five, always.

# Chapter One

*Ben*

BEN WAS on his third walk around Lockstone pond when he heard a strange sound. He'd spent the afternoon inspecting the newt dwellings he and his boss, Jamie, had built weeks before, but that high-pitched squeal stopped him in his tracks. Rain pummeled down, soaking his messy brown hair, and he pulled his hood up absently as he scanned the area around him. There were birds singing and crickets chirping. Everything was so loud. Hoping to hear the noise again, he held his breath and closed his eyes.

There was a rustle of the reeds at the edge of the pond and then a squeak. It didn't sound like mice or frogs... perhaps a pine martin? He opened his eyes and peered towards where the noise came from. He didn't see anything at first, so he took a step closer to the reeds and between the strands of long grass he saw a blur of fur.

Ben placed one foot into the mud near the edge of the pond and moved the long grass out of the way. His boot sank slightly into the mud with a squelch, and he placed his other foot into the reeds carefully. He didn't want to end up in the water.

The creature twitched and Ben frowned as he peered over. He parted the foliage and bent down, still unsure what it was. Not a pine martin. It turned over and a dirty face with a dark mask looked up at him. His first thought was ferret, but then his training kicked in and he looked it over before he got closer. If it was a wild polecat, then he didn't want to put his fingers near its face. He'd never seen a wild polecat, but that didn't mean there weren't any.

There wasn't much difference between a wild polecat and its domesticated cousin, but from what he remembered, polecats were darker with larger heads and ferrets had lighter coats with a more delicate head. He was almost certain it was a ferret.

The ferret let out a little noise that sounded somewhere between a squeak and a whine and then it flopped into the mud and was silent.

It didn't try to run or move. It was so thin and there was no fat over the sharp points of its hipbones. Ben couldn't leave it there. It was obviously in trouble, and even if it was wild, it deserved treatment. He tentatively reached down and scooped it up. It was light and cold to the touch. He quickly saw that it was a boy as it lay lax in his hands. Ben relaxed when he was sure the ferret wouldn't bite or jump out of his arms, and he stepped backwards out of the mud. When he was on even ground, he placed the ferret against his chest. It didn't make any noise or struggle against him. Its eyes closed, and its little mouth was open.

When he peered down at it and saw just skin, bones, and ticks, Ben worried that the ferret had died in his hands. But he gently turned it on his back and watched his chest rise and fall. He let out a breath he hadn't realised he'd been holding.

Poor thing had probably either escaped or had been *set free*. People didn't realise that ferrets couldn't survive in the wild.

Ben texted Jamie to let him know about the ferret and why he was going off-site, then clicked into recent contacts and rang Dane. *"Hey darling,"* Dane answered, his tone light and flirty, making Ben smile. Dane called everyone darling, and just hearing his voice helped with the stress of his upcoming date. His chest untightened and Ben could breathe properly again.

"Hey you. Are you at work?" He walked in the direction of the car park, ferret lying like a baby in one arm, phone to his ear with the other.

"Lunch break. Which is why I could answer my mobile. Anything wrong?" It was unusual for Ben to ring him in the middle of the day without a reason. They shared a few texts and met up at the pub, but Ben never randomly called him in the middle of a workday.

"I found a ferret at work. It looks really emaciated and tick covered—mind if I bring it in? I don't think he's doing so good."

"Of course, darling. Bring him now. I'll be looking out for you."

"Cheers. See you in ten." He ended the call just as he got to his car. He looked at the ferret, who still hadn't moved. He didn't have a box or carrier to put him in, but he didn't think that would matter. He pulled his fleece off and laid it in the footwell on the passenger side, then placed the ferret in it. He didn't move, so Ben doubted he'd get caught in the pedals. He jogged around to the driver's side and got in. Still no movement, just the shallow rise and fall of its chest. Ben started the car and drove the short distance to the vet's where Dane worked.

# Chapter Two

*Dane*

DANE WAS pathetic, and he was under no illusions. Ben called and he'd dropped everything. Or he'd given up his lunchtime so he could treat a ferret Ben was bringing in. He tried to quell the excitement and bit back the smile he couldn't stop—all because Ben had called him, all because Ben was coming over. They'd had a great time at the pub the week before, and Dane knew Ben was only a friend, but it didn't stop the butterflies dancing in his stomach or the warmth in his chest that Ben had called him personally rather than ringing the veterinary practice.

He was bringing in a sick ferret. It wasn't like he was coming because he wanted to spend time with him, but Dane's heart wasn't listening to the logic. He'd take any chance he got to spend time with Ben.

It was more than pathetic, but he couldn't stop how he felt. He'd removed his unrequited affection from *his* best friend and then his *brother's* best friend to a straight man. Talk about going from the frying pan into the fire. It was the story of his life, yet he couldn't stop his heart from melting as Ben walked into the practice with a sick ferret wrapped in his work fleece. There was just something special about quiet tough guys who loved animals.

It didn't hurt that Ben's muscular arms were on show either. *Yum.* He was tanned from working outside, and his hair was wet from the rain. He looked delectable. Dane tried to put that thought in a box at the back of his mind. No good would come of it.

"Come on through the back and I'll take a look at him." His dog, Speedy G, was in his basket in the corner of the room. He wagged his tail but didn't move. He was a good boy and knew to be on his best behaviour when they were at work.

"I found him next to Lockstone Pond. I was looking for newts and found this little guy."

"Trust you to look for newts and find a ferret instead. Put him on the table and I'll take a look." Dane winced when Ben unwrapped him. He was all skin and bones and the ticks were large and blood filled. Even his fur was thin, and there were bare patches along his back and tail underneath layers of drying mud.

He gently looked the ferret over, checking its limbs for broken bones and its stomach for swellings. Its teeth were in bad shape, but he could tell the ferret wasn't more than two years old—its gums were too pale, and its skin didn't bounce back properly when he pinched it.

"He's seriously dehydrated. I'm going to put him on a drip and hopefully that will help and bring him around. I'll get as many of the ticks off as possible as they're not helping with the dehydration." With a small stainless-steel tool that looked like tweezers but were bent at the tip, he removed as many of the large ticks as he could find. The ferret didn't even flinch or protest, and Dane worried that he might be too far gone to save. But he'd try his best.

He set him up on a drip, and one of the nurses arranged a cage in the back room for him. Ben let out a breath he must have been holding. "I'm presuming he needs to stay in?"

"He does. For a week or so. He'll be more comfortable now the majority of the ticks have been removed and he's on fluids. Ferrets can go downhill quickly, but I'm hopeful that there's no underlying problems."

"Where will he go if he gets better?"

Dane glanced up at him then back down to the ferret. "If no one comes forward as his owner, I know of a ferret rescue that may take him in if they aren't at capacity."

Ben grunted. He didn't seem to like that idea, but Dane didn't have any other options.

"I could take him. I mean… if that's okay?"

Dane looked up again, surprise on his face. Could this man get any more adorable? Ben shuffled awkwardly on his feet and stared at a poster about rabbits' teeth.

"If you want him, I don't see why not. I know he'd be in brilliant hands with you."

Ben finally looked his way and smiled. Dane's heart skipped a beat. Ben was so unaware of how wonderful he was. If it were anyone else, Dane would think they were lying, but Ben was as pure as they came.

He coughed to get rid of the extra feels he was getting, forced his signature lip curl, and raised an eyebrow. Yes, that was more like him. Ben was a new friend, that was all. "That's very sweet, darling. I'll keep you informed on how he is. Does he have a name?"

Ben blinked and frowned. "I don't know... I didn't really think about it."

"Just something to put into the system. You can always change it later."

"How about Chase? Because I found him over the Chase."

"The perfect name. Now get going. I'm presuming you're still at work. I'll sort Chase out and give you a bell tonight."

Ben grinned. "Are you playing tonight?" Dane shook his head. He played in a small rock and roll ukulele band called The Ratpack Rangers, but they didn't have any gigs lined up because they were all too busy. Jamie was mostly too busy with Liam and their pet rats, and like him, Markus was busy with work. They needed to get a life—seriously.

"No, I'm on call tonight, but otherwise I'm planning on doing a big fat nothing."

"If you're up for company, I can splash out on Indian... as a thank-you."

"You don't need to do that, darling. It is my job, after all, but I never say no to free food. As long as you're not expecting riveting conversation, you're more than welcome to come round and feed me." It was the first time since they'd become friends that Ben had initiated contact, rather than Dane or Jamie inviting him to join something they were already doing. He hoped that meant Ben was starting to relax and realise he was part of the group.

Ben laughed and Dane tensed as he tried to stop the shiver that threatened to make his whole body tingle. "I'll be round about eight. Who do I pay for Chase's care?"

"Don't be silly darling. He's a stray." Dane would foot the bill himself rather than ask Ben to pay.

"But I'm going to claim him if no one turns up."

"If no owner comes forward, I'll bill you, but not until then." He raised an eyebrow, then grinned when Ben gave in.

"All right, that sounds reasonable. See you soon, Chase. And I'll see you later for Indian?" He gently stroked the ferret's head as he looked up at Dane. Ben's hair had started to dry in wispy short curls, and his lips were pink and plump. It was impossible to look at him and not think of sex.

"Definitely."

# Chapter Three

*Ben*

DESPITE THE dining table in the kitchen, they were both sitting cross-legged on the floor in Dane's living room with takeaway food splayed out on the coffee table between them. The TV was on low in the background, and Speedy G lay his head in Ben's lap and whined until he gave in and fed him popadoms.

"You're a sucker," Dane said with a smirk as he shoveled chicken curry into his mouth like he hadn't eaten all day. He probably hadn't. Ben and Chase had taken up his lunch hour and there'd been a waiting room full of patients.

"You're just jealous because your dog loves me." Ben rubbed Speedy's head, and he turned his muzzle into his hand, thinking there was food. When he realised there wasn't, he dropped his head with an extra huff.

Dane's eyes darkened for a second, and Ben didn't understand why. Then he smiled and gave a shrug. "He loves your food, darling. It's the only way to that boy's heart."

They chatted easily as they ate—about animals, Chase, their jobs, and their friends in general. He and Dane had clicked from their first meeting, and they'd bonded more when Jamie and Liam got together. He was easy to talk to and made Ben laugh. There was no horrible talk about finding some girl to cop off with—one exceptionally good thing about being friends with gay guys. He could cope when they got crude or talked about men, because he knew they didn't expect him to participate.

"Did you grow up around here?" Ben asked. He only knew surface information about everyone apart from Jamie, and that was only because he worked with Jamie.

"Not too far away, my dad owns a small farm." That was a surprise. Though Dane worked with animals, he couldn't see him up to his elbows in shit or milking cows. He was always so neat and put together.

"Really? You didn't want to become a farmer, then?"

Dane wrinkled his nose and adamantly shook his head. "I love animals, and my experience with farm animals has helped with becoming a vet, but farming wasn't my calling at all. My younger brother loves it, so him and my dad run it together. Our mom left when we were little, and we don't see her anymore." Dane offered the information without him asking, and Ben hoped he hadn't forced him to say more than he was comfortable with.

"I didn't know. I'm sorry,"

Dane shrugged and waved it off. "It's no big deal, but sometimes people get confused or think she's died, so I just bring it up if I'm talking about family. How about you?"

Ben nodded but still felt like he'd said something wrong. "My parents are still together. They're… set in their ways, I suppose. Not old-fashioned exactly. Any way that isn't their way is the wrong way. My mum works at a supermarket, and my dad and brother are fishermen. I had to fight to go to uni, because they didn't think a fisherman needed a degree." Ben shuddered as he pictured himself on the boats day in day out with his dad and brother. He was glad he'd put his foot down about university and then left to accept a job as biodiversity officer in Lockstone.

"I hear you. Families can be difficult. I much prefer helping animals. How about you? People usually leave the Midlands to live in Devon, not the other way around."

Ben laughed. "I know, right? I wanted to do something completely different. I got my degree, worked in some of the national parks around Devon, but really wanted to get out of the area." And away from family and friends who did nothing but pressure him. "It's different here, but I like it. Even if I do miss the sea."

Dane nodded. "I guess it is a bit different. I bet your family miss you too."

He nodded and fed Speedy another cracker. "They say they do, but my brother is out at sea for weeks at a time, so it's not that much different with me working here." He loved his family, but he enjoyed being away from them. They were stifling and wished he would settle down to give them grandchildren. He was only twenty-eight, much too young for children and a relationship.

"Oh, before I forget, we're all going to the Drunken Duck tomorrow night, if you want to meet us there."

"I wish I could. I'm sort of going on a date." He forced a smile to his face. He wasn't really looking forward to it, but when a pretty woman asked you out, you said yes, right?

# Chapter Four

*Ben*

BEN COULDN'T help but think how much easier it had been in Dane's living room, sitting cross-legged around the coffee table eating takeaway. He wasn't a naturally social person, and when he was in a setting where he was meant to make conversation with someone who wanted more than he did, he never knew what to say. All he could think about was what Donna might want to do after the date—just a kiss or a kiss leading to sex. Either way he wasn't feeling it.

"Are you enjoying working for the council?" Donna asked.

Ben made a face, and she gave a soft laugh. "I wouldn't say I enjoy working for the council, but I enjoy being outside." He didn't understand why it was so much easier to talk with Dane than it was with Donna.

Why couldn't Donna be a bitch so he could legitimately hate her? She was doing her best to engage him and draw him into conversation, and the more she tried, the more he wanted to run in the opposite direction.

It didn't matter that she went from pretty to gorgeous when her hair was down. She was wearing a flowing flowery top and tight blue jeans, but her looks did nothing for him. He was sure that if she invited him into her bed he'd be able to get off, but he knew he wouldn't feel anything deep inside. Sex was meaningless and messy without a connection.

"Me too. I couldn't stand an office job." She gave a shudder at the thought and he nodded along.

"Very true, although my father wanted me to be a fisherman like him and my brother."

"A fisherman?"

"Yeah, I'm from Devon, so unless I wanted to go into the leisure industry, it was either a fisherman or move away." Being stuck on a boat with his father was enough to give him nightmares. Not that his father was a bad dad, but he couldn't imagine being stuck in such close quarters.

"Wow, I knew from your accent that you didn't come from around here, but I didn't realise you were from Devon. Don't you miss the sea?"

"I do, but luckily I work on Chasewater a lot, so I get to be around water. It might not be the sea, but it helps."

The conversation flowed relatively easily from then on, perhaps because he'd had a similar conversation with Dane? He tried not to analyse that too hard. Donna seemed to be having a good time and that's what mattered.

Unless she wanted more than a date. He hoped not. She was a nice person, but he was knackered from being on edge and trying to be social. He wanted to go home and he wanted to do it alone.

He tried not to look at his watch and wonder when it would be suitable to end the date, because that's not how you were supposed to feel on a date, especially one that was going well. Despite all the attempts not to look at his watch, his eyes were drawn to his wrist and his stomach plummeted when he saw it was only nine-thirty. Why was meeting women so hard? Most blokes saw a woman they fancied and that was it.

Ben took a subtle deep breath and smiled as he tried to concentrate on what Donna was saying. His phone vibrated and he sneakily looked at the screen, his forced smile less stiff when he saw Dane's name flash up. Chase was doing better. He was responding to the antibiotics, the nurses had removed more ticks, and his gums were becoming a healthy pink colour.

"What's got you smiling?"

Ben felt guilty for letting his thoughts sidetrack him. He looked at her through his lashes, expecting to see a scowl or annoyance, but she was smiling and seemed genuinely interested. Why did she have to be so nice?

He cleared his throat and licked his lips. "I found a ferret over Chasewater yesterday. He was really ill, so I took him to the vet's. I just had a text to say he was doing much better."

She gave him a wide grin. "That's great. I can't believe you found a ferret. Was it someone's pet?"

"He's not microchipped, and no one has come forward. He was probably abandoned then." Ben couldn't help but feel happier. He desperately wanted to text Dane back or ring him, but he knew that would be very rude in the middle of a date, so he turned his phone over and tried to concentrate on Donna.

They talked and drank until last orders. Donna slowly grabbed her bag, but he could tell she didn't want to end their date there. He most definitely did, but when he walked her to her car, she hesitated before getting inside and leaned against the door, her face turned up to his.

Ben expected a kiss, but she started to say something instead. "I had a good time, but…" He held his breath. "You're a great guy, but I think we'd be better off as friends. I'm sorry if I gave you the wrong impression. I just…." She sighed and leaned against her car. "My family have been pressuring me into finding someone serious, maybe settling down like my sister, and I thought if I was going to be serious about anyone, it would be you."

He did not expect that. "I understand." And he did, sort of. He wanted to jump up and down for joy as she spoke, but he refrained and let her carry on.

"It's not you, it's me. I'm just not the settling down type, you know? I like to play the field, and the last thing I want to do is date the same man."

Ben laughed in giddy relief and reached over to hug her. She froze, then hugged him back. "I feel the same. Definitely don't want to date— no offence. But my family can be as relentless as yours."

She pulled back and grinned. "Sucks, doesn't it? I have a sister who's been with her boyfriend since they were fifteen. They married at twenty-one and have just given my folks their first grandchild. You'd think they'd be too busy to worry about my private life, but if I hear another 'are you single?' when I go to a family party, I might scream."

"Tell me about it. My brother doesn't have a partner, but he followed my dad in his career, stayed close to home—he's the golden child."

"Families drive you crazy, don't they? I can't imagine settling down and sleeping with the same person for the rest of my life. No offence, but life is too short for me to stick to one man."

"I understand. The part about not being able to settle down with one person for the rest of my life, anyway." He had a feeling it was for entirely different reasons, but it was still nice to find someone who could understand what he felt, even in part.

"We can be friends, though? If you need a girl on your arm to keep the vultures off your back, let me know, and maybe you could do the same for me? I don't suppose you want to be my fake date for a christening?"

Ben blinked. Being a fake date sounded much more appealing than being a real one. "I'm sure I could manage that."

She relaxed and grinned. "Oh good. Because I really want to give the finger to my sister and her husband. I'll buy you dinner as a thank-you."

"No need for that, but I might ask you to return the favour with my family."

"Anytime, Ben. I have to say this has been a great nondate."

He agreed wholeheartedly.

# Chapter Five

*Dane*

DANE'S FAMILY home was nestled in the Staffordshire countryside, down a private country road that led to a large rambling farmhouse with acres of fields and pastures behind. Usually just pulling up to the house relaxed him, but not this time. He parked beside his dad's Range Rover and stepped out onto the gravelled driveway. Speedy G shot out of the car, barking as he raced behind the house to the sheep in the distance. Anyone would think he was a collie rather than a Jack Russell-cross with how he tried to herd the sheep. Luckily they took no notice of him, and the dog was trained well enough not to get too close.

He didn't bother going to the house, because he knew his dad and his brother would be outside working the farm. Both men were workaholics—not that he could complain, he was almost as bad. Despite their busy lives, they usually made the effort to get together every couple of weeks. Either they'd all stay in and eat his dad's famous lambchops, or they'd go to a local pub. They hadn't done that in four months, and he knew it was his fault. He and his brother, Martin, had fallen out, and it was getting harder and harder to hide it from their dad.

Dane sighed, hating that his shitty choices had caused a rift between him and his brother, but not really knowing how to fix it. He tried to forget about it for now. His dad had called to say one of their horses seemed slightly lame, and there was no way he could leave an animal in distress. He lifted his bag farther up his shoulder and walked around the back of the house that led to a large open garden just in front of a couple of barns. He couldn't see his dad or brother yet, but that wasn't surprising. They could be anywhere on the farm. "You in here, Dad?" he shouted and blinked at the dimness of the barn as he waited for his eyes to adjust. A large black horse with a white diamond on his head snorted, and Dane grinned and walked over to him. "Hey there, Zeus, what are you doing? I hope it's not you with a bad leg." He tried to peer into the stall, but Zeus headbutted him and nibbled at his collar. "I've got no treats, you cheeky thing." He carried on stroking Zeus as he scanned the rest of the barn, but he couldn't see anyone, so he shot off a text to let his dad know he was there. Then he waited.

He didn't have to wait long.

"Oh. It's you." He jumped when he heard his brother's voice behind him. Martin carried in tack and placed it on the hooks in the wall on the other side of the barn.

Dane had hoped he could avoid Martin. "Yeah, Dad said one of the horses looked a bit lame."

Martin's brow furrowed, and then his eyes widened as if a lightbulb had gone off. He scowled at Dane, but he didn't stop what he was doing. "Nosy old man needs to mind his own business."

It took Dane a little longer to understand, and when he did, he didn't know how he couldn't have realised the signs of a meddling parent. "I take it the horses are fine."

"Yep."

"Maybe we should clear the air." Things would be much easier if they could pretend he hadn't had a brief relationship with Martin's best friend. He was a horrible, awful brother. But Patrick was hot and fun and had been a good distraction from watching Jamie fall in love with Liam. "Come on, don't be a dick. It was almost a year ago. Let's just forget about it."

Martin was so irritating that whenever Dane tried to apologise, Dane always ended up making it worse. Martin didn't even look his way as he said, "You've made things awkward."

"Don't make me bang your heads together," another voice boomed, making everyone but the horses jump. "I ain't having my boys sitting on opposite sides of the table refusing to talk anymore. It's my birthday soon. I want you both there and happy." Their dad appeared in the doorway as if out of nowhere, tall, rangy and completely unmovable. Dane remembered arguments they'd had as children and how their dad would shut them in their room or the living room or the goddamn *barn* until they made up. He should have realised what was happening when his dad asked him over.

"Your birthday's not for *months*," Martin whined, and Dane had to bite his inner cheek to stop from laughing and making it worse.

"Exactly. So, you two fix whatever's wrong or don't come out of my barn." He moved away from the door and shut them in. *Shit*. The silence that followed was heavy and awkward. Dane didn't know what to say. He knew Martin would want an explanation and not just a generic "I'm sorry."

He was still trying to decide what to say when Martin turned to look at him, arms folded, obviously still pissed off. "Why?"

"Why? We dated for a few months. There's no crime in that. Okay, it was stupid. I'm sorry it messed up your friendship. I wasn't thinking." He'd just needed a distraction and he'd enjoyed being wanted by someone.

"You couldn't leave my best friend alone? Do you know the position it puts me in? It's not like you broke up amicably." No, Patrick had slept with someone else, and Dane hadn't been all that bothered by it.

"I've said I'm sorry to you—has he?" Zeus moved restlessly, and Dane moved closer and stroked him behind the ear in soothing circular motions. It was probably more soothing for him than the horse, but at least it gave him something to do.

"I'm mad at you both." Martin folded his arms and glared at him.

"You're making more of an issue of it than Patrick and I ever did."

"All your relationships end badly. That's why I didn't want you and Patrick to get together. I didn't want to be in the middle of it. And I didn't want to take sides." Martin jabbed a finger in his direction.

Dane ground his teeth and counted to ten. "You don't have to be in the middle. You don't have to take sides."

"Of course I'm taking sides. You're my *brother*. I'm as mad at him as I am at you."

Dane's heart swelled at his disgruntled admission. It was nice that his brother was on his side, even if he had a funny way of showing it. "You don't have to defend my honour. We're grown men, not hormonal teenagers anymore." Martin and his friends were only a few years younger than Dane, but sometimes it felt like decades. "Can we please just agree that I was insane to go out with your friend and pretend it didn't happen? I swear it won't happen again." Martin snorted, but Dane could tell there was less tension in his shoulders. "It could be worse. I could be stealing all the women *you're* interested in."

"You wish." Martin's lips twitched into a smile, and Dane relaxed. He knew that the small movement meant he was forgiven.

Dane walked over to Martin and rubbed his knuckles in his hair. It was a lot harder to do now they were adults, but Dane was still taller. Martin's hair was on end by the time he stopped. "I really am sorry, okay?"

"Just stay away from my friends in future."

"Promise." There was definitely no worry there. He'd learned his lesson. He didn't want anyone but Ben, and he couldn't have him. Why was life so damned complicated?

They turned to look at the closed door. Their dad would be somewhere on the other side. "We're friends again now, can we come out?" Martin shouted. Neither of them wanted to cross their dad when he had a bee in his bonnet.

"Please? I'm still on the clock."


DANE HAD only been home for a short while when Jamie's ex knocked on his front door. Someone must be out to make his life as awkward as possible. He looked at Paul with suspicion. Lately he only turned up when he wanted something or he was causing trouble, and Dane was done with his bullshit. He wanted a boring, stress-free life from now on. He'd created enough of his own drama, he couldn't deal with Paul's too.

"What are you even doing here?" He had no sympathy left for the man. It was hard to believe they all used to be good friends. He'd hurt Jamie twice—once when they were an item and he ran off with Tommy, Jamie's childhood best friend, and then when he became jealous that Jamie had found Liam and tried to split them up.

Paul must be feeling pretty shit, because his hair was flat and soft, with no product in it at all. He also wasn't wearing his usual trademark skinny jeans and shirt. He'd heard through the grapevine that Tommy had broken up with him.

"Can I come in… please?"

Dane shook his head. "I've heard all that I need from you. You were fun to be around when we were at uni, but frankly, you need to grow up, Paul." He flinched and Dane pushed back the guilt. Everyone always pussyfooted around him, Dane included, and he didn't know why.

"I just wondered if you could speak to Tommy for me. Tell him I'm sorry. He won't speak to me."

"Can you blame him?" Dane didn't want to speak to him either.

Paul shook his head slowly, shoulders hunched over. He used to be the life and soul of the party. It was obvious why Jamie, and even Tommy, fell for him. There was something about him that people gravitated towards, but he was also a fucking wanker. "It's not even about Tommy. Did you ever apologise to Jamie for cheating on him? For messing with Liam's rats?" Paul had snuck into Jamie's rat room and placed one of Jamie's male rats in with Liam's female rats. That not only led to them almost splitting up, but to twelve unplanned baby rats, which was completely irresponsible.

Paul snorted and kicked at a crack in the step. "Of course, it has to be about *Jamie*. Everything is with you, isn't it?" His mouth twisted into a bitter grimace. "How does it feel? Knowing I've had him, but you'll always be relegated to the friends' box?"

Dane flinched as if he'd had a punch to the gut. Why were people digging at him about his poor taste in men today? The one thing that could make Paul the life and soul of a party could also make him a cruel bastard. He always found that one detail about someone and used it to his own advantage—whether in a good way or bad. Dane didn't even feel that way for Jamie anymore, hadn't for a long time, but Paul always knew how to dig the knife in.

He stepped over the doorstep, grabbed Paul's arm, and dragged him down the garden path. "What the fuck?" Paul tried to pull himself out of his grasp, but Dane wasn't having it. He might act like a flaming queen on occasion, but he didn't let anyone push him around—especially on his own doorstep.

"There's a reason why your *friends* don't want to hang around with you, *darling*. When you stop being such an arsehole, maybe we can have another conversation. Until then, piss off. If you carry on as you are, you're not going to have any friends left." He pushed Paul out of the garden gate and shut it behind him. Paul stood staring on the other side of the pavement, his mouth open, and Dane resisted the urge to stick his two fingers up at him.

He twirled around and stomped back inside, anger simmering under his skin. As much as Paul was a complete and utter twat right then, there was truth to his words that made Dane sick to his stomach. He would forever be in the friends' box, though that box he was thinking of was with Ben, not Jamie. Maybe he was taking his frustration out on

Paul. He hadn't exactly lied about Dane's choice in men, but that didn't mean Paul was in the right.

"Come on, Speedy, walkies." Speedy's claws made a clicking sound as he ran down the hallway and slid to a stop next to him. He gave a few excited yaps, and Dane put his lead on and quickly exited his house. Thankfully, Paul was gone.

"Dane, Dane!" A young voice shouted at him. He stopped, took a breath, and forced on a smile as he inhaled and looked towards his neighbour's garden.

"Hi Arthur, what are you up to?" The young boy climbed up the short wooden fence and wedged his feet between the panels so he could lean over.

"I found a ladybird, see?" He held a shaky hand out over the fence, and Dane went over and dutifully looked at the small red and black bug that crawled over his finger.

"Wow, it's amazing. Did you count his spots?" Arthur shook his head. "You need to count his spots, so you know how old he is." Arthur scrambled down the fence and started to count loudly.

Dane looked up and saw Arthur's dad, Cal, in the doorway and gave him a quick wave. He wondered if he'd heard all the commotion. Poor bloke always seemed to be around for Paul's bullshit.

Paul really had the uncanny ability to get to them all. Dane opened the gate and set a brisk pace towards the large nature reserve. The closer he got, the easier it seemed to breathe. He stopped at the stile to unhook Speedy's lead and then stepped over into the common.

Like most typical summers, it started to drizzle as soon as he hit the trail that veered around a small man-made pond with a few ducks swimming in it. Bloody typical. Just because he'd not taken his coat.

It was the type of fine rain that soaked him before he knew what had hit him, but it was too late to run back for a coat, so Dane shrugged it off and carried on walking. He'd always rather liked the rain and the smell of wet grass, so if he could ignore how uncomfortable his jeans felt then he could enjoy it.

There weren't many people out. He saw an old couple with a greyhound wearing a wax jacket. They stopped to say hello, and he realised they must be patients of his, or rather, the dog must be. He bent down to stroke him and saw his name on the tag. *Hector*. He remembered who he was then and asked a few questions about Hector and how he was settling in after they'd adopted him from a rescue for ex racing greyhounds. They practically beamed at him as they waxed lyrical about how wonderful he was.

The tension in his stomach eased a little after speaking with them. No matter how shit his private life was, at least he was good at his job. If all else failed, he could become a crazy dog man and relocate to an island with a pack of dogs—no other humans allowed.

Halfway around and his trainers were covered in mud, his dark hair was plastered to his head, and Speedy G was having a grand old time chasing a sodden tennis ball he'd found in the grass. A sheep dog appeared out of nowhere and bounded right up to him. He didn't recognise this one, but he bent down to give her a good scritch behind the ear anyway.

"Shadow, you naughty girl, you have to stop doing that." A woman who had sensibly thought to wear a waterproof jacket ran up to them and pulled her away.

Dane straightened up and gave her a smile. "I don't mind. She's lovely."

"She needs to learn to listen," she scolded but leaned down to give her a stroke. A figure stepped behind her, and Dane looked towards them to say hello. His mouth dropped open when he realised it was Ben.

His heart lurched and he looked from Ben to the woman, realisation dawning. There was a sour taste in his mouth, but he swallowed and forced a smile. "I didn't expect to bump into you here, darling." He cursed himself when he said darling, worrying that Ben wouldn't like it while he was out with someone else—a gorgeous woman who liked dogs and walking. She was perfect for him. He hated her.

Ben's cheeks burned under the rain, and he glanced quickly at the woman who had obviously noted the term of endearment and was confused. "Hi, Dane, this is Donna, a friend from work. Donna, this is Dane, a good friend of mine and the vet I was telling you about." Her eyes widened, and she sent Dane a large smile that made him feel like shit for thinking ill of her.

"Oh, the vet who's looking after the ferret you found?"

"That's the one. How is Chase?" Ben's eyes were so earnest, and although Dane felt awkward at having their friendship defined in such clear-cut terms, he couldn't be mad at him.

"He's doing much better. He's still on the drip, because ferrets are notorious fussy eaters and we haven't been able to tempt him with food yet. But he's definitely perked up."

Ben grinned at him, the corners of his eyes creasing. Dane's stomach tightened and it took a lot not to reach up and brush the rain from his cheeks. "That's brilliant. Can I come and see him tonight?"

"Sure. I'm not working tonight, but I can take you in."

"I'll text you later?" Ben said. Donna reached down and picked up the tennis ball covered in dog slobber and threw it for Shadow.

"It was great to meet you," Donna said.

"You too." Dane hoped he sounded sincere. "See you later." He gave Ben another smile and was about to walk around them when Ben stopped him with a touch to the arm.

"Don't you have a coat? You're soaked." His eyes took in Dane's drenched hair and T-shirt that was almost translucent it was so wet. There was nothing but worry in his gaze. Dane didn't understand why that made his heart swell.

Dane shook his head, droplets spraying them both, and looked up to the sky. "It wasn't raining when I started out. I'll be fine, darling. It's not cold. I'm used to being out in all weather."

"I can give you a lift home if you're ready to go." Dane glanced at Donna, and she smiled and nodded.

"Thanks, but Speedy's still raring to go. I'll see you later, though, darling. Donna, it was good to meet you." He sent her a dazzling smile and cursed silently for repeating himself. He brushed his hand against Ben's arm as he walked by, and carried on down the trail, through the overgrown trees. He shivered as water droplets trailed down his spine. What a day it was turning out to be. First Paul and now Ben with his new girlfriend. He resisted the urge to look back until he'd turned the corner and there was no way he'd see them. He looked anyway.

Officially. Worst. Day. Ever.

# Chapter Six

*Ben*

BEN AND Donna had settled into somewhat of a routine where they'd go for the occasional drink or walk the dog so they could both bitch about their overbearing families, and he admitted that he'd been ignoring calls from his mother and brother. Not his father, because his dad never rang or texted unless it was to his drinking buddies to organise a night on the town. It was nice to talk to someone in the same boat as him, and they'd had a great time hamming it up for Donna's family at the christening. He hadn't been so relaxed with a woman in years, and Donna was quickly making a good friend. But Ben still preferred chilling out with Dane and the guys.

Dane picked him up from his house later that evening and they went to the vet's together to visit Chase. They went through to the back room where the animals recovered. Chase was up and about, lapping up some thick creamy food that looked a little bit like yogurt, though he knew it was some kind of powdered mixture given to help him pile on the calories.

"Hi Chase," Dane said. Chase looked up long enough for them to see the food around his mouth and then went back to it. "I'm glad you're finally eating something."

"Wow, he looks so much better." He was still skin and bones and mostly bald along his back, but at least he was responsive. "Is that nice, Chase?" Ben curled his fingers into the bars as he peered inside.

"Once he's finished eating, I'll get him out," Dane said. "I don't want to interrupt him because he needs the calories."

"He definitely does."

"I was surprised he's bounced back so quickly. If he'll eat some dry kibble or raw meat, he can go home tomorrow—if you still want him?"

"Of course. I'm going to get one of those chicken coops for the garden, but Jamie's lent me one of his rat cages—the Savic Suite or something—so I can have him inside while he's recovering." Chase stopped eating and wiped his face on the blanket next to him, then stumbled over to the door.

"Inside is best while he's recovering. We'll have to keep an eye on his weight and make sure he's eating. Ferrets can be very fussy eaters as they tend to imprint on a certain food when they're young. It's a good sign he's eating what we've been giving him, though. He will have to have some teeth removed when he's up to it, but all in all, he's doing well." Dane unlocked the cage and lifted him out. After a quick kiss to his head that warmed Ben's heart, he handed him over.

He wriggled in Ben's arms, and he couldn't help but grin. It was so different from how he found him. "You are feeling better, aren't you?" He held him close to his chest, and Chase leaned his head against his shoulder, then wriggled sideways, bumped his head against Ben's jaw, and gave his face a lick. If Ben wasn't already in love with him, he certainly was now. "You're such a good boy." He gave him a stroke between his ears, and Chase gave a yawn and tensed for a second. Then his whole body turned to liquid and he closed his eyes and snuggled close to his chest.

"Yep, he's definitely your ferret, darling."

"Is it normal for him to fall asleep like that?"

"Ferrets do sleep a lot, but he's still building up his strength." Ben relaxed when Dane didn't seem concerned and gently placed him back in the cage and curled the blankets around him.

"Shall we head to the pub?" Dane asked, opening the door.

"If you're sure the guys won't mind me tagging along...." Dane rolled his eyes as he went over to a meowing cat in a cage two doors away from Chase to stick a finger between the bars so he could scratch under his chin.

"Don't be silly. I don't know where you've got this idea in your head that you're a guest in our group. Just because you're the newest member doesn't mean you need an invitation, okay, darling?"

Ben eye-rolled back at him and stifled a smile, even though it warmed him inside to hear. "Let's go, then. Bye Chase." Chase was sleeping so hard he didn't reply.

They headed to the Drunken Duck, and Markus was already sitting in their usual booth at the back. It was a Saturday night and not yet 7:00 p.m., but it was still packed. People were already milling around the makeshift dance floor in anticipation of the Green Day cover band that was scheduled to play later.

With a flourish, Dane slid onto the bench opposite Markus and Markus looked up with a grin. "I almost had to kill a man to keep this table," he said, eyeing a group of lads behind them. Ben knew it was a lie because the table was always reserved for them—a perk of being members of a band that played there so often, he guessed.

Dane twisted around to get a good look at the men and snorted. "My money is on you, darling."

"I'll go get drinks. What do you want?"

"I'm on an early shift tomorrow, so I'll just have a Diet Coke, please."

Ben nodded. "Markus?"

"I'll have another bitter. Cheers." Ben headed off, twisting between the crowds and managing to find a small gap at the bar. He leaned against the sticky wood and waited his turn, which came sooner than he thought it would. The barmaid was wearing a tight Green Day T-shirt, her eyes were heavily lined in black, and her hair was dyed black and red. She looked him up and down, and he straightened up, body tensing as he forced a smile in her direction.

"What can I get ya?" she shouted over the noise.

"Er...." What had they asked for? His heart hammered. "Pint of bitter, Diet Coke, and a Bulmers Original, please?" He worded it like a question and winced inwardly as she licked her lips and sashayed away to get glasses.

He paid quickly and carried all three drinks back to the table without dropping one or spilling any. Dane waited until he'd slid them onto the table and then sat next to him before poking him in the ribs, making him jump.

"You were in there." He nodded at the barmaid, and Ben grimaced and took a gulp of his cider.

"I'll pass, thanks."

"You're passing on her? I'm as queer as they come, but even I can tell she's got that hot-goth look going on. Oh," Dane's eyes widened, "unless it's more serious with Delicious Donna than I thought."

Ben didn't want to go into his friendship with Donna, so he made some noncommittal sound and hoped they'd drop the topic.

Markus pretended to gag. "Please, I didn't need to know that." He shuddered.

"Straight sex—is there anything worse?" Dane said, taking a deep drink.

"Well, you're the one who called her delicious," Ben said, trying to keep it light. Markus laughed loudly and tapped his finger on the table and then pointed at Dane.

"He's got you there, ain't he?"

Before Dane could complain, Liam bounded over, Jamie close behind him, bouncing on his heels and practically vibrating with excitement. Markus scooted up the booth and they slid in opposite, and Liam wrapped his arm around Jamie's waist and pulled him close.

A pang went through Ben's heart as he watched them. They seemed so comfortable and happy together. Ben didn't think he'd ever connect with anyone on that level.

"What has you bouncing like a puppy, darling?"

Liam grinned at Dane. "Pride of course. Tickets are on sale. We're all going to go, aren't we? It'll be amazing."

"I had to work last year, so I made sure to book it off this year," Dane said. "It should be fun. Have you been before, darling?" It took Ben a second to realise he was talking to him.

"Er, no. It's not something I've really thought about." He felt his cheeks burning and was thankful that none of them ribbed him for it. Most of the time he could forget they were all gay, not that it bothered him. Hell, he preferred it that way, but there were a few occasions they probably wanted to go off and… do gay stuff without a straight guy cramping their style.

"You should definitely come," Liam said, leaning forward, his odd-coloured eyes bright with excitement. "They put on a great parade. There's music and market stalls, and the Village is packed. So many hot men—not that you'd appreciate that."

"I don't know. You'll probably have more fun without me." He wasn't sure he wanted to watch as Dane hooked up with randoms and Jamie and Liam made out. It was weird enough that Jamie was his boss.

"Don't start that again, darling. You'll be our token straight man. Birmingham Pride is for everyone. Don't feel awkward because you're straight. It'll probably help me find someone. They'll be drooling at your feet, and when they realise they won't get anywhere with you, I'll be there to ease their disappointment."

Ben frowned, not sure he liked the sound of that. "You're not selling it to me."

Dane sighed and patted his shoulder. "Well, if it will make you happy, I'll be on my best behaviour."

"I'm not sure that's a good thing or a bad thing. Okay. I've never been to any Pride before. I'm sure it'll be fun."

"It will be," Liam said.

Before Ben knew it, they'd all booked their tickets on their phones, and he was going to his first ever Gay Pride. He wondered what his father would think of that, but he pushed that thought away for another day. At least Pride stopped Dane grilling him about Donna.

"How's the ferret?" Jamie asked once their plans for Pride were made. "I can't believe you found him over Chasewater. That is *crazy*. How come I don't find cool things like that?"

Liam laughed and gave him a wicked look. "Yeah, he just deals with the knickers in the dogging tree." Jamie groaned and slid down low in his chair.

"Trust you to lower the tone." Markus tapped the back of Liam's head.

"I didn't even know about it until he started to moan about it." Liam rubbed his head. "I had no idea such things happened around here. I didn't think my boyfriend would have to deal with the aftermath of dogging parties. I thought that footballer thing was a one-off." It seemed like sex was on everyone's minds that evening, so Ben was glad that Jamie had to deal with the not-so-nice aspect of countryside management.

Jamie sat back up again and pressed a wet kiss to Liam's cheek. "My poor sheltered boyfriend."

"How did we even get onto this topic, anyway? Let's not talk about work," Ben said. But Jamie looked at him and started to cackle, which made him uncomfortable in case he'd said something wrong. "What?"

"Only *we* could talk about dogging and work in the same sentence."

Ben relaxed, and his mouth twitched before he laughed too.

# Chapter Seven

*Dane*

CHASE WAS well enough to go home, and Dane offered to help set up his cage, which was how he ended up in Ben's bedroom. Dane hadn't been in another man's bedroom without the prospect of sex since he was a teenager still living at home. It felt strange, a little awkward, and he couldn't stop looking at Ben's arse as he bent down to arrange something in the ferret cage. It was impossible not to look, and Dane's cock started to harden. He was in a man's bedroom; that's what it was used to doing. It practically had a mind of its own.

Ben lived in a house share, renting just one room, so he couldn't put the cage anywhere but in his bedroom, which meant Dane got to see a straight man's domain. It was slightly disappointing. He didn't know what he expected, but something a bit more fun. He managed to distract himself long enough for his cock to settle while he sat cross-legged on Ben's bed as if he were fourteen years old, crushing on a boy for the first time.

Dane carefully picked Chase out of his carrier and draped him across his lap. He was still skinny, half bald, but in so much better shape than when he first arrived at the practice. He absently stroked what fur Chase had as his eyes went back to Ben and roamed his strong back as it moved under the thin white cotton T-shirt. Why did he have to be straight…and fucking gorgeous?

"Do you think that's all right?" Ben asked as he stood up and took a step back so they could look at the huge cage that dominated the back wall of the room.

"It's perfect, darling. He's just going to sleep mostly to begin with, anyway. Do you want to do the honours?" He slid his hands under Chase's warm, sleepy body and held him out. Ben picked him up like he was a precious baby, gave him a kiss on the head, and put him in the fluffy house at the bottom of the cage in a nest of fleece blankets.

There was a bowl of water and another for kibble, but Ben also had some extra sachets of Convalescence Support to give Chase until his weight was better. Then he sat on the bed next to him, which made Dane bounce so his knee bumped into Ben's thigh.

A shiver ran down his spine, but he hid it by playing with a loose thread on his jeans and holding his breath. Did Ben feel that? It was like making friends with Jamie all over again, only now he was an adult, and not being able to touch was so much worse.

With Jamie he'd distracted himself by going on the pull, sleeping with any guy who showed a hint of interest, and drowning himself in alcohol and college work. It wouldn't work like that anymore. He was ready to settle down, find someone like Jamie had. He couldn't distract himself with sex and alcohol. Plus, his liver wouldn't like it, and it would be frowned upon to go to work half cut.

"Have you ever had ferrets before?" His ability to converse had disappeared for some reason. All he could feel was Ben sitting so close to him.

Ben shook his head. "No, but there was a petting farm not far from where I lived, and they had ferrets. My college did too. I always liked them." Dane opened his mouth to say something else, but Chase twitched, jumped up to stumble about his cage and explore his blankets, and then moved them around until he got sidetracked by the water bowl, stuck his head in, and splashed it everywhere.

They laughed at his antics. Ferrets were such adorable creatures, and Chase was the cutest of them all. He was light brown with a dark brown mask over his eyes and two little fangs that made him look cute rather than menacing.

"Do you want to watch a film or something? We're probably too late to steal the TV in the living room, but I've got Netflix here."

Dane's traitorous heart skipped a beat. "Sure, darling, but not one of those Marvel films that Jamie and Liam are binging at the moment, not unless it's one with Tom Hiddleston in, anyway." He gave Ben a wink and shuffled up to the top of the bed to lean against the headboard.

Ben turned to look at him, eyebrow raised. "Fancy him, do you?"

"What can I say? I love a svelte charming bad boy." He curled his lip into a mischievous smile. Tom H was definitely his type—not sweet, muscled, outdoorsy men with a mop of unstyled hair and scruff on his chin that was there most likely because he'd forgotten to shave and not because it was fashionable. Nope, not his type at all. He kept repeating it in his mind as Ben settled next to him on the bed and he turned on the TV.

His cock was half hard as Ben settled next to him, and it took all his willpower to look at the TV and concentrate on the film Ben put on. Halfway through it, he couldn't name what it was.

# Chapter Eight

*Ben*

DANE LEFT soon after the film ended, and Ben couldn't understand why he was disappointed. It was late, and they weren't kids who had sleepovers anymore.

Chase woke up before he could dissect his feelings, and he let him out of the cage to explore his room. "Chase, naughty. No. You can't go in there," he said for the thousandth time. He picked him up and distracted him with his toy. Chase stashed it under the bed and then scooted back out and ran to the wardrobe on short stumpy legs.

Ben rolled his eyes and sighed. He didn't know what was so exciting about the wardrobe, but he caved and opened the door. Chase jumped in, dove between his shoes, and did alligator rolls he was so happy. If only people could be so easily pleased.

His phone vibrated and his stomach dropped when he saw it was Donna. Why was he disappointed it wasn't Dane?

"Hey, Donna." He forced his voice to be light and happy. "How are you?" He sat on the edge of the bed and watched Chase root around in the bottom of his wardrobe, curl up, then fall asleep. He was a tad jealous of the little guy.

"Eugh. You'll never guess what my sister just did…" She said in response. Ben relaxed against the headrest and grinned as he listened to her rant. It was fun to hear other people's problems rather than dwelling on his own. He let her carry on, half listening and half watching Chase discover a blanket and pounce on it.

"God, listen to me going on. What kind of shitty friend am I? How's the ferret? You brought him home tonight, didn't you? I really didn't mean to go on and on," Donna said.

Ben looked at Chase. He was now curled up on top of his shoes. It was hard to believe he'd been so sick. "He's doing much better. He's currently asleep in my wardrobe." His words held a hint of a smile, and he relaxed when Donna laughed. She *was* a decent human being, he just wished she weren't so pushy.

"I'm so glad he's better and you decided to keep him. Listen, I know I've talked your ear off, but I'll be over Lockstone Chase tomorrow. Are you free for lunch?"

"I should be, unless I find another ferret of course. 1:00 p.m. okay?"

"That sounds perfect. See you on the morrow!" She hung up and Ben closed his eyes. He stayed that way until his flatmate Ross knocked on his door and poked his head inside.

"All right, mate? We're gonna go to Spoons for a pint or two if you want to come."

Ben was about to turn him down like he had every other time he asked, but something stopped him, and he sat up and nodded. "Sure. Let me just put the ferret back."

Ross's eyes widened, and he jumped out of the doorway. "He's out?" He eyed the cage warily, only just noticing the doors wide open.

Ben smirked at him as he picked up Chase. "Don't worry. He's zonked... you're safe." Chase stretched when he put him back, then snuggled back down into his blankets.

"I can't help it. They scare me."

Clare was putting on her boots when they walked down the stairs. Her eyes widened when she saw him. "Well, I never...." She hadn't expected to see him. His housemates were decent. He'd lucked out when he'd moved to Lockstone, but he'd kept to himself, refusing all offers to socialise outside the house.

Ben didn't know what to say, so he just shrugged and smiled. The local Wetherspoons didn't have the ambiance of the Drunken Duck, but the beer was cheap, and they had an app that meant they didn't even have to go to the bar. It was ingenious.

They found one of those tall tables and sat on rickety chairs. Ross seemed to be doing his best to impress Clare, but she was having none of it. Ben bit back a laugh as he watched her actively ignore him. "So, Ben. Tell me. Are you seeing that cute guy who came around with the ferret earlier?"

His heart skipped a beat, and his mouth dropped open. He quickly took a sip of his lager to give himself some time to think. "Why would you think that?"

She shrugged a shoulder. "He's gay, isn't he? I just presumed...."

"He is gay, but we're just friends." He thought about pointing out that he wasn't gay, but something stopped him.

# Chapter Nine

*Dane*

AFTER HIS last patient left—a house rabbit who needed her claws clipped—Dane slipped into the waiting room and flung himself onto the empty chair behind the desk. He enjoyed the swaying motion as the chair swung sideways.

Laura, one of their receptionists, raised an eyebrow at him as she typed something into the computer without looking at the screen. "Long day?"

He made a noise in the back of his throat. It had been nonstop all day—nothing serious, but one of the other vets had called in sick, so they were short-staffed and quickly backed up. He hadn't taken a lunch and ended up working eight until eight.

"Are you off out tonight?"

"I'm meant to be meeting friends at the Duck, but I think I'm too tired." His jaw clicked as he yawned. Laura powered down the computer and swung around to look at him. He could feel her gaze even with his eyes closed, but he opened one eye and said, "What?"

"You found a boyfriend yet?"

He groaned and let his head fall back. "Let's not talk about my love life." He didn't even want to think about it. It was too depressing.

"I take that to mean you haven't. You should let me set you up with my nephew. He's twenty-four, very good-looking."

"Please, I can find my own dates," he said, although he wasn't quite so sure. The two men he'd liked the most were both unobtainable. And the obtainable one had him falling out with his brother.

"Well, if you don't want to…. *Sean*, how lovely of you to pick me up."

Dane's eyes shot open, and he lifted his head as a gorgeous young guy walked into reception. He looked a little confused by Laura's wide grin and the tone of her voice.

"Not a problem, Aunty L."

She stood up and walked around the desk to give him a hug, then turned to Dane. "Dane, this is my nephew, Sean. Sean, this is one of our vets, Dane."

It would be rude to stay sitting, so Dane stood and offered his hand over the counter. Laura was right—Sean was hot. Tall, lanky with dirty blond hair and pale blue eyes. Dane should definitely stay away. He'd learned his lesson. "Nice to meet you, darling," Dane said, overpronouncing *darling*.

Sean's eyes widened, and his grasp tightened for a second before he let go of Dane's hand. "You too." He looked down at Laura as if he knew what she was up to.

"Sean loves animals too. He's got lizards."

Sean winced and his cheeks started to turn red. Dane bit the inside of his cheek to stop him from laughing. It was becoming more and more obvious that Laura trying to set up her nephew was a regular occurrence.

"I've got an iguana and four geckos."

"Reptiles are such interesting creatures. I had geckos growing up." He'd become so busy as a vet that he had fewer animals now than he did before. Poor Speedy G was an only child.

"Sean's only just moved back to the area. I told him he should bring his lizards in for a check-up or at least register with us." Laura tutted, and Sean rolled his eyes.

"Give me a chance to settle in first." His gaze flickered over Dane, eyes roaming down his chest. Dane's stomach tightened and his cock stirred.

"It was nice to meet you, Dane." Sean's eyes stayed on him while Laura got her bag and took her time getting into her coat as they walked towards the door.

He held it open for Laura, and as she slipped through, his eyes narrowed and he sucked in a breath as he nodded at Dane. *Fuck.*

Dane fell back into the chair, half disgusted at himself and half aroused. It had been so long since he'd been with anyone, let alone anyone that looked at him like that. But he didn't hold a candle to Ben. Life thoroughly sucked sometimes.

When his legs worked, he got up and locked the door, then walked around the back for a last check on the animals that were staying. Angela, one of the veterinary nurses, was already there checking on them, but he couldn't leave the building without seeing them with his own eyes.

He wasn't the vet on call that evening, but he would stay awake worrying all night if he didn't check each animal. Luckily they had no one in too serious condition. Most were routine operations, neutering, and tooth extractions, so he wasn't too worried.

Too knackered to socialise, Dane blew off the guys, and he didn't look at his phone again until he set the alarm to get up in the morning. But he frowned when he saw a text from an unknown number, and he opened it.

*It's Sean. Hope you don't mind Aunty L giving me your number. I don't usually do this, but I like you.*

Dane tried to bite the smile off his lips. Sean might not be the guy he wanted to say those things to him, but it was still nice to hear them, especially from someone so good-looking.

He stared at the text for a long time and then decided what to write back.

*I don't mind, darling. I rather liked you too.*

What if he liked someone else more? They were never going to like him back, and Sean was nice. A bit of harmless flirting didn't hurt anybody. Did it?

*Do you want to go for a beer on Friday?*

Forward, wasn't he? Dane didn't mind. His ego could do with a good stroke.

*A beer sounds good.*

Dane slipped into bed and pulled the covers up to his chin as he waited for Sean to reply. He closed his eyes and pictured Sean's face. His stomach clenched in arousal and his cock started to stir, so he slipped his hand into his boxers and rubbed his erection. He shivered as the heel of his hand pushed against the root.

He imagined that it was Sean's hand, that the heated look he'd given him before leaving the practice was burning into his flesh. He groaned and his eyes rolled back in his head as he grasped his dick and jacked.

Heat coiled in his balls, his thighs tensed, and he came, but Ben's face was at the forefront of his mind. He cursed himself and tried to picture Sean, but his mind couldn't see what he looked like anymore. Eventually he drifted off to sleep with a frown on his face and Ben tattooed on his inner eyelids.

# Chapter Ten

*Ben*

THREE WEEKS after settling Chase in, Ben didn't expect this to happen. He'd gone quiet, but for once it was due to anger and not awkwardness. He glared at their newest housemate, Neil. He'd lived in the house for barely a month, and he was already screwing them all over.

It was one of the many reasons why he was beginning to hate living in a house share. He'd get home from work, and there'd be another stranger moved in. He found it hard to relax like that.

"We are so sorry," Clare said as she clutched Ross's arm and glared at their newest flatmate. "You're such a little bitch," she practically hissed at the new guy, who just smirked and shrugged his shoulder.

He'd been lucky in his house share so far—Ross and Clare were great flatmates, but the smallest room in the house never found someone who would stay for longer than six months. It was annoying that they had no say in who stayed there, considering they lived there, but that was the nature of house shares and one reason he really needed to leave and find himself something a bit more permanent. Now that he knew his job was worth sticking around for, it was worth finding a flat of his own.

He didn't think he would be pushed out quite like this. He held Chase in one hand under his front legs and swayed him slightly so he'd stay calm. Neil looked at him with disgust and fake-coughed into his hand.

"It's in the contract that we can't have pets. I don't know why you're so worked up." He was a conceited arsehole.

"It's not how we do things here. We're all friends." Clare stepped forward, and Ross pulled her back before she hit him.

"Don't worry about it, Clare. I was thinking about finding somewhere else anyway. This has just been a kick up the arse. No way am I getting rid of Chase."

She looked at him mournfully. "We've only just started to get to know you. I like living with you. I even like living with Ross. He's not as bad as he pretends to be."

"Hey," he protested, and she rolled her eyes at him.

"We'll still be friends. You can help me decorate when I move into my new place." If he found one. He was a bit apprehensive about finding something so quickly, but he knew for sure he and Chase were better off out of the house now that the estate agent knew about him. He was lucky he'd gotten away with it for so long.

He'd been told he needed to vacate ASAP or get rid of Chase if he wanted to stay in the house, and that wasn't going to happen, so instead of going out with the guys to Spoons for Sunday lunch, he was going to stay in and trawl the internet for flats to let. *Joy.*

"Go eat lunch. I'll speak with you two later."

"Come and meet us afterwards, yeah?" Ross said, and they left to go to the pub.

Neil laughed and bounced on the balls of his feet. "I guess I get your room when you leave."

"Yeah, I guess you do. I hope I manage to find where Chase stashed his raw chicken last night because I haven't been able to find the bones." He gave a nasty smile back.

Chase bent backwards and stared at him, and Ben hugged him to his chest as he brushed past Neil and made him recoil. He bit back a smirk of satisfaction and went to his room.

Two hours later and he wasn't having much luck at finding anywhere that accepted pets. When had it become so hard to find somewhere? His parents had moved frequently when he'd been a child—all rented properties—and they'd never had any issue because they had a dog and two cats.

He booked in to see a few letting agents, hoping he'd have more luck in person, then sent off a self-pitying text to Dane, though he didn't explain the problem. He didn't want any of them to feel sorry for him, but he didn't feel like going out now. He lay on the bed and stared at the ceiling while Chase rummaged around his room.

A knock on his door made him jump. "What?" he demanded. Only the new guy was in the house, so he didn't know why he would bother him.

The door opened, and Donna poked her head around. "Only me. Your new flatmate let me in. I hope you don't mind…."

He scrambled off the bed and ran to let her in. "Sorry. I didn't mean to snap. The new flatmate has basically got me evicted."

Her eyes widened as she sat on the end of the bed. "What happened?"

"He told the letting agency about Chase."

"Without even talking to you first?"

"Yeah. So now I'm looking for a new place. But most places won't accept animals." She scooted up the bed to sit next to him against the headboard. It reminded him of the time he'd brought Chase home and he and Dane had watched a film.

He checked to see what Chase was doing. He'd fallen asleep in the wardrobe again, silly ferret. It couldn't be comfortable, but he was curled up between his shoes.

He sat back down again, but Donna closed the gap between them and patted him on the arm.

"Have you found another place yet? You could always stay with me… until you find somewhere. Most definitely as friends—just reiterating in case you thought I was putting a move on you." She winked at him. "God, my mother would practically pee her pants if that happened."

Ben laughed but shook his head. "As much as I love to play your fake date, I think that would be taking it a bit too far. But thanks for the offer. It's about time I look for my own place anyway."

# Chapter Eleven

*Dane*

DANE AND the guys had been drinking at the Drunken Duck like usual, but after getting suitably merry, they decided on an impromptu night out in Birmingham. He'd persuaded Ben to come along and was surprised but happy when he did. They'd taken the train and quickly made their way to the Village, where they did a pub crawl and ended up at a bar near the canal. He was buzzed from alcohol and was at the point where he couldn't stop smiling and everything was funny or overly sentimental.

Jamie and Liam were hanging off each other, Markus had bailed a few pubs earlier, and that left him alone with Ben—or as alone as he could be in a heaving gay bar. Men brushed against them, and so many cute guys hit on Ben, but he didn't have a clue. It made Dane feel warm and gooey inside, even though he knew it was because Ben wasn't gay, not because he liked Dane more.

Jamie laughed uncontrollably at something Liam whispered in his ear. Dane rolled his eyes at their sugary sweetness and forced his way to the bar to get another drink for him and Ben. By the time he got back, Jamie and Liam were kissing and Ben stood to the side actively not watching them but obviously not knowing where to keep his eyes trained.

"Here." He handed the neon-blue shot to Ben, who looked at it with a raised eyebrow. "I don't know what it is. It was on offer. Just knock it back." Dane took his own advice and threw the shot back, enjoying the burn as it coated his throat.

"That is vile." Ben abandoned the shot glass on a small table and grimaced.

"You're right. If they're going to suck each other's face off, they should have stayed home." Dane winked at Ben, then shoved Liam's shoulder, forcing the couple to veer sideways, purposely taking Ben's words the wrong way.

"Hey," Liam said with a pout, his arms still around Jamie.

"No one wants to watch you snog each other's face off."

Liam looked around the bar with a smirk. "I don't know about that...." He looked towards the small dance floor in the corner of the room. "I think lots of people would like to see us get it on. Come on." He dragged Jamie to the dance floor, and they giggled and pawed at each other as they danced.

Ben bumped against Dane as people squeezed by, and Dane felt his skin sizzle with heat when Ben's hand brushed against the small of his back. He wanted to lean into the touch, but he forced himself to stay relaxed and looked into the crowd as though he were looking for a guy to hook up with, but there was no way he'd do that with Ben there.

The music got louder, and they had to stand even closer to talk. He tried not to let it get to him, but it was difficult not to. His cock stirred in his jeans, and he didn't even notice Liam coming back a while later with drinks in his hands. "I had to kill a man to get these." It was an in joke, but it never got old.

Dane raised his eyebrow and peered over Liam's shoulder. "Hopefully you didn't kill Jamie, darling."

Jamie appeared behind him then and pressed a kiss to Liam's cheek as he handed him a pint of lager. "Definitely not me. Just three large bears and one twink." Dane tipped his head back and laughed, and his eyes landed on Ben who had smiled but started to look a little uncomfortable. He sometimes forgot that Ben was new to all this, even if he didn't forget that Ben was straight.

"So, does anybody know of a flat or a room going anywhere?" Ben asked, and Dane blinked, realising he'd switched off and missed some of the conversation.

"What? Are you thinking of moving?" Dane frowned and took a sip of his beer. He knew that Ben house shared, but he'd always seemed happy where he was.

"Not voluntarily. My new housemate reported me to the landlord, and they want me to get rid of Chase or leave." Ben shrugged his shoulder and took a gulp of lager. "I was going to start looking for my own place anyway. House sharing was only meant to be while I got settled in to my new job, and I've been here a few years now. I got lazy."

"And you've not found anything yet?"

"Not anywhere decent that will take pets. Apparently I can't get away with calling Chase a 'small caged animal.'"

Dane rolled his eyes. "That's ridiculous. Most people have got pets now."

"I know, but a ferret is a little too strange for most landlords. I don't suppose you'd take Chase in until I find a new place?" He looked at Dane as he worried his bottom lip with his teeth. Dane's cock twitched at the sight, and he had to force himself not to get hard and make a fool of himself.

An idea came to him, and he was drunk enough not to let the obvious flaws in his plan get in his way—flaws like his feelings for Ben and what it could do to their friendship. "Don't be silly, darling. You can both come to mine. I have a spare bedroom, and I don't mind having Chase there. Can't see Chase's daddy on the streets, now can I?" Ben shook his head and started to protest, but Dane leaned over, placed a hand on his firm arm, and gave him his most serious look. "I honestly don't mind. I spend most of my time either at the surgery or at the pub anyway." Dane nodded towards Jamie and Liam who were looking back with interest.

"I don't know…."

It suddenly seemed especially important to help Ben out and have him in his house. He could imagine lazing around the living room, watching shit TV, and taking Speedy G and Chase for walks over the Lockwood Hills. Perhaps seeing Ben leave his dirty towel in the bathroom and unwashed plates in the sink would break him of his stupid feelings.

"It'll be fun. Like uni all over again." He pushed away the horrible thought of how he'd pined after Jamie all through uni. This would be so much worse because Ben was so much more awesome than Jamie. But he could deal. He was used to being The Friend.

"All right… but I'll ask again tomorrow, when we've all not had quite as much to drink."

"Fine, but the answer will be the same." Dane pointed his glass at Ben, then took a drink and swallowed his smile. He was just helping out a friend in need. It didn't mean anything more than that.

# Chapter Twelve

*Dane*

BEN *HAD* asked again, and he was moving in. Dane was low-key freaking out. It was official; he was crazy. It was the worst idea he'd ever had, but he wanted it. More than. When Ben had awkwardly asked again the next morning, he didn't have the heart to say no and he didn't want to.

Who could say no to those eyes?

"You're taking in a lodger?" Martin frowned at him as they set the kitchen table for Sunday lunch. Their dad was busy taking food out of the oven and plating up.

"I'm just helping out a mate," Dane said as he gave Martin his most earnest look. He really was helping out a mate. His feelings didn't matter in the slightest.

"Letting someone you barely know move into your house is more than helping a friend. I hope you're not doing anything stupid. You promised me you weren't going to do anything stupid again, remember?" Martin pointed a fork at him.

"No, I promised not to date your friends—completely different," Dane shot him a smug look as he sat down.

Martin sighed and rolled his eyes. "You're going to regret this."

He probably would, but he wasn't going to tell his brother that. "It'll only be for a few weeks. Two, three months tops."

Martin thought he was insane, and Dane couldn't blame him for thinking things would go wrong, but Dane couldn't stop the rollercoaster he'd started, and despite knowing it could end badly, he didn't want to tell Ben he couldn't move in.

"You're too much like your mother," their dad said as he put huge plates of Sunday roast in front of him. He never usually talked about their mom, so both Dane and Martin stared at him, eyes wide and mouths dropped open.

He didn't look at them while he fetched his own plate and sat between them at the old scarred square table. They'd both done their homework on it and scratched their names into it over the years. He pulled his chair in until he was flush to the table, grabbed his cutlery, and turned his plate so it was in the perfect position. Then he looked up at Dane. "You want things you can't have or shouldn't have. Nothing wrong with that sometimes, but it gets downright depressing if you go from can't to shouldn't and back again, year after year." He looked down at his plate and started to eat, the conversation over. Dane wouldn't know how to reply to that anyway. Was that really why he couldn't find anyone to be happy with? Because he was like his mother?

They ate their dinner in unusual silence, the mention of their mother playing on all of their minds. They never mentioned her again for the rest of the night, but Dane was glad to leave and head to Jamie and Liam's house for a relaxing jamming session. He was just a friend helping another friend. That's all it was, just two mates sharing a house. Nothing at all wrong with that.

It would be so much simpler if he and Sean had feelings for each other. If there was even a hint of a spark between them. But there was nothing. If only he felt for Sean the way he felt for Ben, it would make everything easier all around. Much to Laura's delight, he and Sean had been out a few times. He was sweet and fun and didn't make his insides melt in the slightest. Sean was nursing a broken heart of his own and didn't want anything beyond friendship, and Dane had only agreed to go out with him to convince himself that having Ben live under the same roof wouldn't be an issue.

If there was any heart to break in their relationship, it was going to be Laura's. She was overly excited that they'd gone out on what she called a date. He didn't have the heart to explain, and Sean didn't want to in case she tried to find someone else to set him up with.

He relaxed as soon as he reached Jamie and Liam's house, happy to be away from his dad and his unsettling words. His mother had left them all when he was five years old, and he barely had memories of her, though he remembered longing for her to come back and crying himself to sleep at night for months waiting. They'd had visits for a while, but a few years later they petered off to nothing, and quietly they got on with their lives without her.

His dad never remarried, and he and Martin learned not to mention their mother, not even when all of her photographs were taken down and any knickknacks that belonged to her found their way to the trash. They hadn't needed her in the end. He wasn't sure he liked being told that he was like her.

Dane lounged in Jamie and Liam's living room, catching up and playing a bit of ukulele in an attempt to forget what was said at the family dinner, but not even music would take it away. They were rusty as they played, and Dane's fingers were stiff as he practised chords and tried to remember lyrics. They'd all been so busy lately they'd barely seen each other outside of their usual night out at the pub. Having a few drinks out was fun, but it wasn't the same as a proper natter over a cup of tea at Jamie's. Almost like old times, though Liam hadn't been there back then. No, Jamie had been with Paul, but even he had been absent a lot of the time.

Not much had changed since Liam moved in with Jamie. There were more books, more Marvel figures, and Liam's lone shoe was by the back door. Dane knew there was a story behind it, but he was sure he didn't want to know what it was. Jamie and Liam complemented each other.

Jamie was trying to play the ukulele, but the rat on his shoulder kept climbing down his arm to chew on the wood, so he wasn't getting very far. At least they were both playing badly.

Liam laughed and sauntered over to him, picked the rat up and let her run up his shoulders and hide in his hair. "She loves playing music with her daddy," he said in a baby voice. When Jamie sent him a goofy smile, Dane had to swallow the lump of jealousy in his throat.

Maybe his dad meant he needed to stop trying to find love in the wrong places? It was easier said than done. An image of Ben flashed in front of his eyes, and he groaned silently.

"Penny for your thoughts?" Jamie asked and made him jump.

"Huh? Oh, just thinking about what my dad said today." He gave a light smile and shrugged it off as if it weren't a big deal.

"You're talking to Martin again now, then?"

Dane nodded and licked his lips, mouth suddenly dry. "Dad said I was like my mother, always wanting things I shouldn't have." Dane didn't mention Ben; Jamie and Liam did *not* need to know about his crush.

Jamie frowned. "That's a bit of a shock, plus not entirely true. You already had Patrick. Not your fault he was a cheater." Ahh, poor delusional Jamie. He had no clue about how Dane used to feel for him or how he felt for Ben. Best to keep it that way.

Dane gave his trademark smirk-smile and strummed his uke. "Exactly darling, exactly."

# Chapter Thirteen

*Ben*

BEN STACKED boxes against the wall in Dane's spare room. It was bright and airy with a futon, a desk, and a wardrobe that held some of Dane's younger brother's clothes from his previous visits. He felt weird encroaching on Dane's space and taking the room his family usually used when they visited, but Dane had insisted it was fine and Ben was running out of options.

The room wasn't big enough for Chase's cage, so Dane suggested they keep it in the living room where they'd both be able to keep an eye on him and had swiftly moved furniture around to make it happen. Ben insisted Dane not go to any special trouble, but once he had an idea, nothing could stop him.

"This is the last. Where do you want this?" Dane asked as he lifted Ben's suitcase of clothes up the stairs and wheeled it into the bedroom.

Ben shrugged. "Leave it anywhere. I'll sort it all out later." Despite not thinking he had many belongings, he'd still amassed quite a few boxes more than he'd left Devon with. He supposed once he was settled, he'd have to go home and collect the rest of his stuff now that he knew his move was permanent. "We should put Chase's cage together first," Ben said. It was a brilliant, sturdy cage, but almost impossible to put together without help. Dane had helped put it together the first time, so they were a dab at dismantling and reassembling it.

They went back downstairs, and Ben checked on Chase in his carrier. He was curled up in a fleece blanket and only his two back feet were showing. Ben itched to tickle those toe beans, but he didn't want to wake him up when they couldn't let him explore just yet.

"Let's do this, darling," Dane said as he lifted the box with the cage in it, straining his arms. He was stronger than he looked, but Ben supposed a vet who worked with large animals on a regular basis would have to be.

Ben went to help and pulled out the metal cage pieces while Dane held on to the cardboard. They put everything in neat piles on the floor and between them managed to get the cage built just in time for Chase to wake up and start squirming about in his carrier.

"Hey boy," Ben said as he lifted him out. Chase gave a large yawn and stretched out his small body. "Did you have a good sleep?" The ferret licked his lips and blinked at him.

"Food, water, and blankets are all ready," Dane said as he walked over to them so he could scratch behind Chase's ears. Chase leaned into the touch and twisted around in the way only ferrets could, and launched himself at Dane. He laughed, picked him up, and gave him a large kiss on the top of his head.

Ben tried not to laugh, but it was too cute not to. They made a sweet pair. He couldn't stop the warmth that spread through his body as Dane talked to the ferret. It felt right to be there with him. He was so easy to be friends with that he didn't feel the usual nerves of invading someone's space.

Speedy sniffed at Dane's feet, and he knelt and showed Chase to the dog. He was so well behaved after years of going to and from the veterinary clinic that he didn't even bat an eyelid when Chase leaned over and nibbled at his ear.

"That's a good boy, Speedy. Chase, this is your new brother. You have to be nice to him," Dane carried on talking, and Ben's stomach fluttered at his words. He didn't know why Dane calling Speedy and Chase brothers touched him so much, but it did.

Eventually Speedy got bored and wandered off. Dane stood up again and patted Chase's head. "Come on you rascal. Let's get you settled." He put him in the cage, and he plodded along, sniffed at his kibble, then stuck his head in the water bowl and used his front paws to splash the water out.

"Chase," Ben said, laughter bubbling as both he and Dane got soaked. "I'm so sorry. Bad boy. You should be on your best behaviour." Dane was laughing too, so Ben wasn't worried about the mess.

"You're telling us off, aren't you?" Dane spoke with warmth and affection when he talked to the animals. Not that he didn't speak to his friends with affection, but there was something softer, less guarded when he was with Chase. Ben guessed that was one reason he became a vet.

Chase lifted his head, licked his lips, then sneezed and made them both laugh again. He shot them a disgusted look, walked over to his box full of blankets, and nestled down onto them until all they could see was the top of his tail.

BEN AND Dane fell into an easy routine. If Ben was up first, he'd feed and let Speedy out into the garden. If Dane was up first, he'd put the kettle on. Ben worried about invading Dane's privacy, so tried to keep to his room as much as he was able with Chase's cage in the living room. Dane put a stop to that straightaway.

For the first time in… he didn't know how long, Ben felt relaxed and comfortable in his own skin, which in turn made him comfortable around Dane. He wasn't sure if he was just coming out of his shell, or if Dane and the guys were just easy to be around. Perhaps a bit of both. Hell, maybe it was Chase that made the difference. Either way, Ben felt happier than he'd felt before.

Which unnerved him. He hadn't expected it. He pushed the unease away and opened Chase's cage. "Come on, you. Do you want to explore?" He gave a big yawn, blinked his eyes open, and was out the cage and in Ben's lap like a shot. He laughed, turned him over, and tickled his belly until he wiggled and tried to catch his fingers. Silly ferret.

Once they finished playing, Ben put a harness on him… or tried to. First Chase twisted around so much he got the lead tangled around his hands. Then, once he got it on him, he hadn't tightened it enough, and Chase squeezed out of it in a matter of seconds.

"Don't be naughty, Chase. Don't you want to go outside?" He adjusted the harness to make it a little snugger, then attempted to wrestle the ferret into it again. Finally it was secured, but Chase plodded around the living room, throwing himself on the floor and rolling around in an attempt to get it off. Ben laughed, picked him up, and scritched him behind the ear.

"We're just going to go into the garden. I think you'll like it." He wrapped the end of the lead around his wrist and carried Chase outside.

Dane's garden had a patio where they'd had many barbeques and get-togethers. The rest of the garden was mostly lawn with a border of wildflowers that Dane admitted he'd just thrown down for the wildlife and then let them do what they wanted. Ben liked the look. There were pretty flowers and grasses perfect for bees, and there was a large butterfly tree at the bottom of the garden.

Ben put Chase down, and after a few temper tantrums, he became sidetracked and started to sniff the dirt, stick his nose into the flowers, and rub his belly on the grass. Ben let him set the pace and pottered behind him holding the lead while Chase explored.

He found a small pile of dead leaves and launched himself at them, doing a dance Ben had recently discovered was called the ferret war dance. Ben laughed at him, and Chase stopped what he was doing, still lying on his back to listen. He bent down to tickle him, and Chase started to wriggle again, then jumped around and got them both caught in his lead.

"See? I told you the harness would be a good thing, didn't I?" He carried him back inside and wiped his feet on the mat at the back door. Then he unhooked Chase and let him play under the kitchen table and stash all of Speedy's balls. When Ben went to pour himself a glass of water while he supervised Chase, he saw a green lunch box with a sloth on the front sitting on the work surface. He picked it up, thinking it could be Dane's empty box from yesterday, but there was something in it, though it felt too light to be a sandwich. He opened the box just in case it was rubbish from the day before, and he laughed at the contents—a Mug Shot, a sugar-free jelly pot, a packet of Hula Hoops, and a Snickers. Not exactly the kind of lunch to keep hunger at bay through a busy day.

Ben glanced at the clock. It was half an hour before Dane usually took lunch, if he didn't work through it. Ben had plenty of time to nip his lunch into the practice. Without thinking too much about why he was doing it, he opened the cupboard Dane had given him for his own food, pulled out a loaf of bread, and quickly made him a ham sandwich.

Dane's own cupboards were practically bare, and he'd admitted on several occasions that he kept Mug Shots, microwavable rice, and tinned food in because he was always too tired to make dinner let alone lunch for the next day, and fresh food tended to go off. His idea of lunch was shoving something that needed no preparation into a cute lunch box. Ben tutted and smiled as he folded the sandwich in a cling film and added an apple.

For someone who cared so much about making sure animals were healthy, he didn't apply the same passion to himself. Speedy G had the best organic food and treats, while Dane lived on the soup equivalent of a pot noodle.

Newly packed food ready, Ben called for Chase so he could put him back in his cage before he left the house. The ferret ignored him, and Ben had to crawl on his hands and knees under the table to catch him.

"You are a devil, did you know that?" Chase playfully bit at his hand, not breaking the skin once, and Ben tucked him under one arm, picked up the lunch box, and went to put Chase back.

After only a minor kerfuffle where he put Dane's lunch in the cage and started to carry Chase out to his car, he was ready to go. It wasn't much of a drive, and it wasn't like he had better things to do on a Saturday afternoon.

He didn't see Dane when he reached the surgery just before 1:00 p.m., but he didn't expect to. One of the receptionists was there—an older lady he thought was called Lauren or Laura. She smiled when she saw him, and he smiled back as he walked up to the counter.

"Is Dane free?" He placed Dane's lunch on the counter between them.

Laura's smile drooped slightly, and she looked at him with suspicion. "He's still with a patient. Can I take a message?" Ben shifted uncomfortably, and his gaze flickered to the door behind her and back again. He had a nasty suspicion that he was being given the cold shoulder, and he wasn't sure why.

"Yeah, sure. He er, left his lunch today. Just thought I'd bring it for him." Her lips curled up and she looked him up and down like he was a piece of dog shit on her shoe. He was having second thoughts about turning up out of the blue. Did it make Dane look unprofessional?

She reached over to pull the box away from him just as the back door opened. Ben sighed in relief when Dane stepped out. His eyes widened when he saw Ben, but then he smiled widely and sauntered over.

Ben's heart started to race, and he didn't understand why. "Darling." Dane leaned over the counter to place a kiss on his cheek, and Ben's cheek tingled where his lips had been, and his face started to burn. He'd automatically leaned down so Dane could reach him properly. Laura's mouth was pursed, and she was adamantly not looking at either of them.

"What are you doing here?" He sounded much happier to see him than Laura had.

Ben pulled Dane's lunch back from Laura. "You forgot your lunch."

Dane gasped, grabbed it, and hugged it to his chest. "You're a lifesaver. I hadn't even realised. My hero."

Ben rolled his eyes and bit back a grin. "Didn't want you to go hungry."

"You're a legend. No way would I have time to nip to the shops. We're already behind." Ben noticed how full the waiting room was then and how they were getting a lot of stares. He felt his face heat up again.

Dane shook his lunch box with a slight frown. "It feels too heavy." He opened one corner and noticed the extras. His eyes shot back to Ben, and his smile widened. "You made me lunch."

He shrugged awkwardly, half feeling warmth that Dane was touched, half hating the scrutiny. "Thank you, darling." Dane reached up for a quick hug, and Ben's heart did a little flip.

The door opened behind them, and Ben flinched as a few dogs started to bark. A guy a few years younger than them walked in and leaned over to kiss Laura on the cheek. She beamed at him, and the daggers she'd been giving Ben disappeared.

"Aunty L," the guy said as he pulled back.

"This is a surprise, Sean. Look who's here, Dane. You remember Sean, don't you?" Laura said in a way that made Ben think there was no surprise at all. She practically leaned over the desk to push her nephew in their direction. He was a good sport about it and rolled his eyes at her, but he stepped towards them with a smile that was all for Dane.

Ben's breath caught in his throat as he watched. Had they slept together? Ben was sure Sean's gaze lingered on Dane's body, and Dane's smile spoke of a familiarity that made Ben's stomach twist painfully. The comfort of being with Dane disappeared the longer Sean stood there. Ben looked at the door. He should go, but he didn't know what to say so he didn't look rude.

"What are you doing here?" Dane said to Sean. His voice sounded tense to Ben, but Dane was smiling, so he didn't know what to think.

"Aunty L said your lunchtime was around now. I thought I'd see if you wanted to go out for a quick bite."

Laura's animosity towards him started to become clearer as she avidly watched the two men. It was obvious she was trying to set Dane up, and it didn't sit well with Ben. He didn't understand why, but the thought of Sean and Dane together made him feel sick. It had nothing to do with them being gay, so he didn't get why he was feeling that way.

"I'm sorry darling, I really don't have time. It looks like I'll be working through lunch again." Ben let out a breath he didn't know he'd been holding, and when Dane placed a hand on Ben's arm, he jumped under the touch. "Ben here has been a lifesaver and brought my lunch, but I need to get back to it. This is my incredibly good friend, and now housemate, Ben. Ben, this is Laura's nephew, Sean."

Ben reluctantly stepped forward and shook his hand. They said quick hellos, and Ben gave what he hoped was a decent smile. "Well, I should leave you to it," Ben said, though he didn't want to leave before Sean.

"Nice to meet you, Sean. See you at home, Dane." He didn't know why he added that last bit, but the surprise that crossed Sean's and Laura's faces before he turned around was worth it.

"I'll bring back a Chinese, darling. Ta-ra a bit," Dane called after him, and Ben relaxed when he realised that meant Dane would be coming home and not going anywhere with Sean.

# Chapter Fourteen

*Ben*

BEN HAD been living with Dane for a few weeks, and he hadn't seen Sean again. Dane hadn't brought him back to the house, and Ben had avoided the practice. He was glad. Sean brought back every insecurity he had, but there was jealousy mixed in with it. He didn't understand. Imagining Dane with someone set his teeth on edge.

It had taken him a while to relax again, and he was hyper aware of Dane and the graceful way he moved.

Ben was watching *Hollyoaks* on the sofa, and Chase was curled up in a blanket on the other side when Dane came down, hair wet and face flushed from the shower. He went to sit where Chase was hidden, and Ben had just enough time to grab and pull him over before his butt hit the blanket.

Dane flung his arms out, yelped, and landed half on Ben's lap. Then he pushed himself up with one hand on Ben's chest.

"Sorry, Chase is under that blanket," Ben said.

"Jesus." He gave a breathless laugh, his fingers curling in Ben's T-shirt. Ben's pulse sped up, and his cock started to harden. That was new.

"You gave me a heart attack." Dane slid sideways, and Ben's hand dislodged and slid onto the sofa next to him. He shivered as Dane's hand slid down the front of Ben's chest as he righted himself. Dane was so close Ben could tell he'd used his shower gel.

His stomach somersaulted as though he were on a rollercoaster. It didn't make any sense; it was just shower gel, part of some cheap set his parents had given him for Christmas the year before.

The kerfuffle woke Chase up, and the blanket started to move until his nose poked out of one of the folds. "I almost squished you," Dane said as he reached over and patted his head. Upon realising Dane was home, Chase wriggled completely out of the blanket, pounced on Dane's lap, and grabbed at his hand until Dane gave in and tickled his belly.

Ben watched Chase nip at Dane's fingers, and even though he was excited as he grabbed on to Dane's fingers, he didn't break the skin with his sharp teeth. As quickly as he'd been chasing Dane's hand, he jumped and hopped-slid down Dane's legs until he was on the carpet. Then he danced around their feet like it was the best game in the world. Ben forgot that *Hollyoaks* was on the TV and watched Chase as he pounced on Dane's left foot and bit at the hem of his jeans as though he were a tiger with its prey. They both laughed, and Ben couldn't resist reaching down to tickle his back to catch him by surprise.

He leaped backwards and jumped in the air, his spine like water as he played. Ben could never get tired of watching a ferret play. Dane was so good with him, not that it was a surprise. He'd grown up on a farm, and he was a vet. He was bound to be good with animals, but there was just something so sweet with how they played together. And Chase loved all the attention. He even tried to play with Speedy, but Speedy wasn't so sure and usually jumped onto the armchair that Chase couldn't climb and just watched him with a bemused expression.

"You're such a fierce, fierce ferret," Dane said so sweetly that Ben couldn't stop the burst of laughter that left his lips. His heart warmed as he watched them play, and before he knew it, he was watching Dane as he scooped up a very tired ferret and held him in his arms like a baby. They grinned over his head, and Ben's cheeks started to ache.

BIRMINGHAM PRIDE came around fast, and it was strangely intimate getting ready with a bunch of guys. A large laugh made him jump, and he rolled his eyes towards his bedroom door.

Maybe intimate was the wrong word. He wasn't quite sure why getting ready to go to a parade was such a big deal. Jamie and Liam were downstairs, using copious amounts of hairspray to tame Jamie's curls. He didn't have the heart to tell them that not even using a full bottle would help.

Apparently getting ready for Pride was a tradition Dane and Jamie had started back when they were at university and they made the trip to London for their first ever Pride.

Ben sat on his bed and stared intently at his wardrobe, not because he didn't know what to wear—he'd already dressed—he just didn't understand why it was a Big Deal, so he was pretending to take much more time over it than he needed.

Despite not really understanding the reason they all wanted to listen to loud music and get ready in the same house, he was having fun. Listening to the noise and the fast beat of some generic dance track felt like friendship.

When his door burst open, he gasped and clutched at his heart. "Jesus Christ. Don't you knock? I could have been naked!"

Liam swung from the door frame and cackled as he looked Ben up and down with a mock leer. "I could be so lucky. Is that what you're wearing?"

Ben frowned and looked down at his comfortable jeans and his plain red cotton T-shirt. It was going to be a busy day, and he wanted to be comfortable.

"Yes, why? What's wrong with what I'm wearing?"

"Not nearly enough glam, darling," Dane said as he peered around the open door, a can of what Ben thought was hairspray in his hand.

Before Ben could get offended or feel awkward about his friends not thinking he was good enough, Dane pointed the can at him and pressed the knob. A cloud of shimmering glitter exploded in front of him. It covered his face, hair, arms, and clothes. He was fairly sure the insides of his lungs were sparkling too.

"You bastards!" he said lunging up and trying to grapple with Dane for control of the body shimmer.

"No, it's mine. You can't have it." Dane laughed as he bent over and tried to hide the can up the front of his T-shirt.

Dane might be strong from lifting dogs and trimming rabbits' teeth all day, but Ben was taller and he chopped down trees, dammit. There was no way a sneaky vet was going to get the better of him.

Unfortunately, Dane was like a greased ferret. He knew just how to bend and twist to keep the spray out of his grasp.

But Ben was not above playing dirty. He poked a finger in Dane's ribs and was pleased when he heard a shriek and Dane bowed backwards. He didn't have quite enough confidence to reach up under the T-shirt to grab the can, but he managed to push down on the top of the bottle through the fabric and spray Dane's stomach and the inside of his sleeveless shirt.

Dane gave another shriek and let go. When the spray dropped between them, Liam, who had been cackling behind them, picked it up and sprayed them both until they glimmered like diamonds.

"Now you're suitably dressed." Liam paced in front of them, nodding his head as if he were some kind of sergeant major, though he was covered in even more glitter than they were, and Ben could do nothing to hold in his laugh.

Dane's light brown hair shimmered with glitter, and there were wet patches on his T-shirt from where Ben had gotten him with the spray under his shirt.

Dane held the bottom of his T-shirt and shook it. "I look like someone's spunked on me."

Ben laughed, despite being a little shocked. The thought hadn't even crossed his mind, but the words made his dick twitch with interest.

"Sorry," he said. He held in a breath and let the air out of his lungs slowly, hoping it would calm him down and no one would be able to tell his dick was half hard. This had never happened to him before. Even when he was a teenager.

"You don't sound it." Dane didn't sound particularly mad, and they both grinned as they followed Liam down the stairs and out of the front door.

# Chapter Fifteen

*Ben*

BIRMINGHAM'S FLOOZIE in the Jacuzzi wore a rainbow bikini, and the waves of her hair had been coloured to match. The ornate statue sat in the centre of a large man-made pond at the top of Victoria Square, intercepting the stone steps in front of the town hall. Water cascaded down the centre of the steps into a smaller pool at the bottom where children ran and splashed each other.

It was the first time Ben had seen the fountain full of water. After one leak too many and to conserve energy, they only filled it on special occasions. He looked around at all the people congregating around him. Birmingham Pride was a special occasion.

People crammed together all along New Street and spread up around Victoria Square, waiting for the parade, the official start to Pride. They'd lucked out with the weather, and the sun beat down on them, turning Ben's skin brown. He was from fishermen stock; he didn't burn, he just tanned. Sweat trickled down Ben's back, and he pulled at the hem of his T-shirt to let some air circulate.

He looked longingly at Dane's rainbow sleeveless T-shirt, so baggy that Ben caught glimpses of his bare flesh through the armholes and wished he'd worn something lighter. He told himself he was only staring at Dane due to envy, but that didn't explain why his skin prickled with awareness or why he sought out the glimpses of bare chest as the baggy fabric billowed when he walked.

Ben's heart raced, and he wondered what Dane would look like without the shirt. Would he have chest hair, or would he be smooth? He breathed in and swallowed to get himself under control. Dane was his friend. He was a man, and he was probably the closest friend he'd ever had. That's all there was to it.

His cock was only taking interest because of the buzzing energy around him—men and women celebrating as they waited for the parade to start.

Parents carried babies, and children ran around, shrieking in excitement. The atmosphere was one of inclusion, and even Ben felt part of it.

Dane turned to smile at him, he caught him looking.

"It's bloody hot." He felt the need to explain why he'd been staring so intently at Dane, but his cheeks started to flush. He'd never wondered what anyone would look like naked, no one real anyway. The guy who used to be in *Hollyoaks* didn't count.

Dane nodded in agreement. "You should have been here two years ago. It pissed down all day. We got soaked. Even my boxers were wet."

Ben's stomach lurched as he thought of Dane sopping wet down to his underwear. The erection he'd been trying to stave off came back, and he was glad there were so many people packed in that no one was looking at his groin. Why was this happening now? It was so awkward.

"I shouldn't moan about this heat, then." He wished he'd worn sunglasses like Liam.

"You're from Devon, aren't you? Aren't you a surfer dude? Used to baking heat and frigid waters in the blink of an eye?" Dane said.

Ben snorted. "I'm all right on a boat, not so much a surfboard. Some of my mates are pretty good at it, though." They followed the crowds, dodging in and out of people, trying to follow Jamie and Liam who were just ahead of them, hands loosely clasped, heads dipped towards each other as they talked gently.

The atmosphere soaked into his skin, and for the first time in weeks, he felt like he could breathe. It was hard to be sad with so much positivity around, and he truly felt like he belonged. He'd never had friends like Dane; even Jamie and Liam were better friends than most he had back home.

He tried not to look around with open curiosity, but he couldn't help it. He'd never seen so many people so comfortable with who they were and who they loved. It was eye-opening and inspiring. His glance went to Jamie and Liam's hands again, seeing how their fingers entwined so easily. It was nice to see them so affectionate with each other. Not that they weren't usually affectionate, but there was a level of comfort today that wasn't ordinarily there.

Ben couldn't imagine holding anyone's hand like that. Even after having sex or dating, he never found open shows of affection easy. There was a level of intimacy that came with that kind of touch, and he'd never had it. More people surrounded them as they stopped to wait for the parade. Dane leaned into him, hand on his arm, making his skin tingle as he peered over the crowds and waited for the first float. Ben looked at Dane's hand and couldn't understand the butterflies that fluttered in his stomach.

"The parade should start in the next twenty minutes. It's always late, though, but worth it. We'll go into the Village afterwards, watch the gig tonight and then drink our weight in beer," Dane said. Ben looked up quickly and hoped Dane hadn't noticed him looking at where his hand still touched his wrist. They walked a few more yards, following Liam and Jamie.

Liam finally found what he was looking for—his best friend Selena and her girlfriend were already standing near the barriers at the top.

"Here they are." As Liam flung his arms around them with a laugh, Dawn stole his sunglasses off his face, and Selena ran her knuckles over his head until he let out a strangled laugh and ducked away from them.

"You're such a punk," Selena said affectionately as she turned around to greet them all.

"Hello, darlings." Dane gave them each a kiss on the cheek, and Ben was happy just to smile and say hello, but both Selena and Dawn swept him into tight hugs that made him laugh.

"Did a vampire throw up on you or something? What's with all the glitter?" Selena said, trying to brush it off her arms.

"I don't think that's vomit, Selena—*think* about it." Dawn smirked at her girlfriend and winked, and Selena groaned and shook her head.

"You're such a dork. That joke is at least a hundred years out of date." Liam stuck his tongue out at them.

Ben didn't understand the joke but was happy to listen as they squabbled like siblings. Liam's one arm was slung over Selena's shoulder while she was talking to him, and his other hand was in Jamie's.

Ben envied how relaxed Liam was. He didn't worry about what others thought. Under all the glitter, he was wearing a rainbow-striped T-shirt like Dane's, but it had his favourite singer on the front. The singer was sitting on a ratty old sofa, in typical man pose, legs splayed out, arm stretched over the back, scuffed Doc Martens on his feet, but wearing a black dress that rode up at his thighs. The front of the dress, obviously made for someone bustier than him, billowed open to show a smooth pale flat chest. Liam was so utterly comfortable in his own skin.

He was the exact opposite of Ben. Whereas Liam was carefree and didn't worry what people thought of him, all Ben did was worry. Jamie leaned across Dane and spoke loudly over the hum of the crowd. "Is Donna going to meet us later?"

Ben stopped short; he hadn't even thought of asking her. Did that make him a bad friend? He'd ask her later. He found he could say things to her he'd worry about admitting to anyone else. "I never thought of asking her. I mean we all booked the tickets together ages ago."

Jamie frowned, then shrugged. "I just presumed. I mean, you're a couple now, aren't you?"

Ben didn't want to have this conversation. "We're just friends. She's a hoot." He should have thought to ask her. She'd probably enjoy something like this. Dane snorted loudly in his ear and leaned over to give Jamie an affectionate shove.

"Just because you're all loved up doesn't mean everyone else has to be," Dane said with a roll of his eyes and a carefree laugh. Although Dane's words were light, there was pain in his eyes as they settled on him.

Jamie shrugged, and then Liam pulled on his shoulder and pointed over the crowd. "It's starting." Liam bounced on the balls of his feet, straining to see over people's heads to the bottom of the street. The music slowly got louder as the parade got closer, and the murmur of the excited crowd turned up a notch with anticipation as people strained to get their first glimpse.

There were dancers and groups, people holding banners and giving out sweets, all dressed in elaborate clothing or hardly any clothing, as was the case with a group of muscular guys wearing nothing but body paint and tight swimming trunks. Ben had no idea what they were advertising, but lots of the spectators let out some very loud catcalls.

The first float was a *Wizard of Oz* theme. "Over the Rainbow" was playing and a drag queen, wearing a very grown-up Dorothy dress and sparkly red stiletto heels, lip-synced along. People walked alongside the floats with charity buckets.

Behind one float, a group of people carried a large black, grey, white, and purple flag, and the few who weren't carrying the flag handed out fliers and stickers. A man wearing a purple and grey shirt spotted Selena over the barrier and broke formation to give her a tight hug and shove some fliers into her hand before he winked and walked on.

She passed the fliers around and one made its way back to him as people at the front grabbed them and handed them back. He shoved it in his back pocket and carried on watching. Liam snatched the stickers from her, peeled one off, and stuck it to Jamie's shirt. Jamie just rolled his eyes at him.

The parade was bright, loud, and fun. People were packed closely together, but there was no pushing or shoving, and even the police had smiles on their faces as they made sure everyone was safe.

When the last float waved at them, everyone meandered towards the Village to carry on the celebration.

# Chapter Sixteen

*Dane*

Birmingham's Gay Village was heaving by the time they followed the parade to the end. There were fairground rides, market stalls, and a large stage set up for the evening show. The statue of a rhino made from rhinestones sparkled in the blazing sun above one of the buildings. Dane leaned into Ben and pointed towards it.

"That is more sparkle than what we're wearing," Ben said as he squinted up at it. Dane laughed and agreed.

He'd naturally paired up with Ben, and though they weren't holding hands, they were walking so close their hands brushed with each step. Electricity shot up his arm with each unintentional touch. Dane was sure that men who walked by presumed they were a couple. Any other time that would annoy him—he didn't want potential fucks to think he was taken—but this time, because it was Ben, it warmed him inside out.

"Who's playing on the main stage?" Ben asked as they slowly followed behind the end of the parade. It didn't surprise him that Ben didn't know what bands were playing; he'd been dragged along with them. Not that he didn't want to go, but he probably wouldn't have gone without their gentle prodding.

Dane snorted and nodded towards Liam, who was practically vibrating with energy. "Can't you guess? Liam's favourite singer, Phase. He's a gender-fluid pianist."

Ben nodded. "The singer who originally sang the song Jamie played on the ukulele?"

"That's the one." Jamie and Liam had gone through a rocky patch the year before, but it ended with Jamie serenading Liam through YouTube with a slow cover of one of his favourite songs.

"No wonder he's bouncing like a puppy." They'd reached the Village and continued to follow Jamie and Liam as they walked from stall to stall collecting promotional material from different groups and charities. Liam stopped at each one to talk and to pick up free pens and stickers. Ben wasn't entirely sure why the freebies excited him so much, but they would not run out of pens in the Jamie/Liam household.

Dane went to walk around a group of people and bumped into a familiar face. Markus's eyes widened and he looked a little awkward as he held on to the small legs wiggling over his shoulder.

"Dane, Dane!" the owner of those little legs shouted, and Dane made an effort to shut his mouth and smile.

"Hi, Arthur." Dane looked next to Markus and wasn't surprised to see Cal, Arthur's dad and Dane's next-door neighbour. What did surprise him was seeing Markus with them. What was even more interesting was seeing Arthur so at ease with him, almost like they'd spent a lot of time together.

Dane raised a questioning eyebrow at his friend, but Markus refused to meet his gaze.

"We're going to get sweets and ride the carousel," Arthur said, his hands tightening in Markus's hair, making him wince.

Dane bit the corner of his cheek to stop the grin from escaping. "Not in that order, I hope."

"Definitely not in that order," Cal said. "I didn't realise you would be here." Cal glanced at Markus, but he avoided his gaze too.

"Same here. If we'd known, we could have all come together."

"Arthur!" Liam called as he and Jamie spotted them. He reached up as Arthur launched himself off Markus's shoulders at him, and Dane's heart almost jumped into his mouth, but Liam caught the kid with a laugh and a spin. Cal smiled indulgently at them as though they were both kids.

"Hey, Cal, good to see you again," Liam said as he ruffled Arthur's hair.

"You too."

"Hey, Liam?" Arthur had no problem interrupting the adults and didn't seem to notice the bit of awkwardness coming from Markus. "Did you see the parade? Do you like my whistle?" He wore a pink plastic whistle on a yellow cord around his neck, and when he shoved into his mouth and blew as hard as he could, it made them all wince.

Liam just laughed again. "Wow, that was so loud I even heard it in my deaf ear."

"I made your ear better. Can I get some stickers like Jamie?" Dane couldn't keep up with what the kid was saying, but Liam had no such trouble. He pulled off the stickers he'd stuck to Jamie's T-shirt and covered Arthur's T-shirt instead.

"I figured you'd all be going drinking, and we've got Arthur with us, so…," Markus said as everyone else's attention was on the two kids of the group. Dane had never seen him so awkward, nor had he ever seen him care enough about someone to try, though he didn't understand why he didn't want his friends to know.

"Not until tonight, darling."

"Are you all going to ride the carousel with me?"

That was how they all ended up riding painted horses in a circle, laughing their heads off. He let Markus's secrecy go as Ben's quiet chuckle next to him did something to his insides. He couldn't help but stare at him, and his heart skipped a beat when Ben turned to look at him, his eyes crinkled with laughter and his hair windswept.

DANE WAS pleasantly buzzed by the time darkness fell around them and the lights of the largest stage were switched on. They were in the middle of a sea of Phase fans. Liam was so excited he wouldn't let go of Jamie's hand and eventually he'd steered them to the front. He and Ben stayed further back to watch the show, but the crowd was still teeming.

When Phase finally appeared, the fans all roared and surged forward. He stumbled, and Ben grabbed him around the waist to stop him going down and then pulled him in close to his side. He expected Ben to remove his arm, but his grip tightened.

Dane told himself it was because there were so many people crushed against them, but it didn't stop the butterflies in his stomach or the feeling of how right it was to be in his arms. He glanced sideways, but Ben was staring ahead. It gave Dane a chance to watch him. So many men had ogled him today, and as usual, he hadn't noticed one of them. He didn't realise how gorgeous he was. His firm muscled body came from working outdoors and not from a gym, and his hair was thick and unkempt. Dane's fingers itched to run through it, but he knew friends didn't do things like that. But someone from behind jostled them, and when Ben's grip tightened, he turned to look at Dane and caught him staring.

Dane felt his face heat up at being caught, but he couldn't bring himself to look away. He licked his lips and wished that Ben's lips would touch his. Ben watched his movement, and his eyes darkened. Dane held his breath and for a moment he was sure Ben would kiss him.

Then the stage lights changed from white to neon yellow and the noise of the piano broke their connection as Phase pummeled the keys and sang harshly into the microphone. Ben's head whipped back to stare ahead, and Dane slowly followed and willed his pulse to slow.

Dane sang along to a few songs he knew and cheered when everyone else cheered. Phase moved from behind the piano and grabbed the microphone as he swaggered back and forth at the front of the stage. "How are all you Brummies?" He shouted, and they all cheered back. "I'm stoked to be celebrating Pride with you all today. Is everyone having a good time?" The roar from the audience was deafening. Ben's arm tightened around him, and Dane roared louder. "I'm going to sing a love song for you all. I expect it to end on a kiss. Don't disappoint!" Phase started to sing, and nearly everyone sang along. Dane didn't know the words, but he was familiar with the tune, so he hummed.

When it ended and Phase urged them all to kiss the person they were with, Ben tensed in his arms. But as couples around them started to kiss, Ben turned to look at him. His nose was sunburned, his hair curling at the ends from sweat, and his eyes blazed with a heat that hit Dane in the stomach like a bullet. He was breathless and he hadn't moved an inch.

Ben shifted his body so they were pressed chest to chest, and it took all of Dane's willpower to angle his hips away so Ben couldn't feel how turned on he was. Then, with his free hand, Ben cupped Dane's jaw. His eyes flickered to everyone around him, and he whetted his dry lips.

Dane groaned. Didn't Ben realise how irresistible he was when he did that? And then Ben's mouth got closer to his and his breath hitched. There was no way he was going to kiss him. No way in hell. Dane was still thinking that when Ben's lips found his, and then he was sure he was dreaming.

As kisses went, it was chaste—the press of mouths, no tongue, no exploration—yet Dane was on fire. Electricity shot through his veins and his heart stopped. Cheap beer and overpriced hotdogs shouldn't taste so good, but this was *Ben*.

Phase said something else, but Dane wasn't listening. White noise roared in his ears as he drank from Ben's lips. They opened slowly and Dane shook at the thought of being inside him. Desire flooded his system and his tongue stroked against Ben's teeth. This was it.

Someone bumped into him from behind and his teeth clashed with Ben's, and they paused but didn't pull away. But then they were jarred from the side and the choice was taken from them. Dane gasped and continued to cling to Ben, scared that if he let go, Ben would disappear for good.

The crowds nudged them again, and Ben blinked and shook his head. His cheeks turned red, and he gave an awkward smile and looked back towards the stage.

Dane's lips tingled as he forced himself to watch the encore. Ben still had his arm around him, but it was tense.

When the gig ended, they found Liam and Jamie and wound their way to one of the many bars pumping out music in the Village. Dane pasted on a smile and bought them all shots, falling into the role of life and soul of the party while disappointment and worry swirled inside of him. He hoped he and Ben would be okay.

He hoped he would be able to live with Ben now that he knew how he tasted.

# Chapter Seventeen

*Ben*

DAYS HAD passed since he'd kissed Dane at Pride, and his lips still hadn't recovered. The phantom press of Dane's mouth against his was a constant presence, and it confused the hell out of him. He'd never enjoyed kissing, but there had been something different when he did it with Dane. Usually the act was hollow and kind of gross, but warmth had spread throughout his body and shock hammered in his heart as Dane's lips slid against his.

He was nervous when he finished work and let himself into Dane's house. They hadn't discussed the kiss, and they'd both pretended nothing had happened. They'd kissed in the moment, he knew that, but it was difficult to think of anything else. Every time he was near Dane, he relived that kiss and the confusion that came with it. He did his best to act normally, but he wasn't sure if he was doing a very good job. Dane seemed a little tense as well, and Ben wished he could take that kiss back so they could go back to normal.

They were all going to the Duck again, only this time Dane, Jamie, and Markus would be playing in their band, The Ratpack Rangers. It would mean that Ben could go out and socialise with everyone, but they'd be too busy on stage to chat much, which would be a relief until he could get back to normal.

He went straight into the living room to see Chase first, but Dane was already there, the ferret hanging comfortably in his hand.

"Hello, darling. I've ordered us an Indian, I hope you don't mind. If I don't eat properly, I'll pass out on the stage." He gave a wink and put Chase back as he followed Ben into the kitchen. He'd already placed the food on the dining room table, and Ben frowned. They never ate at the table when it was just the two of them.

"Thanks. You didn't have to."

"Well, there's no point in ordering just for me. Plus I figured you'd be coming to watch us make arses out of ourselves."

Ben couldn't make himself sit at the table and pretend. He pretended with so many people, and he didn't want to lose the friendship they had. "*Hollyoaks* will be on soon. Want to take this into the living room and eat there?" He held his breath as Dane stared at him, then let it out when he smiled and started to gather up the food.

"Of course, sorry. I just thought you might want more room."

Ben looked quizzically at Dane but didn't know how to reply, so he busied himself picking up the remaining containers and following Dane into the living room. They sat around the coffee table like they usually did, and Dane put the TV on low and settled down next to him. Their crossed knees brushed, the hairs on his arms stood on end, and he was hyper aware of where they were touching. Dane didn't seem to realise he was so close. He carried on eating, glancing at the TV, and chatting away.

Ben was reading too much into it and he forced himself to relax. They ended up talking about Dane coming out, and Ben expected a horrible story like he saw on TV, but Dane shook his head. "No, my dad was great. He's s a bloke's bloke, but he's under the impression that what people do in the bedroom is up to them. It was an anticlimactic coming out. I came out after high school, when I decided to go to college rather than sixth form. There were more issues when I decided I wasn't going to take over the farm—though when I said I wanted to be a vet, my dad was all over it—family discount." He rolled his eyes, but Ben could tell he was close with his dad.

He wished he was as close with his parents. On the surface, they were a tight unit. Though he hadn't phoned like the good son he was lately, and he'd ignored their calls to him. He was finding it harder and harder to keep back his frustration when they pressured him into settling down or working with his dad. Why couldn't they just enjoy each other's company? It was one of the reasons he'd moved so far away. They couldn't pressure so much if he wasn't there. "I remember you saying your younger brother is working on the farm. Are you close with him?" Ben remembered the old clothes that were in the wardrobe in his room.

Dane nodded as he ate. "We're both usually busy, so even though we're close, we don't see loads of each other. Working a farm isn't a nine-to-five job, and I've been working crazy shifts at the practice."

"Yeah, tell me about it. My dad and brother work crazy hours. They get good time off, but it's all over the place. I'd hate it. I like the routine of an ordinary job." Their backgrounds were so similar, yet Ben was suffocated by his family while Dane had stood up to his.

They were just getting ready to leave when his phone rang, and Ben frowned as Donna's name flashed up. He'd almost forgotten about her. Dane's smile dimmed, and Ben waved him on. "Go without me. I don't want you to be late meeting the guys. I'll catch up in a moment."

"Hi," he said as he answered the phone. Donna said something, but Ben was too busy watching Dane leave through the front door to pay attention. He wanted to be walking to the pub with him, but he didn't want to chat to Donna on the phone while he did it.

# Chapter Eighteen

*Dane*

THE RATPACK Rangers wasn't just about playing music. It was more of a way to relax and let off steam. They used to practice much more, learn new popular songs, and put a ukulele spin on them, but they'd all been so busy that they were a touch rusty. The crowd at the Duck didn't seem to care, luckily.

Markus was already in their booth when Dane got to the Drunken Duck, a pint of Carling in front of him. He was texting on his phone and didn't see Dane until he slid into the booth opposite him, and he didn't look up until he'd finished his text.

Dane took a sip of his lager and attempted to push Ben out of his mind. It was ridiculous to feel jealous. He must have imagined the connection he felt as they'd eaten earlier. So he peered at Markus and concentrated on his friend instead. That was less depressing. He tried to pinpoint what was different about Markus. He still *looked* the same— long wavy dark hair that was prone to frizz and a large but neatly trimmed beard overtaking his face that was all the trend right then, though Markus had sported a variation of that beard all through university.

When the silence between them stretched a little too far, Markus caved and raised an eyebrow.

"What?" Dane demanded, fighting the urge to cross his arms and pout like a child.

"Seriously? You're going to act like you don't know that I can see you pining away for yet another man you can't have?"

Dane's mouth fell open. He didn't realise he'd ever been that transparent. Markus leaned forward and flicked his forehead, shocking him out of the silence.

"Ouch. I'm not into Jamie or Ben, they're both just friends." That kiss at Pride didn't count. Not one bit. He rubbed at the sore spot on his head.

"I know they're your friends, but that doesn't stop your feelings, does it? I'm just worried, mate. Ben's different to Jamie."

Dane raked a hand through his hair. He didn't want to talk about this. "He's straight, I know that darling. I couldn't see him on the streets, could I? Think of the ferret. You're an animal lover. I'm doing this for the RSPCA."

Markus snorted at him and rolled his eyes. "You're full of shit, mate."

"I don't know what you're talking about. Even if all I ever do is look from afar, you have to admit he makes nice eye candy." Dane tried his hardest to make light of his situation with Ben, but he wasn't sure Markus was buying it, *dammit*. "Anyway, enough about my tragic life. What is going on with you and my sexy neighbour?" Turnaround was fair play.

"There's not much to say. We just like each other's company." Now look at who was being vague.

"Of course." Dane didn't believe Markus at all. He might not know Cal that well, but they spoke and hung out occasionally. They were neighbours, after all. He didn't seem like the type of father who would let any old Tom, Dick, or Markus around his son. "Arthur seems to like you as well."

"Art's a good kid." He didn't explain any further, and Dane could tell that he wasn't going to get any more out of him. He'd always been the brooding quiet one of the group.

They sat in awkward silence, neither of them wanting to talk about themselves, and it was a relief when Jamie got there. Dane watched as he walked towards them, stopping and talking to groups of people, laughing and smiling. He looked happy and hot in that unassuming way that he had. But it didn't hit Dane in the stomach like it used to. Was that because of his growing feelings for Ben? Or had he finally realised he and Jamie would never have worked out?

"Hey guys, what's happening?" He had a pint in one hand and his phone in the other. Could none of them do anything without their phones anymore?

"Nothing," he and Markus both said too quickly at the same time, and Jamie frowned, looking from one to the other.

"Have you two fallen out?"

Dane snorted and flicked his hair out of his eyes. "Don't be silly, darling. Where is Luscious Liam?" he asked a little desperately, knowing that if anything was going to throw Jamie off the scent, it would be his boyfriend.

Jamie's eyes brightened at the mention of his boyfriend's name. How thoroughly sickening. No one should be that gooey. "He's got one more driving lesson, and then he's going to meet us later." Dane couldn't keep up with Liam's hours. He was a driving instructor and worked around school and day-job schedules, which meant he worked most weekends, evenings, and early mornings. It was a good thing Liam had moved in with Jamie, otherwise they'd never get to see each other. The thought made him think of Ben, who was at his house right now talking to Donna. He'd probably go to her house rather than see them play at the Duck. Disappointment hit him full force, and he took a large drink of his lager.

"Come on. It's time to get this show on the road." They got out of the booth and spoke to the manager, Tigger. He'd changed the colour of his Mohican from green to blue, and the studs lining his ears matched.

"Darling, don't you look delightful," Dane said as he draped an arm over his shoulder and gave him a quick squeeze. "Blue suits you."

"Yeah, mate. Matches my blue balls right now." He laughed at his own joke, but Dane heard the undercurrents and could relate. He'd not wanted anyone since Ben moved in. Scratch that. He wanted Ben, but that was it. "I've not seen your boyfriend around for a while."

"He's touring." Tigger waved his arm dismissively. "Come on. It's time for you guys to get up there and sing me a song or five." He winked and slapped Dane on the back. Then he pushed him towards the stage.

Dane chuckled as he walked away and looked at Jamie. "Do any of you know what his real name is?" They'd only ever known the owner of the Duck as Tigger.

Jamie shook his head. "It never occurred to me to ask." The three of them jumped onto the pallet that masqueraded for a stage and adjusted their ukuleles. "Hello, my darlings. Are you ready to rock?" he asked the small crowd gathering in front of them.

# Chapter Nineteen

*Ben*

DONNA KEPT him talking on the phone for far too long, and Ben didn't manage to catch up with Dane and walk to the pub together. He liked walking to and from the pub, chatting and spending time with Dane. On the way there, Dane would be his usual jokey and charming self, and on the way back, he would be tipsy and handsy. Ben enjoyed his drunken hugs and the way he'd hook their arms as they walked back home in the dark.

The Duck was rammed by the time he got there, and Dane's band were already playing. His voice crooned like crushed velvet as he sang. Ben couldn't see him yet, but heat spread throughout his body as Dane's voice got low. His cock throbbed at the gravelly tone, and he instantly became breathless. Ben swallowed as he made his way to their booth and sat down. He forgot about getting a drink as he watched the band perform. Who was he kidding? He was watching Dane and no one else.

Dane swaggered, and his fingers danced over the strings on his uke while he sang a chirpy rendition of Guns N' Roses' "Paradise City." His hair was plastered to his head with sweat, and his T-shirt was translucent with it. Ben almost swallowed his tongue.

Dane had a beautiful body. He was lean yet muscular, and his tight jeans strained over his hips. Ben blinked. He couldn't stop staring and he didn't understand why.

It took him a while to realise Liam was already in their booth, but then he nodded and Liam slid a beer in front of him. Ben grinned in thanks, and then Liam's eyes widened and he swivelled back to watch the band. "I love this one!" he shouted loud enough for Ben to hear. Ben presumed they would start playing the song Jamie had once sung for Liam on YouTube, but it turned out to be a mock-rock rendition of Take That's "Relight My Fire." Ben was ashamed of himself for knowing all the words, but Liam was singing at the top of his lungs, so at least he wasn't the only one.

When they finished their set, the manager handed them all a pint and the band made their way back to the table. Dane smiled and gave Ben a hug. His skin was slick against his and Ben's cock throbbed again. He sat close enough that Ben could smell his aftershave and the salty scent of his sweat. It should be off-putting, but he couldn't help but compare it to Donna's floral perfume.

"I thought you'd end up at Donna's," Dane said as he pushed his wet hair back off his forehead. Ben followed the movement and held on tightly to his pint glass to stop himself from doing it for him. He didn't know why Dane was so fixated on Donna. Ben had never said they were more than friends.

"I already had plans with you." She'd phoned to see if he'd finally spoken to his mother yet and had berated him because he'd ignored her calls for so long. It was so much easier to ignore her now that she wasn't just down the road from him. "Plus, I wanted to see you all play."

Dane tipped his head back and laughed, and like his voice when Ben first arrived, the sound made him shiver. "That's so sweet of you." Dane's thigh pressed in close to his and Ben did his best not to notice. Jamie draped an arm around Liam's neck, and they shared a quick, somewhat sweaty kiss. They were so sweet together.

Was this what friendship was meant to be? The easy camaraderie, gentle ribbing laced with affection? The friends he had back home had never acted like this. They would go out with the sole intention of getting pissed and laid, and they didn't care about each other's lives beyond having someone to go out and compete with. Then again, there would be no way in hell he'd kiss any of them, even if some gender-fluid singer at some gig asked him to.

He was so stuck in his own thoughts that when Dane shrieked next to him, swivelled on the bench, and leaned over the back to hug someone, he jumped at the suddenness of it. Ben leaned in the opposite direction before he got an elbow in the face.

"Darling," Dane said. "I didn't expect to see you here."

It took Ben a few seconds to place the face—the receptionist's nephew. He hadn't seen him since that awkward encounter with his aunt. His good mood slipped, but he forced a smile and nodded hello. Perhaps he *should* have asked Donna to meet him there. His stomach churned, and even though he was sitting at a table full of people he considered good friends, he felt on the outside.

"Aunty L said you were playing tonight, so I thought I'd come along and see. You're pretty good." Ben hated that damned receptionist; she seemed set on ruining his day, night, whatever. It shouldn't matter, but the thought of Dane kissing Sean like they'd kissed at Pride drove him insane with jealousy.

Dane practically preened, obviously not unhappy at the interruption. The easy atmosphere of the group shifted with Sean there, though Ben seemed to be the only one affected. Dane slid closer to him on the bench, but only so he could make room for Sean to sit next to him.

Dane introduced him to Jamie, Liam, and Markus, and then Sean looked at Ben and smiled. "Nice to see you again," he said, sounding genuine.

"You too." Ben wanted to escape. A stranger in their mix changed the whole dynamic, and he half expected Sean to say or do something that would show the others he was a better fit for the group than Ben. It was irrational, but his brain wouldn't stop. If he weren't penned into the booth, he would make an excuse and leave, but if he asked everyone to move, he would only draw more attention to himself. So, he became more and more uncomfortable while Dane leaned into Sean.

He went from sitting so close to Dane that he could smell his sweat to watching Dane flirt and press against Sean. And he'd been enjoying the evening so much.

They stayed at the Drunken Duck long after last orders, drinking with Tigger and the bar staff until the early hours. But Ben only nursed his pint. They were all too drunk to realise he was almost stone-cold sober. His skin was too tight for his body, and every time Dane laughed at something Sean said, it tightened more. Ben's jaw ached from clenching his teeth, and he kept looking at his watch. He could have left hours ago, but he didn't want to leave without Dane, so he stayed and tortured himself.

They split into different directions when they left the pub. Markus had left earlier, so Ben expected the walk home to be just him and Dane. But the relief dissipated when Sean walked in the same direction and he and Dane stumbled along, both pissed, both pawing at each other as they veered off the pavement towards the road.

Ben cursed from behind them, grabbed the back of Dane's jacket, and pulled both of them back onto the pavement. Dane and Sean looked at each other and laughed, their noses so close they bumped together. Ben hated drunks.

He slowed his walk once they were back on track, so he wasn't so close to the laughing couple. But his gut twisted, and he gritted his teeth. He concentrated on putting one foot in front of the other and wished he'd had more to drink. Sean probably lived in the same direction as them. Soon enough he would veer off, and it would just be the two of them. But that didn't happen. They strolled up Dane's street arm in arm, both giggling and swaying as they walked up the pavement to Dane's front door.

A suffocating disappointment settled over him, and he swallowed it down until he could barely breathe. Ben watched Dane struggle to open the door but didn't offer to help. He didn't want to stand that close to them. Instead he folded his arms, looked towards the stars, and cringed at every drunken giggle and laugh until the door finally creaked open. He waited a few moments before forcing himself through and locking the door behind him. Ben and Sean were wrapped around each other on the sofa, hysterically giggling, and the giggling got worse when they fell into a heap on the floor.

He couldn't watch. His eyes burned and his heart hurt as though someone had died.

They laughed again and he couldn't stand it, so he raced up the stairs, flung open his door, and looked around wildly. He didn't know what he was looking for at first, but then something overtook him. He pulled his duffel bag from the bottom of the wardrobe, gave it a shake, and sneezed when Chase's fur billowed around him. Despite being in the living room, Chase still loved to delve into Ben's wardrobe and fall asleep. He shook it again and a crumpled piece of paper floated to the floor. The bag forgotten, he sat on the edge of his bed, picked up the paper, and unfolded it.

A flier from Pride, a permanent reminder of their kiss—as if he needed one. He stared at the flier and then crumpled it up. He had no clue how it had made it from the parade. The background had a purple, black, and grey rainbow effect with a slogan across the front. He threw it towards the bin in the corner, and it hit the rim and bounced onto the floor. Ben couldn't bring himself to care. He shoved a change of clothes into his bag and then tiptoed down the stairs and to his car. He hadn't drunk enough to be over the limit; he just needed to not be in the house with them. So he drove around for a while, his heart thumping against his chest, his stomach twisting until nausea burned the back of his throat.

It took forty-five minutes to get there and the sickness rolling in his belly got worse. His palms were slick and his teeth chattered as though he were in shock. He shouldn't be here, but he hadn't known where else to go, and a part of him hoped it would make Dane feel like he did once he found out. He knocked on the door and the dog barked.

A few seconds later the door opened, and Donna looked at him, mouth open in shock. He gave her a small smile and raked a hand through his messy hair. "Hi. I hope you don't mind me just turning up at this hour." His voice wavered even though he tried to sound nonchalant. It was after 1:00 a.m. Donna probably thought he was crazy.

Donna peered at him with a frown, but it turned into a smile, and she stepped sideways to let him in. "Of course not. What's wrong?"

"I'm fine." He said the words, but his face twisted, and pain radiated his heart. He wanted to burst out that Dane was probably shagging some guy on the sofa right now, but he didn't understand why it mattered so much to him. There was no need for him to feel like his heart was broken into pieces.

"Bullshit. No way would you come here in the middle of the night unless there was trouble." She squinted at him as though she were trying to find some clue on his face.

"Dane's got company. I didn't want to be in the way," he finally blurted out, and her eyes widened as though she understood something that he didn't.

"Get in here." She stood back to let him pass. He was fucked up. He shouldn't have come here. He could have holed up in his room and given Dane and Sean space, but the thought of being there made him want to throw up.

"Thanks," he said.

"Don't be silly. You've basically been my beard to keep my family off my back, and you've asked nothing in return. I can at least offer Nutella out of a jar and a shoulder to lean on." She steered him to the kitchen and pulled out a jar of Nutella as big as his head and handed him a spoon. "Come on. Let's go sit in the living room and eat this entire jar between us."

"Normal people do this with ice cream, you know."

She snorted. "Where's the fun in being like most people." He wished he were as confident being himself as she was.

Shadow ran up to him, tail wagging until Ben laughed and bent down to say hello properly. "Hey girl, did I ignore you? Sorry about that." He stroked her behind the ears and patted her back and then looked at Donna. He didn't know how to explain how he was feeling. He'd never felt it before, not with any of his friends or any of the women he'd dated in the past.

When he and Dane first met, Dane had just been…Dane—his boss' friend, a nice guy and soon-to-be friend. He hadn't looked at him and thought how gorgeous he was. He'd thought he had a nice smile and gentle hands when he greeted all the animals the group of friends had between them, but his heart hadn't fluttered and he hadn't felt this underlying need. Was it their kiss? He couldn't remember. It was as though every day he'd felt more deeply. It didn't make any sense.

"Want to talk about it?" she said around a spoonful of chocolate spread.

Ben shrugged and stuck his own spoon in the jar. "I'm confused."

"About what?"

He licked the spoon to give him a chance to find the right words, but nothing came to him. "I'm jealous." Her eyes froze, then widened, and she blinked.

"Dane?" He shrugged, as if it didn't matter, or he didn't know, but she saw through him and could tell how much it mattered. "Have you told him?"

His mouth dropped open in shock. It wasn't that simple. "Of course not. I mean. I'm not gay… I don't think. And how are you meant to know what you're feeling when you've never felt like it before? Plus, he's seeing this guy. *Sean.*"

"He's crazy if he chooses him over you. You're much more awesome."

"But he only sees me as a friend. Plus, I don't know if I'm jealous or just grateful or mixing my feelings. I've never felt this way, not with women or men."

"Never?"

He shook his head and took the jar of Nutella out of her hands. "Never. When you first asked me out, I was terrified you wanted to date or fuck." He raised an eyebrow at her. He knew she was more of a play-the-field kind of girl rather than someone who wanted to date—his exact opposite, yet the one person he had the most in common with. It made no sense.

"Same, mate. Same. We sure make damn good friends. I'm glad we didn't go there. Come on. let's watch *Emmerdale* on Catch Up and give me that jar. Just because we're friends doesn't mean you get to have more chocolate than I do."

Within ten minutes he was asleep with Shadow's head on his lap.

# Chapter Twenty

*Ben*

FOR SOME reason, his and Dane's friendship became stilted after that night. Neither of them said anything, but there was an undercurrent where there never used to be, and Ben couldn't stop thinking about Dane with Sean. He was thankful Sean hadn't been back to the house, but their usual comfiness with each other was gone. Ben didn't know what to talk about anymore, and he was still as confused as ever about his feelings.

It was that distraction that meant he didn't pay attention to his phone and answered without looking at who it was. "Hello."

"Ooh, so you *are* alive. I've been trying to get hold of you for *months*." His mother's tone was clipped, and Ben winced, but he couldn't blame her.

"Sorry Mum, I've been busy finding somewhere else to live, with work, you know how it is."

"I worked full-time and brought you and your brother up. What would you have done if I'd said I'm busy at work, therefore I'm too busy to mother my children?"

He sighed silently. She was so melodramatic, but there was no change there. "I'm really sorry, okay? How have you been? How's Dad, and Lewis?" The easiest way to get her off his back was to get her talking about other people. He nodded and answered where appropriate as she talked at him. But his head started to thump and he rubbed his eyes and stifled a yawn as she went on and on.

"Good. I'm glad you're coming," she said, and he realised he had no clue what she was talking about. He had a sinking feeling he'd agreed to sell his soul to the devil.

"Uncle Miles's birthday party. I know this lovely girl. She's Cherry's sister's niece. You'll get along like a house on fire." Oh hell no. He was not having his mother setting him up on a date. He thought he'd gotten out of that when he moved to Lockstone.

"No. No blind date. I have a—I'm dating this woman." He hated using Donna like that, but he knew she wouldn't mind.

"You're dating and you didn't tell me?"

"It's very new. We're taking it slow." Glacial in fact. He wondered what his mum would feel if she knew about the confusing feelings he was having for a man he now considered his closest friend? Or he had done until they stopped talking to each other.

"So you'll bring her to your uncle's birthday?"

"I can't promise that. She works, and it's short notice."

"Don't you blame me for the short notice, Ben. You'd know if you answered your phone."

That was true, but she could also have texted him. He knew there was no use in saying that to her. It would cause another argument, and she'd be on the phone even longer. His mum was best taken in small doses. He loved her, and he knew she loved him, but she was exhausting.

"I'll ask, but no promising." Within a few hours of that conversation, he had agreed to go back to Devon for the bank holiday, and Donna was returning a favour and pretending to be his date. He was one part relieved she would be there as a buffer and one part guilty at lying to everyone—including Dane.


UNCLE MILES'S birthday party was exactly what Ben expected it to be. Drunken men chatted in slurring sentences, occasionally breaking out into song, while Irish folk songs played on repeat in the background. His dad was in the thick of it, while his mother and his aunt and their friends were working the room. His mum was in her element as she chatted to everyone and pointed towards him and Donna.

He found it awkward and wished he could fade into the background. Luckily Donna was being a good sport and had won over his whole family. Even his brother liked her, though he didn't seem himself and had disappeared halfway through the night. Perhaps their parents were picking at him like they used to do Ben now that he wasn't there every day for them to concentrate on. He hoped not. He might not be hugely close with Lewis, but he wouldn't want him to feel as pressured and as unhappy as he had.

It was easy to tell that his mum adored Donna, and because she loved Donna, he was lavished with impromptu hugs and kisses. "You should have brought her to see us much sooner than this. I don't know. You'd think he was embarrassed." She smiled at Donna and pulled her into a hug so tight that Donna let out a small yelp.

Donna patted her on the back and extracted herself from her grip. "It really is very new, plus your son is such a hard worker he found it hard to get time off work. It's obvious he gets that from you and his dad."

"We instilled good work ethics in our sons, even if Ben broke our hearts by moving so far away." She shot Ben a look. "Though I suppose he would never have met you if he'd stayed here. Now come with me, dear. Come meet some of the cousins. You're going to love them."

Donna looked over her shoulder and mouthed "Sorry" as he was left abandoned. He went to find a drink, needing something to do with his hands, and went to sit with his dad and his uncle and their friends as they became even more inebriated. "Never thought you'd catch a bird like that," his dad said, pointing his can of Carling at him.

Ben hated being sober while everyone else was drunk, and he didn't like his father calling Donna a bird. "She's a woman, and we met at work." He forced a smile as he wondered how they'd all feel if he'd brought Dane rather than Donna. Would they think he was more than a friend? Is that what Ben wanted?

"I forgot we have to be all PC now." He rolled his eyes, and his friends laughed. "You should marry that one. I don't think you'll do any better. Best trap her now." He hated how his dad spoke when under the influence and surrounded by friends. He got more and more offensive. There was nothing worse than old men showing off. Ben wished he'd stayed in Lockstone and not given in to them.

His only hope was his mother was more tactful than his father, and Donna looked to be having a good time with his cousins. If Dane were there, he wouldn't feel so out of place. But his parents wouldn't approve, even if it was just friends. Ben stood up, and the men at the table all looked at him. "Er—I'm going for a vape," he said. He didn't want to just be friends with Dane. He wanted more.

"You don't smoke," his dad said.

"That's why I'm vaping." Truth be told, he didn't smoke or vape, but he needed to get out of the room for a while. He sucked in the clear cool air when he got outside and relaxed against the wall with a sigh. Being around his family made him claustrophobic. He hoped Donna was doing better in there than he was.

"Five minutes back home and already feel suffocated, eh?"

He jumped and looked to the side. He hadn't even realised his brother was standing there, a cigarette between his fingers.

"I wondered where you were."

He held up his cigarette. "Why do you think I smoke." He didn't seem like the happy-go-lucky guy he usually was.

"Everything okay?"

"Sure, sure." He took a drag and slowly blew out the smoke. "Donna seems nice. Mum and Dad won't stop raving about her." He sounded bitter, but Ben didn't know why, and they didn't have the kind of relationship where they'd tell each other all their secrets.

"She's a good friend," he said instead, and Lewis looked at him with a frown.

# Chapter Twenty-One

*Dane*

DANE SHOWERED and changed into ratty jogging bottoms and a threadbare T-shirt. He scraped his damp hair back off his face with his fingers and, unable to put it off any longer, padded downstairs. Ben was back after taking Donna to Devon to meet his parents. He felt sick, imaging them walking on the beach as a family, throwing the ball for Shadow, and laughing at each other's jokes. He ground his teeth. It was his own fault. His brother and father had tried to tell him this was a bad idea, but he'd assured them they were just friends.

And they were. But now it was more and more difficult to be just Ben's friend, because he wanted so much more. He wanted early morning walks with Speedy and Chase. He wanted to make dinner together and watch *Hollyoaks* after work. He wanted to play at the Duck and have Ben hug him and kiss him afterwards. He wanted their friendship and he wanted more. He needed to stop torturing himself. There was no way he could have more. Ben was straight; he had a girlfriend. Dane didn't want to lose their friendship, so he needed to do whatever he could to get back to that easy camaraderie they used to share. A friend was better than nothing at all.

Nerves danced in his belly, and he took in a few deep breaths to compose himself. The cold shower had done the job with his erection, but the fluttering in his heart at seeing Ben again wouldn't disappear. He'd missed him and was glad he was back, but it hurt to picture Ben taking Donna to meet his parents. They must be more serious than Dane first thought, and he hated it.

Dane stood in the doorway and watched Ben. There was beauty in a person who had no self-awareness of how gorgeous they were, and his quiet housemate had no clue how many people watched him and longed for him. Dane was no exception. Ben had the easy strength of someone used to working outdoors—a body that looked delicious in old T-shirts and jeans made for work and not fashion. Dane shook the image away. He needed to act like his usual charming self, no yearning or panting after somebody he couldn't have. If he wanted to stay in Ben's life, he needed to be content as a friend. So he forced himself over the threshold and gave Ben a smile he knew was much too wide.

Speedy was sitting on the plush chair Dane usually sat on, curled up fast asleep, and instead of moving the pup, he sat next to Ben on the sofa. Any sane person would move the dog off his chair, but he looked so peaceful—and sue him, he'd not seen Ben all weekend and he missed his friend. He was allowed to miss his friend, wasn't he?

"Pizza's ordered," Ben said.

Dane curled his feet up and tucked his bare toes under the cushions. "Brilliant, I'm starving. So how were the family? I bet Shadow loved the beach." See? He could talk about Donna without even actually talking about her. The dog was safe. He liked the dog.

"Yeah, she loved it. Family were the same as ever. Stressful. It was good to see them, but good to get away from them. How about you?" Ben bit at his lip before carrying on. "How's Sean?"

Sean? Why did he want to know that? Dane frowned a little. "He's fine, I'm sure. I've not seen him over the bank holiday. We've both been busy with work. He may come over tomorrow." Now it was Ben's turn to frown.

The pizza delivery person chose that moment to turn up, and Ben practically launched himself off the sofa to go and get it. He sloped back in and put the huge pizza on the coffee table, took a slice, and rolled the stray cheese around his finger. Dane had to stop himself from groaning. Ben didn't have a clue how hot he looked doing that. "Pizza's good," he said around a mouthful, and he still looked good. What had they been talking about before the food arrived? His hunger vanished as his stomach twisted.

"He's an all right guy."

"The pizza guy?" Dane frowned.

"No, I mean Sean. He seems nice."

Dane was so lost. That didn't sound like high praise and he didn't understand why he was even talking about Sean at all. "I guess?" Dane frowned at him, picked a pepper off the top of his pizza, and popped it into his mouth while Ben watched. "Is everything okay?"

"Yes," he said quickly. "No." There was desperation and pain in his voice. Dane put his plate down, not hungry anymore.

"No?" Dane was scared to hear what he was going to say.

"I don't know what's wrong with me." His words broke Dane's heart, but he didn't know what to do. Ben closed his eyes and his forehead creased as though he were in physical pain. "The weekend was fantastic... for them. They loved Donna." Ben stared a hole into the coffee table.

"That's good, isn't it?"

Ben shrugged, and his gaze flickered towards him. "She's a good friend." Dane didn't know what to say. He was relieved that Ben didn't say he loved Donna, ecstatic even, but he didn't know why Ben was so broken up about it. He leaned forward and placed a comforting hand on Ben's arm. But Ben tensed and Dane snatched it away, presuming his touch was unwanted. Ben opened his eyes and they were wild liquid pools of storm-cloud grey.

Ben threw the slice of pizza back into the box, and with greasy fingers, circled Dane's wrist. He didn't squeeze or tug, just held and then slowly pulled Dane's hand back to his arm and planted it firmly there. Dane tensed, his whole body froze, and he held his breath as he waited—he wasn't sure what for. Ben trailed his fingers up Dane's arm and cupped his shoulder, and Dane shuddered as his nerve endings paid extra attention to every touch of his hand. Did straight guys touch like this?

Ben's hand tightened and he leaned towards him. "I fucking hate Sean," he bit out.

Dane didn't reply. He was confused and distracted by Ben's touch. He sucked in a lungful of air and the hairs on his arms stood on end as Ben's face got closer. They were so close his face blurred and Dane was sure Ben could hear each thump of his heart. He didn't know what Ben was going to do, but he was afraid that if he moved, he wouldn't do it.

"I don't even know what I'm doing," Ben said, more to himself than to Dane.

He opened his mouth to reply, but then warm lips greasy from pizza touched his. Dane's heart stopped and he whimpered as he relaxed into the kiss. Spicy tomato sauce, and something sweeter—something he'd never thought he'd taste. Ben's tongue was tentative, licking against his lips until Dane gasped when then he dipped inside.

Dane forgot how to breathe. His cock soared to life, so hard it hurt. He'd imagined this so many times, but he never expected it to happen—never expected it to be so good. It surpassed Pride—they'd only kissed then because the idea had been put into their head by Phase. This was different. Ben had taken the initiative. He didn't know what was happening, but their kiss was electrifying.

Ben gave a strangled moan. His eyes were shut tightly and there were frown lines on his forehead. Dane didn't shut his eyes; he wanted to remember this, to feel this kiss with every one of his senses in case it was their last. Ben's face was masculine lines and sharp angles, softened by full lips. He couldn't believe he was tasting that mouth, but he chased his tongue and Ben gasped, eyes shooting open. They widened as he finally focused on Dane.

In his wildest dreams he'd never expected Ben to kiss him again. His whole world tilted on its axis. They stared at each other, and Dane was sure Ben could hear his heart as it beat wildly against his chest. Ben's hair was ruffled from Dane's fingers, his lips swollen from their kisses, and he'd never looked more beautiful. Dane needed to kiss him again. He leaned forward and cupped the back of Ben's head. He felt him jump under the touch, but he didn't pull away as Dane guided their mouths together. The second kiss tasted as sweet as the first, and he had so many questions, so many worries, but none of them mattered while Ben's tongue tangled with his.

# Chapter Twenty-Two

*Ben*

IN HIS whole life, nothing felt as right as Dane's lips on his—the soft press, the enquiring tongue, the small whimpers Ben swallowed as they kissed. He never wanted to stop, because then he'd have to deal with real life and the confusion he didn't understand.

He'd spent the whole weekend with Donna and his parents suffocating under the pressure to be normal. When he thought of Dane and Sean, it made him try harder to be the person they expected him to be. That should be his life, and he should be happy, but despair had taken over. It was exhausting. His parents loved her—as he knew they would, but he wished it was Dane with him and Dane whom his parents adored.

He'd laid awake every night wondering how different it would be if Dane were there, and he'd remembered the times they'd both sat on his bed watching films. He'd enjoyed the press of his body as they sat next to each other, which led to remembering how they sat cross-legged on the floor around the coffee table and how their knees would brush together. He shivered, skin hyper aware, and that had automatically led him to the kiss he'd tried to forget—the only kiss he'd ever enjoyed. Some people enjoyed kissing for the sake of kissing, but he wasn't one of them. It had been a surprise when he realised he liked it and hadn't wanted it to end.

His whole body became a wired spring, and the tension was only now loosening because Dane was in his arms. The intensity of his friendship with Dane had deepened into something much more than with any other friend he'd had. He didn't know how or why. He'd spent his whole adult life chasing these feelings and he'd never found them, not with any of the women he'd gone out with or had sex with. He groaned, and Dane's fingers in his hair tightened. The bite of pain sent shivers down his spine and he couldn't hold on to any thought other than Dane and what he'd like to do with him.

His vision blurred and his lungs burned until he had to rip his lips from Dane's due to lack of oxygen. Dane's eyes were dilated, his mouth wet from their kiss as he breathed heavily. He was gorgeous. The weight of Ben's confusion came back with each breath. He had no clue what he was doing. He didn't suddenly find men attractive, but there was no denying his attraction to Dane. Tears burned the back of his eyes at the immensity of it. He wished he could sort through his own feelings, but he was as muddled as he always was. More so.

"Nothing makes sense. But I… with *you*…." His voice was wobbly, bordering on hysteria. Dane tensed but didn't put any space between them, which he appreciated. He couldn't stand it if Dane moved farther away from him. Panic bubbled up in his throat and he laughed while he shook his head. "I've never liked anyone the way I like you."

"Same, darling, same," Dane said in agreement, but Ben wasn't sure Dane understood exactly. Ben peered at his face and wished he could read his mind. Dane worried at his lip. "I never expected this. I don't know—I didn't think you were gay."

He froze. That word again. It wasn't a bad word; he just didn't think it labelled him. Not completely.

"Or bisexual," Dane said quickly, taking his silence the wrong way.

"It's not that. I don't know what I am. I've never known what I am." Dane frowned, and even though he didn't move away, there seemed to be more distance between them.

"You have a girlfriend," Dane said.

"What? Donna? She's just a friend. Her family are as obsessed with her settling down as mine are. We just use each other to keep them off our backs. There's nothing more." He hoped Dane believed him. He understood how bad it looked, because he'd taken Donna all the way to Devon to meet his family. Perhaps he wouldn't have done that if he hadn't been so upset about Dane with Sean. "Anyway, you've been seeing Sean."

Dane's eyes widened and his brow furrowed. "Since when?"

"You brought Sean back here." They'd been wrapped around each other on this very sofa. *He hated the fucking sofa.*

"That time we were drunk? He'd been having trouble with his ex; we drank a lot. He slept on the sofa, and I slept in my bed, *alone*. I know where you were, though. You went to Donna's."

"I did go to Donna's. I shouldn't have. But I didn't want to watch you with him, so I went to Donna's. We ate Nutella out of the jar and watched *Emmerdale* reruns. She's a good friend." She really was. Along with Dane, Jamie. They were all good friends, and he wasn't used to having that.

"You should have told me how you felt," Dane said, and he hooked their pinkies together. It was such a small movement, but it made Ben's chest expand with warmth.

"Truth be told, I didn't know that's what I was feeling. I've never wanted anyone before." His mouth was dry, but he forced himself to carry on. "Until you."

Dane laughed softly and shook his head, but there was a smile on face and their fingers were still hooked together. "What a pair we make. I'm not sure you've noticed, but I'm not good with men. I always choose the wrong one. I figured I was doing that again, so I kept quiet because I never want to lose your friendship."

Dane bit at his lip, and it was like the wool had been pulled from Ben's eyes. He'd spent so long worrying about himself and his own feelings or lack of them that he hadn't even noticed that Dane wasn't always the confident out-and-proud guy he portrayed. "You won't lose my friendship. I have a feeling your run of bad luck has come to an end."

Dane laughed. "Confident, are you?"

Ben noticed the flecks of green in Dane's eyes, the length of his eyelashes and the faint freckles over his nose. He was breathtaking. "Confident in you."

"Jesus, Ben." Dane groaned as he pulled Ben close to him and pressed his face into the crook of Ben's shoulder. Ben shuddered, not just because he enjoyed their closeness, but because he enjoyed closeness at all. It was all so new to him, and he was loving it.

"Not so confident in myself. I'm still a mess, but I know I want us to be more than friends."

Dane caressed his cheek with gentle fingers and Ben blinked. Dane's eyes were clear and bright with something that looked like hope. When Dane leaned towards him and bumped their foreheads, Ben gripped the back of Dane's head to keep them together and sighed.

"I'm sorry for making you think there was more to me and Donna than there is. I really wished it were you with me in Devon."

"No one has ever chosen me before." Dane's words wavered, and Ben's heart broke for him. How had he not seen how insecure Dane really was?

"I'm choosing you, Dane. You might not want me to once you realise how fucked up I am, so just be patient." What if sex with Dane left him feeling as empty as sex with the women he'd dated in the past? He didn't want to hurt Dane's feelings.

"Is this for real?" Dane asked.

"It's real."

"You might need to pinch me."

Ben leaned closer. "How about a kiss instead?"

"I'd be crazy to say no to that." Ben's mouth slid against his and he licked against his lips until Dane groaned. When they finally pulled away, Ben was light-headed.

# Chapter Twenty-Three

*Dane*

BEN WANTED him. Dane alternated between ecstatic euphoria to blind panic. There may even have been a little dance. As scared as he was, he had to see where it would lead them. He couldn't stand to be an experiment, but he'd regret it forever if he pushed Ben away. He didn't want to lose his friendship, yet now he'd tasted him, had his hands on him, his mouth against his, he couldn't think of anything else. If anyone could ruin his run of bad luck with men, it was Ben. He was a breath of fresh air, and Dane wanted to breathe him in.

There was no way Ben had lied about his friendship with Donna, but Dane was still antsy as he waited for Ben to come back from her place. Ben felt she deserved to know the truth and to be told that he could no longer be her pretend date for family functions. Dane cleaned the kitchen, fed the animals, and then tried to watch TV, but he couldn't settle. His whole body tingled from thinking about that one small kiss, and it scared him how much he wanted to do it again, to feel Ben's work-roughened hands on his arms, his lips against his.

Panic bubbled in his stomach as more and more outrageous scenarios went through his head. What if Ben hurt his head, got amnesia, and decided he loved Donna? What if she decided she wanted to be more than his friend? What if she was a downright bitch? It was nearing the point where he was going to start making stupid promises to gods he didn't believe in as long as Ben came back. He desperately wanted to talk to Jamie, but it would be wrong to speak to him knowing he was Ben's boss and one of Ben's only friends in the area. Instead he eyed his phone, and before he could think too much, he rang Markus. He was always a voice of reason.

"Come on, answer the phone," he muttered.

"Yep," Markus answered.

"You busy?" He heard a muffled conversation. and Dane walked over to the window to look out onto the street and saw Markus's car next door.

"No, I'm at Cal's. Is everything okay? Want me to come round?"

Dane closed his eyes and flung himself onto the sofa with a groan. "I have no idea, and yes, would you mind? No, wait. Second thoughts. Would Cal mind if I came to you?" All he needed was Ben to walk in on a conversation about what had happened. That would be just his luck.

There was another muffled voice while Markus talked to Cal, and then Markus was back. "Cal said no problem, come on round. The kid's sleeping over at his nan and granddad's." Dane winced as he realised he was probably intruding on a rare night alone together for them.

"Are you sure you don't mind?"

"Of course not, get on round here." That was Cal's voice. Markus had obviously put him on speaker. He gave a little laugh.

"All right darlings, I'll be there in a jiffy." He hunted for his keys and shoved his feet into his trainers. "Be good, boys," he called to Speedy and Chase. In response, Speedy gave a grump and closed his eyes. Chase was already fast asleep on his back with his paws in the air.

Cal's door was open when he jumped over the tiny brick wall that separated their front gardens. He knocked on the door as he walked through. Then he kicked off his trainers and closed the door. They were sitting on the sofa together—close, but not too close. Like they were fooling anybody.

"I'll leave you both to talk," Cal said. "Coffee, tea?"

Dane sat on the two-seated sofa opposite and grabbed a large plush teddy that obviously belonged to Arthur from the seat next to him and hugged it to his chest. "You don't need to leave. Two brains are better than one. Isn't that what they say?"

Markus raised an eyebrow. "Something like that. What's wrong?" Cal settled back down, just a few inches closer to Markus than he'd been before. Dane didn't think Markus even realised he'd placed a comforting hand on Cal's knee.

"Ben kissed me," he blurted out, unsure how else he could say it. Markus's eyes widened and his mouth dropped open. "Come on. Don't be that surprised. Technically we kissed during Pride at the gig. There's this song Phase sings, and he asked everyone to kiss the person they were with. We did. But he kissed me again yesterday. Don't look like that. I'm not that ugly, am I?"

Markus started at him like he couldn't believe what Dane was saying. "Don't be ridiculous. Ben's not gay. Are you sure he kissed you?"

Dane's grip on the teddy tightened, and it started to play a creepy nursery rhyme. "Jesus," he said as he shoved it off his lap and eyed it was as though it were the devil.

Cal hid a laugh behind a cough and reached over, silencing the noise. "Sorry about that."

"I'm one hundred percent sure he leaned over and kissed me. He wants more than kissing. He wants a relationship." He fought the urge to lick his lips and relive the feel of their lips sliding together.

"Isn't he dating that woman from work?" Markus asked.

"No, they're just friends."

Markus didn't look convinced. "I'm sure she took him to a family christening, and didn't he take her to meet his parents in Devon? I'm not too sure this is a good idea."

"That's not it at all. They both took each other to family functions to stop family from setting them up. Ben's not attracted to her at all." He hoped Donna wasn't attracted to Ben either.

"If you say so. Is Ben even gay?" Markus raised an eyebrow. He wasn't nearly as happy for him as Dane wanted him to be.

"I wouldn't say he's exactly gay, but who cares about labels?" It was obvious to him that Ben was confused about his sexuality, but Dane hoped they could work through it together. He'd taken the first step, after all. "But what if she persuades him not to date me?" He pictured Ben hitting his head again, and Donna coming to the rescue. His brain was running amok, and not even his friends could distract him. He could picture her now, all doe-eyed and sweet. She'd cry and cling to him until he patted her hair and told her not to worry. God, he hoped not.

"I doubt that will happen. If he says he wants you, then he does. He's a to-the-point kind of guy. And if she's just a friend, you've got nothing to worry about anyway," Cal said thoughtfully.

"You're right." He trusted Ben, and there was no need for the worry he was feeling.

"You've had a thing for Ben for ages, so why aren't you happier?" Markus added.

Dane shrugged. It was hard to believe anyone would choose him, and Ben wasn't gay. What if they had sex and he hated it? What if he was shit at sex? "I'm scared that we won't work out, that he doesn't really want me. Perhaps he's mistaking lo-ust for friendship? Let's be real. Look at my track record. When has it ever gone well for me? I'm terrified we won't work out, because I've never felt like this for *anyone*." He stressed the word anyone.

"Anyone?" Markus knew about his secret crush on Jamie back when they'd been at university.

"Stop stressing. Drink your tea and try to relax," Cal said as he leaned over and patted Dane's knee. Dane wished he could be so calm.

They talked a while longer, and then Dane's phone rang. He scrambled for it and almost dropped it when he saw Ben's name flash up. "Hey," he said, hoping he didn't sound as scared as he felt.

"Hey." Ben sounded happy. "I'm going to be a little late. I went to meet Donna for a coffee, like we discussed, but she was back-ended by some kid without a licence, so I don't want to leave her until everything's sorted."

Dane silently cursed the person who back-ended Donna, but he couldn't be upset that Ben would do anything for his friend. "Of course that's okay. She's not hurt, is she?"

"No, just a sore shoulder. She's more annoyed about her car and the insurance."

"I'm glad she's not hurt," Dane said, though he was disappointed Ben wouldn't be back anytime soon.

"She really is just a friend, you know. And she's perfectly happy to stop our fake-date arrangement."

Dane let out a breath he hadn't realised he'd been holding. "I know. I'll just miss you." Ben chuckled and it went straight to his cock.

"See you at home."

He ended the call and turned to Markus and Cal who were watching him with interest. "She got in a car accident. She's okay, but he's helping her sort insurance and stuff."

"You can't make it up, can you?" Markus said.

"I think we need something a little stronger than tea," Cal announced, using Markus to push himself off the sofa. He came back a little later with vodka and three shot glasses.

He should probably stay sober for Ben, but his nerves were fried, and when Cal poured him a shot, he knocked it back.

# Chapter Twenty-Four

*Ben*

BEN SLID his key into the lock, slowly pushed open the front door, and winced when the hinges creaked. He was later than expected, but he wanted to make sure Donna was settled before he left her alone. He hoped Dane understood. He sounded fine on the phone, but it was difficult to tell without seeing his face. The lights downstairs were off, so he presumed Dane was already in bed. Disappointment settled over him. He looked forward to seeing Dane, now he'd had a bit more time to process his feelings and talk to someone who he could actually trust.

This was the first time he was doing something just for himself, and it was almost as terrifying as it was freeing. He was used to his nerves getting the better of him. His anxiety played a large role in his life, and he'd needed time to sort through it.

He went to switch on the light in the living room, but his foot caught on something, and he went flying. He saved himself from hitting his head on the coffee table using some kind of cross between a tuck-roll and a contortionist move. While his heart jumped into his mouth, he lay on the floor until he could tell he hadn't broken a limb. He sat up slowly, figuring he'd slipped on one of Speedy's rope toys, but as his eyes adjusted to the darkness, he saw a shoe and attached to the shoe was a long sprawling leg that belonged to a very passed-out Dane.

He half lay on the chair, his back awkwardly arched, one leg over the arm and the other out straight. His head was tipped back, and his mouth was open as he snored silently. Ben knew that was how he lay when he was too drunk to make it to his bedroom. They'd gone to the pub and come back pissed often enough for Ben to know the signs.

He leaned down and gently shook Dane's shoulder, his fingertips caressing the warm skin he could feel through the thin fabric of Dane's T-shirt. Electricity shot up his arm and he shivered and wiggled his fingers when he pulled away. Dane whined but didn't open his eyes. He looked so sweet in his sleep, his usual sarcastic manner hidden.

"Dane, you should go to bed." Ben's lips twitched into a smile as Dane grumbled and his eyes rolled under his lids. He frowned. "Dane, come on, let me help." He started to move him into more of a sitting position, and Dane stirred.

"Sssleeping," he slurred, head tipping forward. "And waiting for Ben." He didn't open his eyes.

"I'm here, but it's late, so let's get you to bed."

"Bed." His eyes shot open and his gaze was heated as it zeroed in on him. Ben's breath hitched in his throat. "Bed with Ben."

Ben groaned and his cock was instantly hard. Sex had always been something to get over with. This amount of attraction for someone was new, and he was afraid it would disappear. He wanted to kiss and be kissed. His cheeks burned with a mixture of desire and embarrassment as he imagined more, and he was glad for the semi-darkness even if Dane was too drunk to notice.

Ben licked his lips, his throat dry. "Yeah, I'll help you to bed." If his voice was an octave lower, he chose to ignore it. Dane didn't argue at the obvious way he'd taken his words wrong but allowed Ben to get him to his feet and up the stairs. Dane was handsy as Ben attempted to keep him upright enough to get to bed, but he wasn't coordinated enough to do more than grab his arms, almost head-butt him in the face, and then walk into a wall. Ben bit back a laugh.

"Gonna fuck you into the mattress," Dane slurred as Ben managed to hook an arm around his waist and open the door to his bedroom. He was as drunk as a skunk, so the words shouldn't have an effect on him, but his stomach tightened and heat coiled in his groin like a spring waiting to go off.

Dane flopped backwards onto the bed and bobbed like a rag doll, his feet hanging off the end. He didn't attempt to get undressed, which Ben was grateful for. He wasn't quite ready for the full monty yet.

Dane crooked his finger at him in a come-hither action that made Ben laugh. In response, Dane frowned at him, closed his eyes, and flung an arm over his eyelids. Ben hesitated, then bent to slip off Dane's trainers. He left him in his shirt and jeans but pulled the throw off the edge of the bed and draped it over him.

The only light was from the landing, and it caught the planes of Dane's face. Ben's breath caught. How come he'd never noticed how beautiful Dane was? His hair curled messily around his ears, his brows were ever so slightly tweezed in such a way they framed his large eyes, and his body was lean yet muscular. He shook his head to dislodge the image in his head. If he didn't get to his own room, he'd weaken and end up in bed with Dane. Neither of them were quite ready for that, despite Dane's earlier words.

It was difficult to walk away from Dane's room, but he forced himself to push open the door to his own bedroom. He turned on the bedside lamp to give him enough light so he didn't trip over something yet again, then he stripped down to his boxer shorts and slid into his unmade bed. He closed his eyes, but he imagined Dane's lips against his, and he couldn't drift off.

Heat pooled in his groin as his eyes fluttered closed and he bit his lips. His limbs became heavy as he thought of Dane, knowing he was on the other side of the wall. His cock hardened and he shifted his hips restlessly and shivered as his erection brushed against the quilt. Finally he groaned, reached under the blankets, and pushed his boxers down his hips to free his erection. He circled his fingers around his shaft and thrust his hips up into it, imagining it was Dane's hand, and his balls drew up. He couldn't remember a time when he'd touched himself and thought of an actual person—the occasional celebrity, but usually he got himself off as quickly as possible, happy to get to the end result.

This time he didn't want it to end. He wished it really were Dane touching him. His breath sped up and his hand tightened as he touched himself. He came so suddenly he had to bite back a cry, scared of waking Dane. Then he gasped as he lay in bed, come cooling on his belly and smearing against his quilt. He should have had the foresight to kick off the blankets, but he couldn't bring himself to care.

# Chapter Twenty-Five

*Dane*

DANE WOKE on a gasp; he was so thirsty he thought his throat had been cut. He rolled sideways and his head pounded, so he stumbled out of bed to the bathroom and turned on the cold tap. He leaned over and stuck his mouth under the faucet and drank until he was full. His stomach rolled and he cursed drinking so much with Markus and Cal. To be fair, he hadn't expected to be there that long. As hour after hour went as he waited for Ben, he drank away his nerves until he couldn't feel anything and then stumbled back home and passed out on the sofa—not waiting for Ben, just too drunk to go to bed. He frowned and tried to remember when he'd made it upstairs. He had vague images of Ben and hoped he hadn't blown it. That's if Ben still wanted him. Donna could have changed his mind. Hit him over the head and caused that amnesia Dane was so worried about.

His reflection in the mirror was wide-eyed and pallid. He had serious bed hair, and his eyes were puffy from the alcohol. Although he felt half human when he brushed his teeth and took a quick shower, his stomach growled. He needed grease to soak up the alcohol.

Once he was dressed comfortably in an old T-shirt and jogging bottoms, he started to cook a greasy fry up. Ben hadn't appeared from his room yet and Dane tried not to worry. He heated the oil—this was no time for a healthy breakfast—and cooked enough sausage and bacon for both of them.

"Morning." Dane jumped at Ben's voice. With pillow creases on his cheek, his hair standing on end, and wearing a faded green T-shirt with a hole at the neck and Teenage Mutant Ninja Turtle pyjama bottoms, Ben looked gorgeous. His feet were gloriously bare, and Dane had a hard time looking away from them.

He sucked in a deep breath and forced his eyes up to Ben's, afraid of what he'd see there. "Breakfast?" It wasn't the question he wanted to ask, but he was afraid of the answer he would get if he asked another.

Ben nodded, his eyes intense. Dane's skin prickled under the intensity and his palms started to sweat. Oh god, this was it. Ben was going to tell him that their kiss was a mistake and that he was going to stay with Donna. He'd have to agree, smile, and pretend as though it didn't break his heart, but he'd do it for Ben.

He had to get out of there. It didn't matter that he had food frying or that he'd asked Ben if he wanted anything. He bolted... but Ben stepped into him and gripped Dane's upper arms. And then their lips were touching... more than touching. Ben's mouth crashed into his and the bite of his fingers on his arms made Dane's eyes roll in his head.

Relief flooded over him and his knees gave out, but one of Ben's arms snaked around his waist and pulled him against his chest until there was no space between them. If he'd been worried about Ben not wanting him before, then all those thoughts disappeared as Ben's erection ground against his. Ben pulled back, and Dane whimpered, but when Ben chuckled, Dane blinked open his eyes. Ben traced a callused fingertip over his cheekbone and down over his mouth.

"I think you're burning breakfast," he said, and Dane cursed and turned around to the stove to pull the frying pan off the heat. Ben was still at his back, and Dane could feel the laughter.

"This is your fault." He prodded the sausages with a fork. They weren't that bad. "I hope you like the fat on your bacon crispy." He turned around, and Ben was smiling. Dane's heart jumped. He'd convinced himself that Ben wouldn't choose him; no one ever chose him. Tears burned at the back of his eyes for some reason. He was overwhelmed in the best possible way.

Ben leaned over and brushed a kiss to his forehead, and Dane wanted to fling his arms around his neck and never let go.

"Put the toast on. I'll make tea." Dane fed bread to the toaster and got out plates, then fried a couple of eggs while the bread was toasting. Ben worked around him, pulling the PG Tips out of the cupboard, grabbing their preferred cups. Being in the kitchen with Ben made him warm inside.

A few minutes later, they were sitting at the kitchen table eating their breakfast. Dane's hangover had disappeared, but he was sure that was more to do with Ben than the breakfast.

"I'm sorry it took me so long to get home last night. Donna was pretty shook up."

Dane pressed his leg against Ben's under the table. "That's okay. You're a nice guy. You're a good friend."

"I told her about you and us—I hope you don't mind," Ben said.

"Of course not, darling. I'm glad you felt comfortable telling her."

Ben shrugged. "I'm not so sure comfortable is the right word, but I didn't want to lie."

"What did she say?"

"She was shocked, not because I like you, but because I made the first move." Ben grinned and his cheeks turned a delightful shade of red. "I think me turning up on her doorstep at 1:00 a.m. all sad and pathetic because I thought you were with Sean told her everything she needed to know."

"You are so sweet." Dane couldn't stop smiling around his breakfast. "I'm sure the guys will actually be shocked. Perhaps not with me, but you, definitely."

Ben ran a hand through his hair and then paused with his bottom lip caught between his teeth. "I'm not sure I want them to know—not right away. I know that's shitty, because I told Donna, but with the guys, I'd feel more pressure, and I just want to figure us out first, you know?"

Dane was disappointed. He'd been out since he was a teenager, and not telling their friends about their relationship would be difficult. They hung out all the time, and he hated keeping things from them. But he knew this was all new for Ben, and he wanted him to be comfortable. "We'll go at your pace." Ben relaxed and smiled at him. Who could resist his smile?

"I know this is probably hard for you. You've figured everything out, and I'm fucked up."

Dane hated hearing those words. He reached over the table and covered Ben's hand with his. Ben seemed surprised at his actions and turned his hand over so they could thread their fingers together. "You're not fucked up." Ben raised an eyebrow at him, and he relented. "No more than anyone else."

"I don't know about that. Different, then. If you don't like the phrase 'fucked up.'" He ran his free hand through his hair and pulled on the strands until Dane saw pain flicker across his face. "I'm twenty-eight years old, and it's taken me this long to find someone I'm attracted to."

That shocked Dane, but he tried not to show it. "Lots of men come out later in life."

Ben shook his head. "I don't think I'm gay. But I am one-hundred-percent into you. Don't doubt that." Dane sucked in a breath and relaxed. "I don't know anything else, but I do know that."

Dane stood up, still holding on to Ben's hand, and walked around the table. He sat on Ben's lap and shivered when Ben slid his arm around his waist. "We'll figure everything else as we go." Dane traced Ben's eyebrow with a fingertip and gently moved down his nose and to his lush lips. Ben opened his mouth and sucked on his finger until Dane went cross-eyed. He groaned as he pulled his hand away and used it to steer Ben's face to his.

They eventually came up for air and to eat their breakfast, legs pressed against each other under the table like they were teenagers. Dane couldn't stop grinning around his bacon. "Oh, I forgot to say that we're both invited to Dawn's thirtieth birthday party. Selena is recreating a children's birthday bonanza for her, and we all better be there and willing to eat, drink, and be very merry."

Usually Ben would try to get out of something like that or say he wasn't really invited, but he did none of those things. "It sounds like fun. You'll have to help me pick out a gift for her."

"We'll get her something together." Dane kissed him and smiled as he pulled back. "Changing the subject, did you know that there's a Farmers Fayre over in Staffordshire, near where my dad and brother live?" Ben shook his head, and Dane couldn't resist combing his fingers through the messy locks. "It's pretty fun. Lots of stalls, animals. The local ferret charity is usually there, and they have ferret racing."

"Ferret racing?"

"We can take Chase on his harness with us and watch the racing. It's all very laid back and it's for charity."

"This race doesn't entail men putting ferrets down their trousers and seeing who can last the longest, does it?" Dane laughed at the old-fashioned image and shook his head.

"No, there's usually about five tubes. You put the ferret in one end, and whoever gets to the other end first wins."

"Sounds like fun, let's go."


DANE'S HANGOVER disappeared as they walked around the fayre. He held on to Chase's lead and wished he was holding Ben's hand. Chase had no sense of direction and ran from side to side and back, tangling between their legs until he almost tripped up and Ben was in stitches laughing at him. He bent down and picked the wriggling ball of fluff up and stroked down his spine to calm him as they carried on walking.

There were horses, cows, and sheep, all in different pens, and there were market stalls selling food and crafts. Kier, who ran Pan Ferret Rescue, had a large tent full of information about ferrets and the rescue, but there was also a stall to buy things, and in the centre, there was a large pen set up for racing. Dane knew him through work, and he easily spotted his tall frame above everyone else. They'd made it just in time to put bets on for ferret racing, and he and Ben went to look at the ferrets taking part.

"Which ferret shall we bet on?" Dane asked. Ben studied each entrant—one was fast asleep, another was eating kibble, and another was showing off in front of the bars.

"Definitely that one." They placed their fifty-pence bets and watched, along with a small crowd as Kier placed each ferret at the start of their tubes. "Are you all ready," Kier said to them all. "You have to cheer them on, because ferrets need to feel the love." He opened the doors, and the ferrets all disappeared into the PVC tubing.

Dane cheered for the ferret they'd placed money on, and Ben joined in. The ferret who'd been asleep skittered down to the end, bombed out of the tube, and turned its body around until it backed into the corner, lifted its tail, and did a large poo that made all the children laugh. The other two ferrets didn't come out of their tubes, and Dane bent down to peer into them. "Look at this." He pulled on Ben's sleeve until he bent down as well and pointed towards the ferret they'd bet on. He'd curled up into a ball and had gone fast asleep.

Ben laughed, and Chase wriggled in his arms, not understanding the fuss. "We bet on the wrong one."

"If we'd thought properly about it we would have known to bet on the sleeping ferret. They always need the toilet as soon as they wake up." Each ferret had food, water, and blankets at the other end, and they all revelled in the attention they got. Kier handed out prizes to those that won and handshakes to those that didn't. He spotted Dane and smiled in recognition. Dane had spayed and neutered many of the ferrets that came Kier's way and helped all he could to make sure they were all healthy and happy.

"Dane, good to see you here." They shook hands. "This must be the ferret that was found over Lockstone." Kier nodded at Ben, and they shook hands too.

"Yes, this is Chase. And Ben." Kier stroked Chase's head and laughed when he tried to nip at his fingers.

"Good to meet you. It's great to meet others who love ferrets. You'll have to come to the rescue when you get a chance. I'll show you around." Dane knew what Kier was trying to do, but he didn't say anything. He enjoyed watching Ben come out of his shell.

"Feisty little thing, isn't he?" Kier said when Chase wriggled and reached up to lick at his chin. "He's looking great." They chatted for a while, and Kier cuddled the wriggling Chase, unfazed in the slightest by his movements or how he went from giving kisses to love bites. Most people didn't understand ferrets at all, but Kier was an expert. He'd run a ferret rescue for the last six years, and it showed.

"Is it okay if I give him some salmon oil? I bet he'd love a treat," Kier asked Ben.

"I've never given it to him before, but sure. If it's safe."

Kier smiled at him and reached for a bottle of amber liquid. "It's all right for a treat. I usually use it when I cut their claws or clean out their ears."

Ben frowned as he watched Kier hold Chase in the crook of his arm and squirt some of the oil onto his belly. Chase instantly curled round, stuck his nose in it, and licked it up. Ben's mouth dropped open in amazement, and Dane couldn't stop watching Ben as Ben watched the ferret lick his own belly as if he didn't have a spine at all.

"I can cut his claws for you, if you'd like?"

Dane patted Ben's arm. "Please do. We always have a wrestling match at the vet's. Let's see how the expert does it."

Kier nodded at them. Then he sat on a stool and placed Chase carefully on his knees. He gave him a little more oil and then, while Chase was distracted, he took each paw in his large hand and snipped the ends of his nails off with tiny nail scissors. "This is a game changer. And you do the same thing to clean his ears out?" Ben said.

"Yeah. I usually use a baby wipe over the tip of my finger and gently clean in the ear shell. No need to go deep or stick anything down there. Not that you need me to tell you. You live with a vet."

"Just because I'm a vet doesn't mean I know the easiest way to do things. This is good education for me too." Dane learned more about ferrets from Kier than he ever had from university.

"Yeah. I'm really amazed."

Dane was amazed. They never used salmon oil at the vet's, and it was eye-opening to see how Kier cut Chase's claws in under a minute. Chase carried on licking his belly long after the oil had disappeared, his back legs twitching in the air.

"We've got a few ferret books for sale, if you're interested. I recommend *Ferrets for Dummies* unless you want to use him for ferreting. If he's just going to be a pet, the Dummies book has great information in it."

"I'm going to buy it now." Kier was very good at what he did. He informed them on better animal care and made money for his rescue centre. Dane loved to see Ben so happy and carefree as he immersed himself in ferret care.

"I bet little Chase would love a friend, you know." Dane tipped his head back and laughed. He knew that was coming. Kier always tried to get him to adopt ferrets.

"I don't know about that yet. I'm still getting used to one ferret," Ben said.

"Ferret Math will catch up with you soon enough," Kier said. "Come see me then."

Ben looked between Kier and Dane. "What is Ferret Math?"

Kier gave them both a knowing smile. "One is not enough. One will turn to two, and two will turn to ten." He winked. Chase became a little restless as they talked. "If you guys want to carry on looking around, he can stay here with me. I've got an extra pen, food, and water. Who knows? He might find himself a friend." After Kier assured Ben that he wouldn't lose or sell Chase—he didn't adopt out ferrets when he was at an event—they quickly looked around the rest of the fair.

"Want some candy floss?" Ben asked as they passed a food vendor. Dane's stomach grumbled and his mouth watered at the smell of spun sugar.

"Most definitely."

# Chapter Twenty-Six

*Ben*

SELENA AND Dawn's flat was filled to the rafters with people, and the music was an array of cheesy eighties one-hit wonders that Liam kept randomly singing along to—loudly. There was a huge banner over the fireplace that said *Happy 30th Birthday*, and there were embarrassing photos of Dawn tacked up on every surface. If the grin on her face was anything to go by, Dawn didn't seem concerned that there was a photo of her passed out on a toilet in pride of place above the party banner.

Ben stood near the window holding a bottle of beer while Dane ate a mountain of party food off a pink paper plate. The whole gang was there, apart from Cal, who hadn't been able to get anyone to babysit, and there were others that Ben had never met or only recognised in passing.

"You're quiet. Is everything okay?" Dane asked leaning in next to Ben's ear so he could hear him over the music.

"I'm fine, honest." He gave a small smile, but Dane didn't look convinced. "Really. There's a lot of people here." He was used to their small group of friends now, but when there were so many other people, he found it hard to socialise. He was glad Dane was with him. If he weren't, he'd be standing by himself in the corner, wondering when he could disappear.

Dane bumped their shoulders together, and the tension relaxed. He loved how Dane didn't belittle him or tell him there was no need to feel like that.

"I know what you mean. I don't know how we've all fit in their tiny flat."

"Like sardines," Ben said dryly, motioning around them. There was nowhere to sit and no free floor space. Dawn had a lot of friends.

"Do you want a chicken drumstick?" Dane held out his flimsy plate and Ben couldn't help but grin. If they weren't hiding their relationship, he would lean forward and kiss him. Instead, he took that drumstick and watched Dane watch him.

Dane carried on talking, and they both ate off his plate until Ben's nerves disappeared and he didn't even clam up when people he didn't know wandered over to speak with them. He was enjoying himself.

"I'm just going to put this in the bin. Do you want another drink while I'm in the kitchen?" Dane asked.

"Sure." Ben smiled and watched Dane's arse as he pushed in between people to get to the table.

"Ben! Dance with me," Dawn slurred as she stumbled over to him and threw her arms around him. "It's my birthday. I want to dance." She dragged him the two steps from his window spot to what had been dubbed as the dance floor, and then Selena changed the music, and the familiar tune of *Agadoo* by Black Lace came through the speakers.

There was a collective groan, and Ben panicked, worried everyone would be watching him as Dawn made him dance. He glanced towards the kitchen, but there wasn't enough room to escape.

Dawn sang badly as she bounced her knees and did the actions. When he didn't join in, she nudged his hip with hers and started to bop up and down and point. Liam quickly joined in, and Ben didn't feel quite so exposed, and before he knew it he was pushing pineapples and jumping up and down.

By the time the song was finished, half the people in the living room were dancing from wherever they were, and Ben was laughing.

"I had a party just like this when I was eight. I love this band so much," Dawn told him with actual tears in her eyes. "Only less alcohol. It was the best party." She sighed happily. "This is the best party." She made a heart motion with her hands at Selena, and she did them back.

"Selena, put the *Hokey Cokey* on!" she shouted, but one of her friends came out of nowhere and placed a hand over her mouth.

"Definitely not. Only one Black Lace song per evening. Remember our deal?" Her friend winked at him. "There is definitely not enough room in here to do the *Hokey Cokey* without someone losing a leg."

She sighed but agreed. "They're a good band. I don't know what's wrong with the lot of you."

"They're a great band when you're eight." They squabbled like siblings, and Ben had to agree with her friend.

"Yeah, you need to be eight or you need to be hammered." And he was not hammered enough to listen to more cheesy party songs.

"That's it, gang up on me, on my birthday. It just means neither of you are drunk enough, so you need to go get a drink."

Her friend laughed and rolled his eyes at her. Then he turned back to Ben with a smile and held out his hand. "Hey, I'm Christian. You look vaguely familiar, but I'm not sure if we've officially met."

They shook hands and Ben tried to place him as well but couldn't. "You look familiar too."

"Here you go, darling." Dane appeared at his shoulder and handed him a bottle of beer.

"Thanks. This is Christian." They shook hands, but Dane stood so close to Ben he could feel every movement.

The cheesy dancing was liberating. Ben felt much freer after Dawn made him dance, and he and Dane chatted, talked, and even danced some more for the rest of the night.

The party was winding down and those who were left had congregated in the kitchen even though it was smaller than the living room and not nearly as comfy.

Jamie was sitting on Liam's lap next to the table that held the remnants of party food while Selena and Dawn were on the other chair. Dane pulled himself onto the work surface near the oven, and Ben stood next to him and leaned his butt against the edge.

There were more of Dawn's friends there who Ben didn't know, but he was merry enough and comfortable enough standing next to Dane that he didn't feel awkward.

Christian crawled out from under the table with a groan, and Dawn yelped when she spotted him. "What are you doing under my table?"

"I fell asleep." He rubbed his eyes, then made himself comfortable on the floor with his back against the fridge.

They were all talking nonsense, and Ben was knackered but too lazy to move. His eyes were closed, but he was still half listening to one of the conversations going around when Christian mentioned he'd walked in the parade at Pride.

Ben's eyes shot open, and he blurted out, "That's where I know you from."

Christian's eyes widened in surprise and then recognition. "You were with Dawn and Selena. I think I remember you. You were one of the guys covered in glitter." They all snickered and Ben nodded.

"You were handing out fliers in the parade." The purple and grey ones, the one he still had in his room somewhere.

Christian nodded. "I was walking with my asexual meet-up group." Ben blinked in surprise. He wouldn't have guessed Christian was asexual. He'd seemed so friendly, and he'd done his fair share of grinding on the makeshift dance floor.

"Christian's been running a group in Lockstone for three years now," Dawn said, sounding proud.

He nodded and they carried on talking. Ben had to bite his lip from asking what would probably be inappropriate questions, but it turned out he didn't have to—Christian had no problems talking about himself.

Ben listened quietly and took it all in, but something he couldn't pinpoint churned in his stomach. He wasn't quite sure what it was, but Christian's words resonated with something deep inside of him.

"Greysexual. What's that?" Everyone turned to look at him, and he tensed. He should have stayed quiet.

"It's someone who experiences romantic attraction only occasionally. I tend to hover between asexual and greysexual. My boyfriend identifies more as demisexual."

Ben had never heard some of those terms before. He'd only ever heard of asexual, and that had always been in a derogatory context that his old friends used to use.

"I didn't realise there were all these different terms." Ben shrugged his shoulders and tried to appear blasé and relaxed, though his mind was racing.

"Ben is straight and had very straight, vanilla friends before he found us," Jamie explained as he poured himself another shot of vodka.

"Pour me one. What kind of friend are you?" Dawn pouted, and then everyone asked for shots and the conversation was dropped. But Ben couldn't stop thinking about it.

While everyone was distracted, Dane leaned towards him. "I'm glad he said he's asexual, because I was ready to throttle him when I saw you both dancing together."

Warmth spread throughout Ben's body and he couldn't stop the smile. "We danced to 'Agadoo.'"

"I don't care." Dane's mouth brushed against Ben's ear and he shivered.

# Chapter Twenty-Seven

*Dane*

THEY WERE taking their relationship slowly, though living in the same house meant it probably wasn't as slow as if they were dating and living in separate places. But compared to other people they knew, they were taking it at a snail's pace. They hadn't had sex or even slept in the same bed, though there had been plenty of kisses and cuddling.

Ben wasn't comfortable telling anyone yet, and Dane respected his wishes because he knew how new this was for him—not just because Dane was a man, but because he was still finding himself and what he liked and didn't like.

They were planning a night in together watching a film. Ben cooked and Dane was showering the smell of damp dog off him after a busy day at work. The hot water pelted over his head and shoulders, and Dane sighed as his muscles loosened. He quickly shampooed his hair and washed his body. The thought of sitting pressed up against Ben's hard body made his cock stir. He groaned, shut his eyes, and angled his head under the spray. He'd been in a state of semi-arousal since he and Ben got together, and he wasn't complaining, but it was like the longest foreplay ever. The slightest pressure on his dick or one hot thought about Ben and his cock was hard instantly.

He hissed as he soaped himself up, and before he could think much about it, he slid his fingers around his erection and thrust into his palm. His heart raced and he closed his eyes as the water cascaded down his back. He pretended it was Ben's hand touching him as he squeezed, thrust, and ran teasing fingers across his length until his balls tingled. With one lone swipe of his thumb across the weeping head of his cock, he came with a gasp. He'd be ashamed at coming so quickly if it hadn't felt so good. His heart rate slowed, and he rinsed the soap and come off his body and turned the water off.

He dried himself quickly. Now he'd taken the edge off, he wanted to go downstairs so he could be with Ben. He towel-dried his hair and turned around to grab his underwear.

"Shit." Since Ben moved in, he usually brought his clothes into the bathroom so he didn't have to trek to his bedroom in a towel, but he'd been so distracted today that he'd forgotten. He gave his hair one last rub to soak up as much moisture as he could and tied the damp towel around his waist so he could go get dressed in his bedroom.

He stepped out of the bathroom, steam wafting out around him, and yelped in a very manly fashion when he walked straight into Ben's chest. Ben's hands came up to steady him and cupped his shoulders.

"Sorry," they both said at the same time, then laughed. Ben didn't move his hands, and Dane's laughter drifted off as he realised Ben's eyes were roaming his chest. His skin started to flush, and his cock filled despite the relief he'd found in the shower.

A droplet of water fell from his hair and trailed down his neck to his pecs. Ben's gaze filled with heat as he watched it travel down his body, and Dane stood still.

Ben let go of his shoulders and Dane thought that would be it, but Ben leaned forward and tentatively licked the errant droplet away. Breath hitched in Dane's throat and his heart skipped a beat as the heat from his tongue scorched his skin.

The water droplet was long gone, but Ben's mouth was still pressed to his chest. Dane wanted desperately to touch him but worried it would scare him off, so he kept his hands at his sides, the palms pressed tightly against the towel over his hips.

Dane could feel Ben's indecision, and he almost said that he didn't have to, but then Ben moved his mouth and pressed a kiss to the slight dip between his pecs, then another one over his heart and his collarbone. Then his face was pressed tightly into the crook of Dane's neck.

He shuddered and closed his eyes as Ben's five o'clock shadow scraped along his neck, followed by biting kisses, then something else— something hot and wet. Dane gasped and his knees shook as Ben tasted his skin and kissed and suckled at his neck until he was dizzy.

A small whimper fell from between his teeth, and Ben paused. Dane thought he'd messed it up, but Ben just pulled him in closer and caressed Dane's arse through the towel with one of his large palms. He sucked deeper, and Dane ground against him, unable to keep still.

The knot on his towel unravelled, and Dane felt the cool air chill his one hip and leg, but they were so close the towel didn't fall. He wasn't sure Ben knew the towel had come undone, but as he was about to reach for it and say something, Ben's mouth moved from his neck and caught his lips in a slow, deep kiss. He forgot about the towel.

Ben cupped his head, fingers threading through his wet, tangled hair, then trailed downward, leaving a damp trail down his back. His hands went to cup his arse again, and when they hit bare flesh, they hesitated and pulled away. He sucked the breath from Dane's lungs, and then his hands were back, cupping his cheeks and pulling him so close Dane could feel Ben's erection through the jeans and towel. Nothing he'd ever done so far felt as good as Ben's work-rough fingers digging into the flesh on his arse.

They kissed until Dane felt dizzy with lack of oxygen, and Dane pulled his mouth away and sucked air in. Ben dropped his forehead onto Dane's shoulder, his breathing ragged. "Fuuuck," he said, and Dane smiled and pressed his cheek against Ben's head.

His heart rate slowed as they stood in the hallway near the bathroom door, and he shivered when the heat of their encounter cooled enough for him to realise he was mostly naked. Ben's hands were still cupping his arse, and he flexed his cheeks. Ben whimpered, but he didn't move away.

"I should put on some clothes," Dane said, though he'd like nothing better than to take Ben to bed and show him how much better it could be. They'd kissed many times since they'd gotten together, but never with such intense heat. And neither of them had even come.

Ben caressed him one last time and took a step backwards as Dane just managed to catch his towel and hold it against his groin. Ben's face became red and he looked at Dane's crotch like he'd looked at that water droplet earlier. Dane's stomach quivered at the image that came to mind. His cock started to harden again, and it took all his willpower to stay where he was. "You need to stop looking at me like that, darling."

Ben blinked and his eyes finally raised to meet Dane's. It was an ego boost to have him look at him with such blatant desire. "I can't even remember what I came upstairs for," he said with a laugh.

Dane smiled and leaned over to press a kiss to his cheek. "I'm sure you'll figure it out. I'm going to put some clothes on before I forget I'm a gentleman." He winked, and Ben laughed as he walked away, arse on show.

# Chapter Twenty-Eight

*Ben*

He and Dane finally had to leave the comfort of their home before their friends got suspicious. As usual they were at the pub in their booth with Jamie, Liam, and Markus. There was an all-women Bon Jovi tribute band called Bonnie Jovi crammed onto the stage, and they had the whole place singing and dancing—Liam the loudest of them all.

He, Dane, and Markus were sharing one side of the booth because Liam and Jamie kept randomly making out and no one wanted to sit next to them, though sitting opposite them was just as bad, especially when Dane was pressed so closely against him.

It was odd to be out and have no one know about their relationship, and it was strange to act like they weren't more than friends. It had been awkward at first, but once he realised no one could tell what was happening between them, he relaxed. And it was kind of fun to have a secret that only Dane was in on. Every innocent touch was electrified, and when Dane purposely switched their drinks and placed his lips on the glass in the exact same place his had just been, he almost came on the spot.

It was heady. He'd never been so turned on before, not with another person. Masturbating had always been better than sex because there was no pressure, no person to please. He'd worried that he wouldn't want sex with Dane, that it wouldn't be good, but even though they hadn't gotten that far yet, everything they had done had been amazing. He thought about sex with him, what it would be like, who would do what and what would make Dane wild. It left him on the brink of arousal constantly, and he revelled in it.

He wanted sex with Dane, whichever way it happened. He knew he wasn't experienced, that he probably wouldn't be as good as others Dane had been with, but that didn't worry him. The excitement and the slow burn in the pit of his stomach overtook any worry he had. Dane not only made him think of home and comfort, he turned him on until he couldn't see straight.

It took Ben about an hour to get the courage to tentatively move his hand from his own leg to Dane's under the table. He stumbled over his words as he talked to Markus, but otherwise didn't act any differently. Dane's hand covered his, and Ben had to bite his inner cheek from smiling.

"I hear you and Donna split up." Jamie leaned over the table towards him so he could hear over the music.

Dane's hand tensed over his, and he turned his hand over so he could thread his fingers with Dane's. "Yeah. I mean no, we weren't really together." Jamie looked at him with disbelief. "We weren't right for each other."

"Not right for each other? I thought you were perfect together. She's perfect for you, she even works in our field." Dane was talking to Markus, but Ben could tell he was listening to Jamie.

Ben rolled his eyes. "That just meant all we had in common was work. Not overly exciting." Not like being with Dane. He could make watching the soaps exciting.

"I guess you're right. On the surface, me and Liam have nothing in common. He's a self-employed driving instructor who vlogs, and I'm a countryside officer who plays badass ukulele."

"You and Liam have loads in common—rats, music, terrible B-horror films, and an obsession with Marvel."

"I guess we do have a lot in common." Jamie's eyes turned misty, and he turned to Liam with a smile.

"Much better than only having work in common," Ben added. He had so much more in common with Dane. Their work was different but overlapped slightly and they both loved animals and watching TV snuggled on the sofa. They loved Chinese food and long walks over the Chase. With Dane, he didn't have to try at all. He might still be confused about his sexuality and where he fit, but he knew he fit with Dane.

# Chapter Twenty-Nine

*Ben*

BEN HAD never been to the Black Country Museum, and Dane was shocked that he hadn't even heard of it, considering it was a place he and his family used to visit every summer holiday as children. And he used to go there regularly with school too.

"I didn't grow up around here, remember?" Ben laughed as they got out of the car and walked shoulder to shoulder to the museum. He expected it to be a large building full of glass cabinets. He enjoyed a good museum, but he didn't understand why this was such a good one.

"You don't understand, Ben. You need to eat the fish and chips from the fish-and-chip shop, you need to try the sweets from the sweet shop, you have to have a pint from the pub."

"Are you sure this is a museum? Most museums don't have a pub."

"It's technically a living museum. It's a whole town, with shops, houses, the canal, and the coal mines. Which we get to go down as well." Dane paid for their tickets, and they walked through the door back in time, onto a street of cobblestones with quaint shops and storefronts as well as little cottages set up like they'd been frozen in Victorian times. There weren't many people because they'd gone early and managed to miss out on the herds of families and screaming children.

Dane was buzzing with excitement, and Ben grinned at his enthusiasm. "Oh, this is a schoolhouse. Let's take a look, darling." He pulled on Ben's arm to change direction and then they were holding hands. Blood rushed to Ben's head, and he looked around, sure that everyone there would be looking at them, but no one paid them a blind bit of notice.

"Sorry." He went to pull his hand away, but Ben held on to his fingers until he was sure he wouldn't.

"It's okay. I like it. I want to hold your hand." It was one of the things he'd always wanted—to hold hands with a partner he felt connected to.

He'd imagined it so many times, though he'd never pictured that partner would be a man. It made him a little uncomfortable because he wasn't out and it was all new to him, but he didn't know any of the people around them, so what did it matter if they held hands?

Dane beamed at him, and his hand relaxed into his. "Come on. Let's have a look in here. There's usually clothes we can dress in too."

Ben rolled his eyes, and they entered the schoolhouse and nosed around at the small desks and overly large rulers. They let go of each other's hands and joked around, putting on flat caps and taking photos of each other in the tiny chairs.

When they left that building, Dane steered him around the back to a large open area that housed an old-fashioned fairground and what looked like miniature pirate ships, swings, and a huge wooden red-and-white helter-skelter.

"We have to go on that." Dane grinned and dragged him to the person manning the entrance to the rickety spiral staircase that led to the top. Ben wasn't so sure. It wasn't that it was too high, but it was old and wooden, and he pictured it buckling under their weight.

"Is it safe?"

"Of course it is. It's only made to look rickety. It's tradition. If you're at the Black Country Museum, you must go on the helter-skelter, and you have to ride the narrow boat along the canals. Bonus points if you're picked for legging." He was afraid to ask what legging was, but he followed Dane up the inside of the helter-skelter and watched as he pushed himself down on his butt and spiralled towards the bottom so fast that the photo Ben tried to take of him was blurred. He skidded out of the bottom of the slide and slid across the grass before he came to a stop. Ben watched him stand and dust himself off with a laugh, and when he looked up towards him with a thumbs up, Ben sat at the top and pushed himself downwards.

He was dizzy as he spiralled around and around, his butt numb from the wooden planks the slide was made out of. As he shot out of the end, Dane was there to pull him to his feet, and he laughed as they stumbled along the grass, holding hands all the way.

Next they went on a trip down the coal mines, which Ben found fascinating. Their guide was dressed as a coal miner and made it all come alive. The whole group had to wear hard hats as they walked through. Black rock surrounded them, illuminated only by soft lighting. Ben tried to imagine working so far underground, and the carved-out corridors closed in on him. Ben was thankful when he almost hit his head on a few of the wooden posts that held up the ceiling, and Dane snickered. Ben gave him a mock glare and prodded him in the ribs, which resulted in a tiny yelp that made the others stare their way. Ben didn't even care they were centre of attention.

Ben was glad to be back above ground once the tour finished and took in a deep breath of fresh, crisp air. Dane pulled him along to The Bottle and Glass Inn, the quaint little pub in the middle of the square, where they each had a pint of famous Bottle and Glass ale. It was nice to do something just the two of them, neither afraid of who might see them.

Ben knew that was mostly his own issue, but walking hand in hand throughout the museum grounds gave him more and more confidence.

"How are you enjoying it so far?"

"It's pretty great. I can't believe how large this place is."

"I used to love coming here as a kid. We'd come every summer. They have an electric tram we can take a ride on when your feet start to ache." Dane winked. They were both avid walkers, and he couldn't imagine either of them getting tired, though a ride on an electric tram where they could sit next to each other and hold hands sounded good to Ben.

They ambled down the cobbled streets looking at mining cottages and shops. Dane practically drooled when they stopped in front of the sweet shop. It had jars of old-fashioned sweets in the window, and Dane ushered Ben inside, where there were even more jars behind the counter and an array of hardboiled sweets in displays. Ben's mouth watered at the smell of spun sugar and chocolate.

The man behind the counter was dressed in Victorian clothes and greeted them with a flourish. Dane asked about different sweets, and they ended up buying many different flavours, all which were made on site.

When Dane told him that he was taking him on a date to a museum, Ben hadn't expected this. "Try one of these?" Dane held out a red-and-white striped paper bag full of sweets, and Ben took a small round one with pink and cream swirls.

"What's this one again?"

Their server answered, "Rhubarb and Custard."

Ben popped it in his mouth, and the flavour exploded over his tongue. His eyes widened and he groaned. "Wow, that is so good." He'd had them before, but they didn't taste half as good as these. Perhaps it was the freshness of the sweets, but Ben secretly thought it was the company.

They walked towards the canal, and Ben had a moment of déjà vu as they came to the small ornate bridge. He glanced at Dane, who grinned at him. "Why is this so familiar?"

"You've watched *Peaky Blinders*, right?" Ben nodded and his eyes widened as he looked around, now picturing it with 1920s' garb, Cillian Murphy, and dodgy dealings. "It was filmed here?" Dane nodded. "No way. That's so cool."

"It is. They've filmed a few different scenes around here. We'll have to watch it together and see if we can spot what scenes. Now. Are you ready for a bit of legging?" Dane waggled his eyebrows, and Ben's cock took interest. He completely forgot about *Peaky Blinders* as his mind was filled with something much more delicious.

"Don't think I don't know you're pulling my leg about something." He pointed his finger at him, and they laughed all the way to the canal. The narrow boat was red and green, and the captain ushered them all on with a wide smile. The scenery was beautiful, and Ben relaxed with the motion of the water as they were taken around the canal. It was definitely now one of his favourite ways of exploring the countryside. He and Dane were still holding hands but they were quiet so they could listen as the captain told them the history of the Black Country. They came to a tunnel, and Dane shoved him in the shoulder excitedly.

"This is it!" He jumped up and walked towards the front of the boat. "We'll do it, come on." He didn't even give the captain a chance to ask the question, but his enthusiasm won everyone over, and they were both picked for legging… whatever that was.

"All righty, then. As I'm sure you can tell, there aren't any walkways in this tunnel, and the only way to get the boat from one end t'nother was for men to lie on their backs at the front and walk the wall. Think you can get us there safely?" He winked at them, and Ben looked dubiously at the two planks of wood nailed to the front of the boat.

"I don't know about this…."

"It's much safer now than it used to be." Before he knew what was happening, he was lying on his back with his legs off the side of the boat and Dane was doing the same on the opposite side. "There's some divots in the stones. Try and get your feet in them and push," the captain said. Ben gripped the side of the board he was lying on, even though he was strapped in, and he pushed his feet against the slippery wall. Between them the boat moved at a snail's pace through the tunnel. They were lucky it was a small tunnel.

"Good job, boys!" the captain boomed when they got to the other side. He unhooked them both and took over the reins. Ben's legs were burning as they sat back down.

"This is not the kind of legging I was picturing," Ben said into Dane's ear.

Dane twisted around to face him, his smile widening. "Oh, kinky, are you? Perhaps we can do your version of legging when we get home." Ben shuddered and could barely concentrate for the rest of their trip.

Once they got off the boat, they each had a cone of chips wrapped in newspaper and walked back through the main street. Dane popped a chip into his mouth and sucked the salt and vinegar off his fingers. Ben's stomach muscles tightened, and he groaned, forgetting about food as he fixated on Dane's tongue as he cleaned his fingers. He acted like his actions weren't doing anything to Ben at all and just smiled at him.

"It's almost perfect. If we had a bit of rain right about now, then it would be one-hundred-percent perfect. Chips wrapped in paper always taste so good when you're walking in the rain."

Ben laughed. He'd never heard of such a thing, but he'd be willing to get wet for Dane. "I'll take your word for it."

After watching him eat chips, Ben couldn't stop looking at him. He was overly aware of everything Dane did, and every time they touched or held hands, electricity would race up his body.

When they finally got home, his skin was tingling all over and his pulse was racing. Dane let Speedy out into the garden and fussed over the ferret, but Ben was out of it. He could only follow as though he were in a dream. His eyes drank Dane in—every movement he made was elegant, his voice was smooth as he spoke, and it curled around Ben until he was so turned on, he didn't even know how he'd got there.

Dane hadn't done anything overtly sexual. He was just being himself, but Ben couldn't stop thinking about what his skin would feel like under his fingertips. He remembered the fullness of Dane's arse in his hands when they'd kissed after Dane's shower. Whether it was a peck on the lips, a brush of the mouth, or a deep kiss filled with heat and the promise of more to come, Dane's kisses were intoxicating.

Nerves fluttered in his belly, and when Dane finished sorting out the animals and turned back to him, he obviously realised Ben was on the edge. His eyes darkened and he licked his lips as the air around them sparked. Dane held out his hand, and Ben took it without question or worry. He luxuriated in the tingle of his hand in Dane's, in the race of his pulse and the erratic beating of his heart. He couldn't hold back any longer—the arousal burned bright and his blood was like molten lava in his veins.

"I really want you." He wished he could be more profound, say something that would match the significance of the occasion, but words were beyond him, and he knew that Dane would understand and look past their simplicity. He'd never wanted anyone before, and he wanted Dane.

"Will you come upstairs with me?" Dane asked. The nerves raged, but Ben didn't run away. Nerves about wanting someone were completely different to the nerves he'd always had because he *didn't* want someone. He nodded, and Dane led him upstairs.

For the first time in his life, he wanted someone romantically… sexually. His brain threw questions at him, tried to plant the seeds of doubt, but he listened to his heart, and his heart wanted Dane. His heart and body were in perfect sync about that.

Dane's bed was large, the duvet slightly wrinkled, and one pillow lay on the floor with a dog-shaped dent in it. It hit him then that he was in another man's room and that he wanted to be there. The intimacy of being in Dane's private space wasn't lost on him, nor was the fact that he would be on the bed and among the sheets Dane slept on the night before. Ben's cock hardened and pleasure coiled in his stomach like a spring.

Dane was unusually quiet, worrying his bottom lip between his teeth again. "We only do as much as you feel comfortable doing. If you change your mind or don't want to do something, tell me, okay?"

Ben nodded. "I'll tell you." He didn't have to hide from Dane, and that made him want him more. There were the usual nerves about sex, but they were mixed with want and heat, which was a heady combination. Skin peeked out from beneath Dane's V-neck, and Ben hesitantly reached towards him. He pressed a finger against the V and then dipped his finger beneath and felt the smooth skin over his collarbone.

Dane gasped and then sucked in a breath. "Take it off?" Ben's voice broke, and Dane swallowed but did as he asked, pulling the shirt over his head, and dislodging his hand.

The rise and fall of his chest kept Ben entranced. He was pale and mostly smooth—so different to a woman. His mouth watered at the thought of licking one of Dane's nipples. Would it be sensitive against his tongue? Could he suck it into his mouth, and would it drive Dane wild? Need hit him so desperately he almost came without even touching Dane. Was this what other people felt when they had sex? This mixture of comfort, warmth, with a bite of heat and danger? All Ben knew now was that Dane became more beautiful every day, and for the first time in his life, he genuinely wanted sex.

"I want you," he said, mouth dry. "I've never really wanted anyone before." Ben gave a breathless laugh and ran a hand through his hair.

"I'm glad you want me."

"I do, I really do, but I don't know what I'm doing. I usually pretend and lie until whoever I'm with is satisfied and hasn't got a clue I want to be somewhere else. I don't want to pretend with you."

"Then don't." Dane strode over to him and pulled his head down into a blazing kiss that took away his breath and all his nerves.

Perhaps he should feel scared—not because he didn't usually like sex, but because this time would be with a man. The nerves didn't come, just a blanket of comfort because it was Dane and nothing could be wrong between the two of them.

He clenched his arse cheeks at the thought of Dane inside him, and it stirred something deep and primal within him. He wanted to be as close as he could to this man. He wanted Dane to crawl inside of him and brand him as taken. Nerves weren't enough to take this from him, and the panic he usually felt about everything in his life didn't appear.

The hairs on his arms stood straight with awareness so strong he let out a shudder and crooked his finger at Dane. "Please," he said, not recognising the needy breathless voice that fell from his own lips.

Dane had obviously been waiting for permission, and he smoothed his hand over Ben's chest. Ben hadn't even realised he was shaking.

"It's okay." Dane's words were barely a whisper, but they flowed over Ben like silk.

"I know." And he did. He'd never been more sure of anything. "I need your hands on me." His voice was raspy and full of need so strong his eyes closed with want.

He needn't have worried about Dane. He was so in tune with Ben that he knew exactly what he needed.

Dane pressed a shaking hand to his cheek, which made his eyes fly open. The scorching touch of work-rough fingers rubbed against him, and Ben moved into the touch, Then Dane slid his hand towards his mouth, where Ben was able to press a kiss to the palm.

"Like this?" Dane asked, his voice like liquid heat. Ben whimpered, and then Dane grasped the back of his neck and pulled him in for a desperate kiss.

Ben moaned into his mouth, the taste of ale and chips strong. He'd never kissed like this before—or maybe he had but he wasn't into the woman kissing him and that made all the difference. The lips pressed against his were full, slightly chapped from where Dane bit at his lip, and his tongue was insistent as it ran along the seam of his own mouth and dipped inside to taste him as if he were something special.

It was like waking from a coma. His nerve endings were so sensitive they felt like flames everywhere Dane touched him. That elusive spark he'd tried so hard to find was there. It had nothing to do with Dane being male, nothing to do with the straining erection rubbing at his hip through layers of denim, and everything to do with Dane himself—every detail of him, inside and out.

No one else had ever made him feel like this. He could try sleeping with other men, dating them, but the old familiar dread raised its ugly head at the thought. He wanted Dane because of the person he was, because he was a good friend and a wonderful man.

He needed to be reminded that his body was good for more than lies or half-truths. It felt amazing to feel desired and to desire. If he didn't rein in his hunger, he would come right there, and they hadn't got beyond kissing. He wanted to get further.

Ben felt a comforting sense of peace as he ran his hand over Dane's back so he could follow the notches of his spine with his fingers. There was no need to find excuses to get away, no need to stress about spending time with someone he wasn't that into—not with Dane, never with him. The passion was an extension of their friendship, and the warmth of it almost brought tears to his eyes.

Perhaps that wouldn't sound exciting to others, but the deep intensity of his feelings went beyond physical attraction, beyond friendship and fleeting lust. He didn't have the words to explain it, not even to himself, and so he opened his mouth wider, pressed his tongue against Dane's, and lost himself in the kiss. They stopped long enough for Dane to try and get him out of his shirt. It took Ben too long for his brain to catch on to what he was doing, but when he did, he quickly wiggled his arms out of the sleeves and they both worked to pull the shirt over his hands until it dropped forgotten on the floor. The cool air made him shiver, but Dane's warm hands slid over his arms and pulled him close.

Dane didn't have much chest hair—just a smattering of invisible blond hairs between his pecs and a swirl around his belly button that trailed down into his waistband.

He was lean and had good muscle definition, like a swimmer or a runner. Without even thinking about it, Ben pressed a hand over Dane's heart, then smoothed both hands downwards, from chest to stomach to waist, luxuriating in the softness of his skin and the tickle of coarse hair.

Ben hooked his fingers into the loops on Dane's jeans and pulled him forward until their straining cocks rubbed against each other through their trousers and their bare chests pressed together.

Goosebumps raced up his arms, his already hard cock pulsed, and Ben leant his forehead against Dane's shoulder as he tried to get hold of himself. He never contemplated that touching would ever be this intense. It was almost too much, but he never wanted to move.

"Bloody hell," he said into the crook of Dane's neck, the faint taste of salt and spicy cologne on his lips. His insides felt like jelly, and he was sure if Dane's arms hadn't wrapped around him, he would have slid to the floor.

"It's all right. Just feel," Dane said between small kisses to his cheek. He nibbled a line up Ben's cheekbone to his left earlobe. then sucked the small sliver of flesh into his mouth, rolled it around on his tongue, and nipped playfully at the edges. Ben's eyes rolled into the back of his head. It was such a small action in reality, but the heat of Dane's mouth, the movements of his tongue brought images to mind of that tongue sucking other things and he couldn't stop the needy whimper that escaped his mouth.

The thought of Dane's mouth on his erection almost made him come. Blowjobs had always been stressful before Dane, but now he couldn't stop thinking about it. He wanted to feel Dane's mouth stretch wide around him, and what's more, he wanted to do the same to him. There would be no worry about maintaining a hard-on.

They were similar in height, but different body types. Ben was thicker, his muscles made from felling trees, hiking, and working outdoors daily, while Dane's muscles were less defined. The planes of his chest fit perfectly against Ben's, yet it wasn't enough. Ben moved restlessly, creating as much friction as he could.

Dane leaned backwards, his pupils blown, lips swollen as he stared down at him. Ben didn't know what he was going to do until he dropped to his knees, hands skirting the waistband to Ben's jeans.

"Dane," Ben pleaded, though he wasn't sure exactly what he was pleading for. Dane rubbed his cheek against the denim that covered Ben's erection, and stars exploded in front of his eyes. He staggered backwards and whimpered as he fell into the chest of drawers. He tried to hold the noise in, but he couldn't contain it. It was too much and not enough.

Dane rolled his eyes up at him and smiled—a wicked tilt of his lips that made Ben think of things he'd never wanted before.

Dane unsnapped the button, gently pulled the zipper down, and then leaned forward and pressed a tender kiss to the quivering flesh just beneath his belly button as he hooked his fingers into his boxers and pulled them down his hips. Ben's cock sprang free, hitting Dane's chin, and he gasped. He didn't get a chance to get used to the feeling before Dane clutched his buttocks, pulled him forward, and swallowed him down until his nose was pressed against the neat thatch of Ben's pubic hair.

He never thought he'd be a screamer, but Dane's mouth was like a scalding furnace around his sensitive flesh, and the way he moved his tongue sent shots of adrenaline right through his balls until they drew tightly up against his body. He clutched at the edge of the dresser with one hand, fingernails biting into the wood as his legs started to tremble. Dane hummed, and Ben grabbed a tight hold of Dane's hair to steady himself.

He tried not to thrust forward, but he wasn't in control of his own body.

"Sorry," he gasped when Dane gagged. He expected him to pull away, but Dane gripped Ben's hips and pulled him towards his face, showing him a rhythm to move in. He was inexperienced, afraid to go too fast, but unable to stop himself, yet that didn't deter Dane. He knew what to do, and Ben trusted him. His thrusts became erratic, the intense heat almost too much to bear. Then Dane slowed him down with a hand on the hip and sucked until just the tip of Ben's cock remained in his mouth. He teased the head with the point of his tongue, and Ben felt his balls tighten.

Their gazes caught, and Ben's vision started to blur. He didn't want to come yet, didn't want this to be over. Dane, so in tune with him, knew what he was thinking and circled the base of his cock to stave off the orgasm.

Ben sucked in air until his vision cleared, and then one of Dane's hands was on the move. While the one hand kept a loose grip on his cock, the other slid between his legs until Ben felt a hot palm rub against his testicles and trail further backwards to circle his sphincter as if trying to gauge his reaction.

Ben wasn't quite sure *how* to react. He knew this was coming, obviously, but he'd refused to let his thoughts delve too deeply into it. He let his mind go there now, thought of what it would be like to have Dane inside him, and realised he not only wanted to find out, he needed to find out. The finger felt out of this world as it gently massaged him, and that small teasing touch made Ben ache for more. It was shocking—taboo— but that just made his body react even more. Precome dribbled from his cock, and his whole body was on fire as he let himself feel everything.

Breathing became difficult as he lost all ability to control his body. It belonged to Dane now, and whatever he did to it turned the pleasure up further until Ben was dizzy with it.

Dane didn't try to penetrate him. Instead he lowered his mouth to his cock again and sucked, moving his hand in time with his rhythm. Sweat dripped into Ben's eyes as he watched Dane move, watched his erection slide into his mouth. It was the most erotic thing he'd seen in his life. He could come like this, but he didn't want to. He desperately wanted to touch Dane.

He pressed his hand against Dane's head to stop his movements. Dane rolled his eyes up in question, and Ben licked his lips. "Don't want to come like this."

Dane stood up and kissed him. It was weird to taste himself for a second before he got lost in the kiss. Ben didn't really know what he was doing, but he knew he wanted Dane on the bed. So he steered Dane backwards and gave him a slight push. He was still in his jeans and there was something highly erotic about seeing Dane with ruffled hair, swollen lips, and bare chested.

"Take 'em off." Dane's eyes widened, but he did as Ben asked and slid them, along with his boxers, until he was naked. Ben stepped out of his jeans and then tripped over them and crawled onto the bed, over Dane until they were face to face. He chuckled softly, and Dane smiled and reached a hand up to cup his cheek.

"I don't know what to do," Ben whispered.

"What do you want to do?" Dane's words were just as quiet, as if there was someone else in the house who would hear them, and it didn't feel right to break the spell between them.

His eyes roamed over Dane's perfect body, not really knowing where to stop. "Touch you." He leaned down and pressed his open mouth to Dane's, taking control. Dane wrapped his arms around Ben's neck and curled a leg up over his hip, applying pressure. Ben learned quickly, and he lowered his whole body against Dane's until their naked flesh touched. They groaned together, and Ben rubbed against him until they found the perfect position, his cock nestled into the crook of Dane's groin and Dane's cock hard against his stomach.

It probably wasn't the best position for him to give his first hand job, but neither of them wanted to be any further apart. Ben managed to squeeze his hand between them, and he circled Dane's cock and flicked his thumb over the head. He swallowed Dane's cry and enjoyed the movement as Dane's hips rose off the bed towards him.

If sex was like this, then he wanted it all the time.

They had to breathe eventually, and Ben ripped his lips from Dane's. Dane was still gently thrusting against his hand, their sweaty flesh sliding together perfectly. Ben gave a muffled groan and burrowed his head in the crook of Dane's neck. He had an idea and shifted his hips up enough to create more room. Then he slid his cock next to Dane's and gripped them both.

"Oh, God." Dane gasped and thrust up into his hand. Ben shuddered. He squeezed them both, and Dane bit into his shoulder. Short gasps coming from his mouth as Ben jerked them both together. Ben's skin tingled and his balls drew up tight. Their leaking cocks made the movements easier, and their flesh glided against each other as they thrust into Ben's hand.

His orgasm was a surprise. Intense pleasure pushed him over the edge and, without warning, he came between them. Dane was only seconds behind, and their come mixed as Ben continued to jerk them both as their cocks softened.

Only then did he collapse on top of Dane, their sticky groins sliding together deliciously. Dane wrapped a leg around his and threw an arm around his neck as they both gasped for breath and waited for their heartbeats to return to normal.

"I really love your idea of legging better," Dane said between breaths. Ben laughed and kissed the closest piece of skin he could find.

# Chapter Thirty

*Dane*

BEN WAS sprawled out, legs akimbo, the duvet Dane had pulled over them before they fell asleep kicked to the end of the bed. Dane's face was pressed into the crook of his neck, and he had one arm flung over Ben's chest and a leg thrown over one of his. His groin was pressed into one of Ben's hipbones. He groaned in pleasure and nestled back into Ben as he drifted back to sleep.

An incessant beep pulled Dane back from sleep and he was so foggy he couldn't understand what the noise was until Ben woke up and rolled sideways to fumble for the phone on the bedside table.

"Hey," he mumbled into the phone. Dane traced a pattern on Ben's chest and enjoyed the rumble as he spoke. He was too relaxed and sleepy to worry about who it was until Ben tensed beneath him. Then he rolled his eyes up to look at him and watched the colour flush his cheeks. Dane shivered at the sight of all that skin and pressed a lazy kiss to his jaw. "Jamie. Err. Hi. Yes, this is Dane's phone, he asked me to answer his phone. We—fell asleep watching a film in the living room."

Dane lifted himself up on one elbow as sleep left him. Ben sent him a silent grimace and mouthed, "Sorry." He'd obviously answered the phone half asleep, not realising it was Dane's.

"You were looking for me? My phone? It's… in my room probably. I didn't hear it. Sorry."

Dane tried to make sense of their conversation, but it was impossible. "Is everything all right? Is Liam okay?" Jamie wouldn't call them in the middle of night without good reason. Dane's heart started to thump painfully.

Ben raised his eyes to look at him and nodded, though he was still listening to what Jamie was saying. "A fire? Where? Jesus. I'm on my way. I'll meet you there." He switched the phone off and turned to Dane. "I've got to go. There's been a fire over Lockstone Chase. Jamie just got a call from the police. He's there now." He got out of bed and started to dress, his face strained with worry.

It took Dane a moment to untangle himself from the sheets, but he started to grab clothes too. "I'll come with you."

"You don't have to—"

"I want to." He pulled Ben to him for a quick kiss. "And you answered my phone, so Jamie will know I'm awake. I'll not be able to relax knowing you're both there. Come on, I'll drive." It wouldn't take long to get there, but Ben was too agitated to drive.

Despite the darkness, Dane spotted the billowing smoke just five minutes away from home. There was a fire engine on site, and they seemed to be controlling the fire, although he guessed it had done considerable damage. He glanced at Ben, who paled in the darkness as he took in the smoke and the flames.

There was an ambulance there too, and Jamie was there with a couple of teenagers being given oxygen. *Shit*. He and Dane glanced at each other and came to the same conclusion about the teenagers. Lockstone was rife with kids who thought it was a great place to hang around, smoke, and set a fire or two at night.

Jamie was there with his boss, and Liam was close by, talking to a policeman, a good distance away from the fire as the fire brigade carried on dousing it with water. Ben jumped out of the car and hurried towards Jamie, Dane only a step behind. It was unspoken between them that they wouldn't advertise their relationship, not until Ben was comfortable— and not while a fire blazed right next to them.

"You can't go there." A policeman came towards them, arm out to stop them going any further.

"I work here," Ben said, eyes going over his shoulder to Jamie and Liam.

"We're with them." Dane placed one hand on Ben's shoulder and pointed towards Jamie. They jogged over and Jamie gave them a wan smile and then coughed. "Are you okay?"

He nodded and glanced at the teenagers, both looking sheepish. They shivered even though they'd been given blankets and their eyes were wide with shock as the fire continued to fight the spray of water. The water was winning and the flames had fizzled to practically nothing.

Ben didn't look as though he believed Jamie as he pulled him into a gentle hug. "What did you try to do? Put the fire out yourself?"

Jamie snorted, then coughed again. "Nah, they won't even let me get close. They were already putting it out by the time I got here." He nodded towards the firefighters. "I get like this if I stand too close to the bonfire on Guy Fawkes Night." He looked out into the smoke with a frown.

Their boss was still talking with the police, and Jamie moved away with a small smile and walked back over to them. "I should see what they're saying."

Ben brushed his hand against Dane's, and Dane shivered. He hadn't expected such an intimate touch. Even though he knew no one was watching them.

"I better...." Ben pointed towards Jamie and their boss. Dane nodded and squeezed Ben's fingers tightly before he let go.

Dane and Liam stood apart from Ben and Jamie as they talked officially with the police and their boss. He couldn't hear what was being said, but they were all frowning. Dane wondered how much damage the fire had caused. Despite how late it was, an audience started to appear behind the tape that cordoned off the area from the main street. There was still smoke in the air, but the fire was eventually doused until there was nothing left.

"What the hell are they doing?" Dane grumbled as they stared. Their conversation looked finished, so he and Liam joined them all. The evening was dry and unnaturally warm with a slight breeze. Dane could taste the smoke on his tongue. The police spoke to the onlookers until most of them disappeared. Dane jumped when Ben threaded his hand through his and squeezed again. It only lasted a few seconds, but it warmed him more than the fire ever could.

"How bad is this fire going to set you back?" Dane asked. It was dark, but he could see burned-out trees and shrubs where there used to be life.

Ben winced and gave a drawn-out sigh. "We won't know until we can assess the damage, but I'd say bad. I know we occasionally use burning as a method to control the heathland, but that is planned meticulously and well thought out. This is anything but."

# Chapter Thirty-One

*Ben*

IT WAS after eleven when Ben finally stood in the doorway to Dane's bedroom. He'd left the landing light on, so Ben could see him sleeping peacefully under the covers, only his wavy light brown hair showing. Ben's eyes didn't move away from him as he stepped into the room and undressed. He pulled his work polo shirt over his head, shoved down his jeans, and toed them and his socks off at the same time. He left his clothes where they fell. His heart was swelling with something warm and permanent as he hovered next to his side of the bed. His side. He had a side.

In the weeks after the fire, Ben was so busy with work that he barely saw Dane, or when he did, he was knackered and all they did was fall into an exhausted sleep together. There had been one awkward night where he'd gone to his own bed, but Dane had slipped in between his sheets in the early hours, and since then, Ben went straight to Dane's bed and curled himself around him. They always wore boxer shorts. Ben felt uncomfortable sleeping completely naked, even after sex—one of his many hang-ups.

Dane gravitated towards him straightaway, flung an arm over Ben's chest, and threaded his leg between Ben's, although his eyes were closed and he didn't wake. Ben pressed a gentle kiss on top of his messy head and relaxed into the feel of having Dane in his arms.

Ben was exhausted and all he wanted to do was fall into a dreamless sleep, but his brain wouldn't switch off. For once, it wasn't the fire that was running through his brain. It wasn't even Dane.

Christian's words replayed on a loop, even though Dawn's party had been over a month before. He'd ignored it the first time he thought of it, but he was too tired to ignore it anymore, and the panic he thought might rise with it was blessedly absent. Christian hadn't said much at Dawn's party, but what he revealed was so similar to how Ben felt before he'd fallen for Dane that he couldn't ignore it in the early hours of the morning when the rest of the world was asleep.

Ben knew he wasn't asexual, but maybe he was something else. The thought that he could be somewhere on the asexual spectrum—a spectrum he hadn't known existed until Dawn's birthday party—didn't scare him like he thought it would, not now that he had Dane and friends who accepted and celebrated people's differences. Perhaps being different wasn't so bad.

His eyes were gritty from lack of sleep, and he'd forgotten to turn the light off in the landing, so he could watch Dane as he slept. His mouth was slightly open, his bottom lip plump and kissable. It took everything in Ben to resist kissing him. He didn't want to wake Dane up just because he wanted a kiss.

It was such a new experience for him to want to kiss somebody, but he was also enjoying the moment and the feeling of that new experience, so he was happy to wait until Dane woke for his kiss.

Heat slowly filled each of his limbs until his skin was hot to touch. His cock hardened slowly, and his balls were heavy as he watched Dane sleep. He turned on his side, so he faced Dane, and he carefully placed a hand on the swell of his hip. Dane didn't wake, so Ben closed his eyes and soaked in the feel of him so close. He slipped a finger under the waistband of Dane's boxers, wanting to feel more skin, and finally fell into a deep sleep.

IT WAS still early when he woke, but he felt rejuvenated. Ben's whole hand had slipped inside Dane's boxers during the night, and his hand cupped the swell of his arse. He bit back a groan, not wanting to wake him up. Dane's face was pressed against the crook of his neck and one of his arms was draped over Ben's chest. He could get used to waking up like this. They fit so perfectly together that Ben couldn't ever imagine waking up alone now. It seemed laughable that he'd tried so hard to get this with the women he'd dated in the past, yet it had happened with Dane without his knowledge.

Ben smoothed his hand down Dane's arse, and Dane moaned and stretched like a cat. Ben froze his movements, and Dane tipped his head backwards and opened one sleepy eye. "Don't stop," he mumbled and closed his eye again.

Ben smiled but did as he asked, slipping his hand further into Dane's boxers and scraping his blunt nails along his arse cheek. "Sorry I woke you," he whispered.

Dane pressed his mouth into Ben's neck and licked a strip of skin. "I'm not."

His words made Ben brave, and he moved his fingers in circular motions until the tips brushed the crack and followed the pathway down. Dane whimpered, and Ben's breath caught in his throat as his fingers explored. His cock throbbed when the ring of muscle fluttered underneath his touch, and Ben broke out in a hot flush as he imagined pushing into that tight heat. It was a wild thought, one he'd not let himself think of too much just in case it scared him or he got so nervous that he did something stupid, but touching Dane like this was all he could think of.

Dane adjusted himself, and when his cotton-covered cock brushed against his, the small unassuming touch made Ben see stars. Dane circled his wrist and pulled his hand out of his boxers. Had he done something wrong? Touched him in a way he didn't like? Nerves twisted in his stomach but then Dane steered his hand to his mouth. He pressed a kiss to his palm and then slowly licked his forefinger.

Ben gasped, and his eyes zeroed in on Dane's mouth as he sucked his fingers. His tongue was hot and wet, and Ben's breathing became harsh as he watched Dane suck on them until they glistened. He pulled away with a pop and then nudged Ben's hand back under the covers to his arse.

"Do it again," Dane said as he leaned in for a kiss, his tongue curling into Ben's mouth. As Dane took control of his lips Ben gripped his arse cheek. His spit-slick digits slipped into his crack and everything clicked in his brain. He knew what Dane wanted him to do. As he ran his fingers along Dane's crack, his heart thumped wildly in his chest.

He circled the small ring of muscle, and Dane whimpered into his mouth until Ben was dizzy with need. He pressed down, and the cooling spit helped the movement, but he didn't breach the muscle. Nerves set in, and he was too afraid of hurting him, though Dane was acting anything but hurt. He kicked one leg over Ben's hip and used the heel of his foot to force Ben closer. Their erections pressed together, and Ben shuddered.

"Please." Ben swallowed the words, and when Dane's hand tangled in his hair to deepen the kiss, Ben pressed his finger down until it breached Dane's body. He was scared he had hurt him when Dane ripped his lips away to take in a breath of air, but instead of returning to the kiss, he turned his head to nip and bite at Ben's shoulder.

Ben didn't think anything like this would turn him on. When he'd thought about sex, it had always been clean, vanilla—romantic. This was more than he ever thought possible and definitely not vanilla, not in his head, anyway. He'd never thought fucking and romance could go hand in hand, but Dane was proving him wrong.

Dane bore down on his finger, and he slipped further inside. There was something decadent and taboo about what they were doing, but instead of turning him off, it turned him on. Dane was so tight around him, and he imagined him around his cock and shuddered. Dane snapped his hips up, pushing their cocks together, and then pressed back onto his hand. Ben nudged Dane's head with his cheek and steered him back to his mouth.

He licked at Dane's lips, slipped between them, and soon found a rhythm where his fingers and tongue moved in sync. Dane unravelled in Ben's arms and twisted his body around Ben's in such a way that Ben found himself on his back with Dane straddled over his thighs, curled over him so not to dislodge his fingers.

The movement freed Ben's other hand. It automatically went to Dane's neglected arse cheek, and he used it to pull him closer.

"Not going to last," Dane said as he gasped against Ben's mouth. Ben grunted, unable to speak. He bent his legs and dug his heels into the mattress, thrusting his hips upwards, looking for friction. Dane leaned backwards and braced himself against Ben's legs.

Ben's eyes widened as he took Dane in. His head was thrown back, and his chest moved with each fast breath. His chest was smooth and pale, his abs tight. Ben moved one hand to his thigh while his other finger pushed into him. His arm was aching from the awkward position, but he refused to move his hand. Dane was beautiful as he lay draped in his lap. His erection peeked out of his boxers, and Ben hooked a finger into the elastic and pulled him out. Dane gasped and his eyes shot open. His pupils were blown, and he bit at his lip as he watched Ben. He'd never felt so powerful before. Dane made him feel so many things—all of them good.

"Yours too." His voice was strained as he looked between them. Ben knew what he wanted, and he pushed the elastic of his own boxers down so he could free his cock. The cool air on his heated flesh made him shiver. Precome glistened, and he wiped his palm against it, smearing the clear liquid. Then he sat up taller and grasped Dane's cock, mixing their excitement together.

Dane pushed away from his knees and leaned in to take his mouth in a brutal kiss that had him rocking backwards onto the bed. His fingers slipped free, and he clutched Dane's butt until there was no space between them. Even that wasn't close enough.

His hand was caught between their bodies, and there wasn't much room to move, so he trailed his fingers down to Dane's balls. His own cock moved next to Dane's, and their bare flesh slid against each other until Dane erupted between them. That was all it took for him to go over the edge. His balls drew up, and he came harder than he'd ever come before. White noise roared in his ears, and his pulse raced. Dane collapsed, their slick flesh sticking together. He enjoyed the weight of Dane on top of him, and as their breathing got back to normal, he ran his fingertips along Dane's spine.

"God, Ben. Jesus," Dane mumbled against his collarbone. Ben could feel him smile, and that made him smile too. "Best way to wake up."

"Yeah," his voice was breathless, and he'd lost the ability to talk in actual sentences. They lay together, come cooling between them until Speedy started to whine and they had to get up to let him out, then let Chase have a play in the living room before they had to get ready for work.

He was cleaning out Chase's cage when Dane ventured back inside with Speedy at his heels, cheeks rosy from the cold. Chase ran over to him and raked at his trousers, then tried to shove his nose up his trouser leg.

Dane laughed and bent down to scoop him up. "I don't think so, Chase. I know you're an ankle biter, no way am I letting you up my trouser leg." He attempted to stroke the ferret's head, but Chase was in too much of a playful mood and he tried to catch Dane's fingers with his mouth instead. Dane just laughed some more and put him back down, then reached for the Pride flag on the back of the chair. He waved it at Chase, who went mad with happiness and jumped high as he tried to grab the edge. He twisted and ran, then rolled onto his back as Dane threw the flag over the top of him.

"The amount of toys he has, and the flag you got from Pride is his favourite thing ever," Ben rolled his eyes at him but still leaned over and tickled the lump he saw under the rainbow.

"We should ferret-proof one of the spare rooms so he has more space when we're at work. Of course, your room would be the best, as it would give him more room."

Ben blinked and looked up silently at Dane, unsure what he was really saying, but hopeful. So hopeful.

"You could move your clothes and stuff into my room. Permanently." He stood awkwardly as if he was unsure of Ben's reply. Surely, he should know. Ben stood up and went to hug him, then realised he had rubber gloves on and peeled them off before he reached for Dane.

"I'd love that." He'd been sleeping in Dane's bed anyway, but he always went to his room to change. and he'd never left any clothes in there apart from the ones that littered the floor before bed. Ben kissed the smile from his lips, stealing it from himself. The kiss deepened before Dane ripped his mouth away and hopped backwards.

"You little devil!" He bent down, and then Ben noticed Chase had managed to get up the leg of his work trousers and he was biting at Dane's ankles. For whatever reason, most ferrets liked to attack feet, but Chase? He had a penchant for ankles, specifically Dane's. Ben didn't blame him.

# Chapter Thirty-Two

*Dane*

DANE GOT to work in a haze of sexed-out bliss, and with one sore ankle. He and Ben had been sharing a bed for weeks, and Ben had never initiated sex before. Cuddles, comfort, and sweet, sweet kisses, yes, but it hadn't gone beyond that. He got goosebumps just thinking about what they'd done, and his cock stirred. They hadn't even gone that far, and it had been out of this world, better than any full-on sex he'd had. He clenched his arse as he remembered Ben's fingers, and he felt oddly empty. It had been so powerful, he'd been so intent on him, that Dane hadn't had the brainpower to touch him back. He mourned that fact, but he couldn't mourn their encounter; it had been too hot. Hot and sweet because being with Ben couldn't be anything but.

Dane's cock was still semi-erect from just thinking about that morning, but he willed his body to behave and took a deep breath as he bent to put his lunch in the staff fridge. He couldn't work with a hard-on. That would be weird.

"You're looking a bit spaced out today?" Laura said from behind.

He jumped. "Jesus. You scared me." He filled the kettle enough for both of them and plonked teabags in two cups.

Laura was still laughing at him when one of the veterinary nurses arrived.

"What's so funny?" Clare asked.

"Dane was in a world of his own and almost peed his pants when I came in," Laura said.

"I did no such thing, darling." He rolled his eyes and handed each of them a cup of tea. Then he made himself a new one. His phone vibrated in his pocket and he pulled it out, unable to stop the smile when he saw Ben's message pop up.

*Are you free for lunch?*

*Unless any emergencies come, why?*

*I'm going to be at a site near you all day. I thought I could meet you for lunch.*

Dane grinned even wider and replied.
*That sounds good. I'll let you know if anything pops up. One o'clock okay?*

*One is perfect.*

Dane was still smiling when he realised the room was quiet. He looked upwards and both women were staring at him. "What?" He hoped they couldn't see him blush.

"Texting someone special, are you?" Clare wiggled her eyebrows at him.

"Just a friend." He felt the need to over explain, but that would just make it worse. "Anyway, I need to go set up for morning appointments. I'll leave you two to gossip." They laughed as he walked away from them. When he got to his room, he looked at the clock and hoped the morning went fast so he could spend some time with Ben. Speedy was settled in his bed in the corner under his desk as Dane turned on his computer to check what appointments he had that day.

The Appointment Gods were obviously on his side when it got to lunch time, so he was able to take the time off. He grabbed Speedy's lead and walked out the front so he could wait for Ben, but he was already there talking to Ronnie, one of the part-time receptionists, while Laura sent overt daggers his way. Silly woman. Even if Ben weren't in the picture, he and Sean would never have been anything but the occasional fuck buddy to each other.

Ben turned to him but carried on his conversation with Ronnie. He walked over to Ben and Ben bent down to stroke Speedy as he wagged his tail and jumped at Ben's legs. "Hey there Speedy, I missed you." He rolled his eyes upwards to Dane as he said the words, and Dane's heart expanded. Everyone would assume he was talking to Speedy when he said that, but Dane could see the truth in his eyes.

"Ready?" Dane wasn't sure where they were going, but they needed to get away from the vet's because he was afraid everyone would be able to tell what Ben was to him by the look on his face.

"Yep. I thought we could get chips and walk in the park." Chips sounded much better than the lunch he'd packed.

"Sounds great." Ben opened the door for him and Speedy, and they walked the short distance to the chip shop. Dane asked for a wrapped cone and then ripped a hole in the top of the paper so he could get to the chips, just as he'd done when they went to the Black Country Museum. Ben laughed at him. "Why didn't you just get an ordinary cone?"

"You heathen. Everyone knows chips taste better this way."

"Oh really?" Ben leaned towards him, and his heart started to hammer. Fast as a thief, he nicked a chip from Dane and popped it into his mouth. "Hmm… you might be right, although it could be all the vinegar you drenched them in."

Dane gave him a playful shove as they walked towards the small square at the bottom of the high street. Everyone called it a park, but it was more of a war memorial with a few benches around the outside. They sat at the furthest one, and Ben let Speedy off his lead so he could explore. "Vinegar and chip-shop paper make chips taste great. All we need now is for a downpour. There's nothing like eating chips in the rain."

"You're an odd man, Daniel Vincent."

Dane raised an eyebrow and ate another chip. "You've only just realised that now, darling?" Ben grinned, and Dane wanted nothing more than to kiss that grin from his mouth, but he refrained. "When I was about fourteen, Jamie and I used to go to this youth club every Tuesday. They had a pool table, cheap food, and drinks. It was mostly a way the adults tried to keep the kids off the street. When it closed for the night, we'd get a wrapped cone of chips on the way home. It poured with rain the once, and we got drenched. But those chips were the best I'd ever tasted."

Ben smiled wistfully at him. "I wish I'd known you back then. Perhaps I wouldn't have felt so out of place if I'd had friends like you and Jamie."

Dane popped a chip into his mouth and chewed. "I'm not sure about that. I was a tad selfish and had a chip on my shoulder because I was just discovering I was gay and I was positive my father was going to make me stay on the farm." He shuddered.

"I bet you weren't that bad. I always felt out of place, different to my family and friends. I told you I've never really found women attractive?" Dane nodded. "I've never really found anyone attractive until you, which is just confusing." Ben hadn't expected to have this conversation right there and then, but it seemed like the natural progression to what they'd been chatting about, and he wanted Dane's opinion. "Ever since Dawn's birthday when Christian talked a bit about being asexual, I've wondered if I might be demisexual or something. I'd never heard of that word before then, but I don't know. I think it fits. Or bits of how I feel fit. What do you think?" He shrugged and shoved another chip in his mouth to give him something to do.

"I guess it could make sense. Plus we've been friends for a long time, so we already had a connection. I admit I'm not much of an expert when it comes to asexuality, but we can always do a bit of research or talk to Christian. It doesn't make a difference to me, though. In case you were worrying." Dane was overwhelmed at how much Ben trusted him. He hoped that Ben knew he'd never hurt him or turn him away because of how he felt.

"I know. But it would be nice to not be confused about my past."

"Whatever you want, whenever you want it," Dane promised.

"Good. We should all try and get out soon. Do something. Drinks or a hike or something."

"You're right. Dawn's birthday was the last time we all got together, and that was a bit crazy." Dane had a flashback to the party and watching Ben dance to awful party songs with even worse actions. He smiled. Ben was a good dancer once he relaxed and stopped worrying what people would think. Dane wondered what it would be like to dance properly with him—some slow number that meant they could get as close to each other as possible while people looked on with jealousy and wondered what Ben would be like without so many clothes. He shuddered. Ben's brow furrowed as he looked at him. "What?"

He was going to lie, say it was nothing, but the words slipped out before he could sensor them. "I was imagining us at a club, dancing pressed together on the dance floor, people surrounding us but not being able to touch, the music beating down on us as our hips moved to the rhythm."

Ben's eyes widened and his lips dropped open. "Shiiit," Ben said.

"Would you like that?"

He cocked his head to the side as though thinking carefully about the question. "Yeah. I think that sounds good."

"One day soon, darling," Dane promised. Their eyes bore into each other until Dane could barely breathe. As soon as Ben came out, Dane was dragging him to a club and dancing with him all night long until they were both crazy with desire for each other.

# Chapter Thirty-Three

*Ben*

THEY'D TAKEN Speedy and Chase on a long walk, though Ben ended up carrying Chase most of the way around. He was more relaxed than he'd ever been. He'd even talked to Dane about his suspicions about being demisexual, and Dane hadn't batted an eye. Dane made him feel warm inside, made him want to smile just because. For the first time, he wanted to hold someone's hand, though he wasn't quite brave enough to make that move so close to home. Dane didn't judge or push. He went at Ben's pace, and just knowing that turned Ben on in a way he'd never been turned on before. He wanted Dane so much—it was insane to him how he could want someone when he'd spent his entire life wanting no one.

They still hadn't gone all the way, but Ben thought about it constantly. He'd worried that the attraction would disappear once he and Dane were together—the same way he'd crush on a girl back home and then lose interest almost instantly if she showed interest. But that hadn't happened with Dane. It was still a lot to wrap his head around. But now he couldn't stop thinking about sex, more specifically sex with Dane.

What would they do? How did it work? When? He knew the basics, of course, but he wanted it to be good for both of them. He was still new at all this, and Dane had experience.

Ben lay on the sofa with his head on Dane's lap as Dane absently ran his fingers through his hair with one hand while he played Merge Dragons on his phone with the other. Ben was flicking through a worn copy of *Ferrets for Dummies* he'd bought from the farmers fayre a few weeks ago and doing his best to concentrate on the words and not the hand on his scalp.

"Do you think Chase is happy?" Ben asked, breaking the silence, trying his best to distract himself from sex. Dane's fingers stilled.

"I think he is. He's had his bad tooth extracted, he's been neutered, and he has a good home—why do you ask?"

"Kier mentioned getting another one to us. I know he was being nice, but I think he was trying to give us good ferret advice. Plus, I've watched loads of YouTube videos of ferrets playing together, and this book says they should be kept in groups... or pairs, at least."

"It's true that it's recommended they're kept with a friend or two, but I don't think he's unhappy."

Ben frowned to himself. "Am I being selfish keeping him when it means he has to be alone?"

Dane put his phone down so he could look into Ben's eyes. There was a small frown on his face. "You're the least selfish person I know. You *saved* Chase. He'd probably be dead if you hadn't found him."

"But still... I'm not a ferret." The thought of giving Chase up made Ben feel sick. He'd become attached to him instantly, but he needed to think of what was best for him. Chase should have ferretty friends to play with.

"If you're that worried, we can always go get another ferret."

Ben snorted and rolled his eyes, slightly irritated. "I can't do that. It wouldn't be fair on you. This is your house. I've been here much longer than we originally agreed." He'd forgotten that he was meant to be looking for his own house, and he didn't much like reminding himself or Dane. They were so good together, but that didn't mean he shouldn't be looking for somewhere else.

Dane narrowed his eyes. "Seems to me that you've got a place here. I already asked you to move into my room. And the owner of this house doesn't mind getting another ferret with his boyfriend."

Ben's stomach churned for a second, but then warmth spread throughout him. They'd not said that word before—even after Dane asked him to move his stuff into his bedroom. Ben hadn't allowed himself to even think it, but beneath the nerves those words brought, it felt right. He twisted into a sitting position so they could have this conversation the right way up.

"I didn't want to presume. We've not talked about it, and this was meant to be temporary." Dane tensed, and Ben realised what his words sounded like. "I mean living here—not us, not you." He relaxed again, and Ben let out a nervous breath.

"We're getting along pretty well—"

Ben leaned forwards and interrupted his words with a quick kiss. "Very well."

Dane laughed. "Very well, indeed. I don't want to lose this." He motioned to them on the sofa, and Ben's eyes moved to Dane's crotch. It was a novel move for him; he wasn't usually so—horny, but with Dane, he couldn't get enough.

"Hey, eyes are up here, perv," Dane said with laughter. "Don't get me wrong, sex with you is out of this fucking world, but I'd miss just sitting here in the same space as you. Stay. Get a ferret with me. You told Kier you'd go check out his rescue. Perfect excuse."

Ben's eyes welled with tears. Dane not only understood him, he enjoyed the parts of the relationship that Ben did as well. Ben was boringly ordinary, and he'd always thought he had to conform and fit in, but with Dane he did fit in—just him, no conforming. Sitting with Dane, even doing nothing, was his favourite thing.

Not that he didn't enjoy the sex—for the first time in his life he truly did, but a big part of the reason he enjoyed it so much was because of all the other stuff.

Sitting next to each other on the sofa, each doing their own things, walking Speedy and Chase over the park, taking turns cooking—even washing their clothes together—there was just something so intimate about all of that.

"I'd miss this too." Neither said the boyfriend thing again, but it was out there, between them, coiling around them, and Ben found he liked it.

"Good." The corners of Dane's eyes creased as he smiled. Ben couldn't help but trace one of those with a fingertip. Dane shuddered and closed his eyes as though to contain himself.

When he opened them, they were glistening and bright. "Are we getting a brother or sister for Chase?"

"Yeah. I like the sound of that."

"We can go around on our next day off."

"As long as we go late afternoon. I'm meeting Christian for a chat, remember?"

"I'm sure that will be fine. If not, I'll book on our next day off together."

"Brilliant. We should get more fleece. And more kibble—is the cage big enough? Shit, I should probably buy my own cage—can't keep borrowing Jamie's spare, can I? He might need it back eventually."

"Don't worry darling, Jamie would have let you know if he needed the cage back. If we convert your old room, we might not need a cage at all. Jamie won't mind us hanging on to it until we've sorted everything out."

Chase was fast asleep over a pile of Speedy's toys, as if he were a dragon hoarding gold. His back leg twitched, and he stretched but never woke up. Speedy was lying on the rug in the middle of the room, his comfortable dog bed mere inches away from Chase. Ben loved them as much as he loved Dane. He adored coming home to their sweet faces, taking them on walks, and playing with them in the garden. This was as near to perfection as he'd ever found.

Maybe soon he'd be brave enough to come out to all their friends and tell them he was in love with Dane. He looked back at Dane and couldn't breathe for wanting him. His insides were warm, but the heat was cranking up as his cock stirred. His mouth watered as he lowered his gaze to Dane's lap and saw the hardness strain against the denim. What did he taste like? He rubbed the front of Dane's jeans with the heel of his palm.

A long, drawn-out groan fell from Dane's lips as he tipped his head backwards and his eyelashes fluttered closed. Need coiled in his belly, and he put more pressure as he rubbed. Dane panted and rolled his hips upwards to find friction. Dane's pleasure was in Ben's hands and the intensity of his own excitement skyrocketed. He hadn't touched himself yet, but each noise Dane made, each push of his hips was like a hand grasping his own dick. He unsnapped the button on Dane's jeans and lowered the zipper.

Dane gasped, his eyes shot open, and he looked expectantly at Ben. He didn't have to wait for long. Ben's hands shook—with nerves or need, he wasn't sure which—as he pulled Dane's erection from the confines of his boxers.

"Ben," Dane said on a shudder. Ben glanced at Dane's face—his lips were glistening from where he'd licked them, and his eyes were dilated. He lowered his gaze back to Dane's cock and watched as his fingers traced the length of him. His skin was hot and hard as he explored. The tip was leaking precome, and Ben pressed his thumb into it. Dane cursed and pushed up.

Ben couldn't take his eyes off the liquid coating his thumb, and before he even thought about it, he sucked his thumb into his mouth. It was faintly bitter as Dane's taste exploded over his tongue. His own cock roared to life and he groaned.

He dropped to his knees next to the sofa and ran his hands up Dane's thighs. Dane was dazed as he sat there, and he whimpered when Ben pulled his jeans and boxer shorts further down his legs so he had better access.

Nerves fluttered in his belly, but it wasn't enough to snuff out the excitement as Dane's beautiful cock bobbed towards him. He'd never done this before; he'd probably be bad at it. But that didn't stop him. He lowered his head, chased Dane's cock with his mouth, and licked a strip across it until that unique flavour burst against his tongue again.

He swirled his tongue around the tip as Dane's hips lifted and pushed him further into his mouth. Ben opened his mouth wider and sucked as hard as he could. Fingers found his hair, but they didn't try to take control, which Ben was grateful for. He explored Dane's cock with his tongue, mouth, and fingers until he had it committed to memory.

He rolled his eyes up and watched Dane as he lowered his mouth further. Dane's brow creased and his mouth dropped open as keening sounds fell from between his lips. Ben gagged when he tried to take too much, so he pulled off enough so he could grip his length with one hand and suck on the sensitive head. Teasing soon became his new favourite pastime, and with his free hand he cupped Dane's balls. Dane jumped and parted his legs further.

"Christ," he breathed. Ben didn't say anything, just put more pressure on his cock until he could feel Dane's balls draw up.

His heart stuttered and his own cock swelled in his jeans, but he didn't even think about pleasuring himself. This was all about Dane and discovering his body in a way Ben had never wanted to do with anyone else. Dane's pleasure was his pleasure, and when he came, Ben was seconds behind him. With Dane's fingers raking through his hair, his essence coating his tongue, and Dane's softening cock in his mouth, Ben had never felt closer to him.

# Chapter Thirty-Four

*Ben*

CHRISTIAN SAT at a small table in the back corner of Lock Over the Chase tea shop when Ben arrived. He recognised the long black hair and easy smile from the party, and Christian stood when he saw Ben hesitate in the doorway. Ben forced himself to walk over, nerves overcoming him.

"Hi, Christian. Thanks for meeting me so quickly. I hope I didn't interrupt your day."

"Of course not. I'm happy to help any friend of Dawn and Selena's. Shall we order tea? I waited for you to get here first." They walked over to the counter, and Christian ordered a pot of tea and a carrot cake. Ben didn't think he could eat anything, so he just ordered a coffee. His palms were clammy when they walked back to the table, and he rubbed them down his thighs. Admitting his feelings to Dane hadn't been as awkward as this. It was one thing to tell his boyfriend something in confidence, but to talk about it to a near stranger made it more real, somehow.

They didn't talk until after their drinks were brought over. Then Ben shifted in his seat and looked at Christian. He was normal. Ordinary. Nothing odd, weird, or strange about him. He was around their age but had an air of confidence that Ben lacked. He seemed self-assured and unashamed. He reminded Ben a bit of Liam in that way.

"So," Ben started. "You probably realised at the party that I don't know much about asexuality." It was hard for him to say the word, but he forced himself.

Christian nodded and took a bite of his cake. "Not many people do. It's getting more widely accepted, but most people off the street probably don't even know there's a spectrum of asexuality."

"Yeah, that was definitely me. But hearing you speak… you said a few things that felt familiar, and it made me wonder about myself. I don't think I'm asexual. I've had sex before."

"It can be confusing. I consider myself asexual for the most part. I sometimes slide over to greysexual, with a little bit of sensual attraction thrown in, but I'm mostly asexual."

"I don't get how you can change. Surely you're one or the other?"

"Feelings are fluid, ever changing with the tides. Why would sexuality be any different? Most of the time, I don't want or need sex with my boyfriend, but occasionally I'll get the urge to be closer to him than cuddling provides. Doesn't mean I'm not asexual."

Ben tried not to let the shock show on his face. He didn't get how he could be asexual and have a boyfriend, but Christian acted like that was nothing out of the ordinary.

"This is so confusing." He ran a frustrated hand through his hair. He'd hoped this conversation would clear up things for him.

"It's difficult when you're still figuring it out. Plus no one is the same. These terms are just here to help us. You can use one or another, you can decide not to use any of them, and it won't be wrong. I find that they helped me find my place and helped me find others like me so I'm not so isolated. But I know some people who don't want to be labelled at all, and that's fine too."

Ben had hoped that Christian would be able to tell him that he was one thing or another and he'd be able to tell himself that was the reason he'd felt different for so many years, but nothing was ever that easy.

"Can I ask you a personal question?" Ben nodded. "Why are you wondering about asexuality now?"

"I've met someone." He didn't mention names because he didn't want it to get back to the group. Not that he thought Christian would gossip, but he'd asked Dane not to tell anyone, so he should do the same. "A man. I've never—with a man before." He could feel his cheeks burning, so he took a sip of his coffee to distract himself and hide a bit of his face. "I've always been with women before. But I've never been attracted to anyone." God this was embarrassing. "I wanted to want them, and I could"—he looked around to make sure no one was listening—"get off, but I never liked it beyond the physical release, you know? Jerking off was a lot less complicated."

Christian's kind eyes widened in understanding. "I understand. I went through something similar when I was first discovering my sexuality. Luckily, a friend's older brother came out as gender-fluid, and it introduced me to a whole new set of people and a way of life that I wouldn't have known about otherwise. It made it easier to find a place to fit in and to be accepted."

Ben nodded that he understood. The friends he'd had growing up were all heterosexual and none of them socialised with anyone different. The only time he'd heard the word *asexual* was as an insult along with the term *frigid*. They drank in silence for a few minutes, as though Christian knew he had a lot to process.

"I don't understand why any of this matters to me, anyway. I've found someone I'm attracted to, so I should be happy," Ben said.

"It's confusing to always feel one way and then, for whatever reason, you start feeling another way. We want to make sense of it. Stop beating yourself up. How new is your relationship?"

"Very. But we've been friends for a couple of years."

Christian pointed his fork at him, then licked the frosting off it. "Sorry to throw another term at you, but you could be demisexual."

"I thought about that, but part of me feels like I'm just trying to find a word to use so I can fit in. Twenty-eight years is a bit old to suddenly decide, don't you think?" He must have been living under a rock. That was an accurate description of the small fishing town he came from, he supposed.

"You're never too old. It basically means the person doesn't feel attraction until they form an emotional connection. Sounds like that's what you've done with your man. Age has nothing to do with it."

They spoke for nearly an hour, and as blown away as Ben felt at what was a whole new way of life for him, it also soothed the raw edges of his nerves. He'd always thought he was the only one who felt like he did, but to find out there were others who felt similarly made him feel less like a frigid freak. He still wasn't one-hundred-percent sure he was asexual or demisexual, and part of him felt ashamed at trying to find a label to make himself feel less alone. But that was his brain playing tricks and twisting things again, so he tried to ignore every negative and concentrate on the positives. And as much as he now felt like he might have somewhere to belong, he knew it made him different.

Maybe normal was overrated.

# Chapter Thirty-Five

*Dane*

BEN STILL wasn't exactly sure if he wanted to put a label on himself, but after his talk with Christian, he seemed to be a bit more confident and was more comfortable in his own skin. Dane didn't care either way, so long as he was happy. He'd gotten everything he ever wanted. Ben was an attentive boyfriend and they got along famously. The only issue he had was keeping it a secret from their friends. They wouldn't care at all, but Ben was still afraid.

He'd gone from only dating women to living with a man, so Dane had to rein himself in and let Ben set the pace. He could be patient.

He'd booked an appointment with Kier, the owner of Pan Ferret Rescue, to see the ferrets there. They were both excited, and Dane felt grown up. He had a successful job and a house, but there was something about getting a new pet with his boyfriend that just cinched the deal.

The rescue was located on the outskirts of Lockstone, in the large garden of an old farmhouse. It wasn't a farm any longer, but there was enough land around the house to have a warren of interlinking sheds and runs that housed over fifty ferrets looking for a new home. And there was a room inside dedicated to ferrets with medical needs who couldn't stay outside and needed extra attention.

Kier was in his early forties and greying slightly, but he didn't have an ounce of fat on him. He was hot but gave a hands-off vibe that Dane wouldn't cross. Dane first met him when he started working at the veterinary practice in town and Kier brought some ferrets in for spaying. They'd worked together on the rescued ferrets ever since. They got along well but never moved past acquaintances. Kier kept to himself and rarely left his property. He had a few people who volunteered, and he took part in different fundraisers, but Dane had never seen him do anything that didn't involve looking after ferrets.

Dane parked on the gravel driveway and waited for Ben to pick up Chase's carrier. Extremely put out at being confined, Chase raked the bars at the front in protest.

Ben walked up to him and Dane didn't even think; he reached for his free hand but yanked it back when Ben tensed.

"Sorry," Dane muttered, his cheeks burning. He wasn't used to being with someone so… new.

"It's okay, just not used to it." Ben brushed the back of his knuckles against Dane's hand in an apology. "Give me a bit of time, yeah?"

Dane smiled and Ben knocked their shoulders together, lightening the mood. "Let's go add to our family."

Dane reached over and unlatched the gate. The gravel crunched under his boots as they walked over the pathway to the front door. He rang the bell and they waited.

Kier came from around the side of the house, and an old dog padded slowly behind him. Dane greeted Diego first—Kier would only be offended if he didn't.

"Who's such a good boy," Dane said as Diego sat on his foot and leaned against his leg for a scratch behind the ear.

The dog looked over at Ben and gave a small yap, as though demanding more attention, and Ben must speak dog, because he placed Chase's carrier on the floor and bent down to scratch Diego's other ear.

"He's such a slut," Kier said affectionately. "Come on Dee, that's enough. They're not here to see you," he chastised, but the dog only moved when he was good and ready. He pottered in the direction of a well-loved tennis ball, picked it up, and then lay down.

"Hi Kier, how are you?"

"Not too bad, glad you've finally decided to see sense and adopt a ferret from me." He looked at Ben, smiled, and held out his hand. "It's good to see you again."

Ben shook his hand. "You too. We're looking for a friend for Chase."

Kier bent down and investigated the carrier. He stroked the paw that poked through. "I knew it wouldn't take you long."

"You and that book persuaded me," Ben said.

"I'm glad you've persuaded this one to get a ferret." Kier looked at Dane with a grin. "I've been on at him for years to adopt some."

Dane snorted. "It's much easier to have more than one animal when you've got someone else in the house to help."

Kier smiled and shook his head. "I wouldn't know. Come on round the back. I bet you're dying to see the ferrets."

They went around the back of the house to a warren of worn but well-kept sheds with windows and runs attached.

"I've got a run we can use in here. You can let Chase out and we can see if they get along."

They walked through the first section of a large shed, though shed seemed the wrong word for it. It was much sturdier and larger than any ordinary shed. Ferret pens lined the back wall, and there were windows on the opposite wall. There was an area with kibble, blankets, and clean food bowls just as they entered.

"We just had a donation," Kier explained.

"Wow," Ben said as he looked around, his eyes immediately fixing on the ferrets in the pens.

Kier shot him a grin. "I recently expanded. I made the runs tall enough for us to stand in because crouching constantly was hell on my back. Come on in. There are two free-range areas. I kept one free for you guys so we can see how Chase is with them."

Dane was impressed with the layout of the sheds. The ferrets weren't overcrowded but every inch of space had been used thoughtfully.

"There is no way I can choose one." Ben sounded a bit shell-shocked.

Kier grinned, crease lines forming at his eyes. "That's okay. I'm here to help. You're relatively new to ferrets, so I can show you some of our more laidback residents. We've got a few kits in, but they tend to be extra work—not that I'm trying to put you off. Plus, you're living with a vet, so you've got an added advantage.

"There are five in this pen. They're all relatively easy-going, ranging in age from one to three years."

Ben stood in front of the pen and peered in. Then he glanced back at Dane. "What do you think?"

He blinked out of his daze, but he was as lost as Ben was. "I'm not sure, darling. Do you have any ideas who would be the best fit for Chase?" Dane asked Kier.

"If you don't mind albinos, then I think Squidge might be a good fit. He's around two years old, got handed in by inexperienced owners who got bored of him. He's a bit of a chunky monkey but very friendly with other ferrets."

Ben frowned. "Why would we mind if he's albino?"

Kier shrugged. "Some people are put off by the red eyes. Albinos are harder to home than polecats."

Dane already knew that, but his heart hurt anyway. Ben's face was full of horror and sadness, then determination.

"We have to have an albino, then."

Dane laughed, joy bubbling over. That was his Ben.

"Let me get him for you." Kier reached into a pen and crooned softly at the sleeping ferrets inside. They didn't wake, so he softly stroked the nose of one until he yawned, stretched, blinked, then scrambled to his feet and launched himself into Kier's arms.

"Hey there, Squidge. You ready to make some friends? Be on your best behaviour." He pressed a kiss to the ferret's head and ushered them into the empty run. Then he shut the door, pushed a bolt across, and locked them all inside.

The run had clean shavings on the floor, a few cat beds towards one side, lots of tubes, and a cat tree.

"If you let Chase out first so he can get familiarised, then we'll see how they are."

Ben put Chase's carrier on the floor and unlocked the door. Chase pushed it open with his head and ran off, so happy to be free that he did a little war dance and ran into one of the beds. They all laughed when he just wriggled on his back, and they watched him explore the new place and sniff out the new scents before Kier put Squidge down. They didn't go near each other for a few moments, but then it was as though they both realised the other was there and they tensed, hackles rising.

Ben held his breath and unconsciously gripped Dane's arm. The small touch in public made Dane want to announce his feelings for everyone to see. Dane touched his lower back in comfort, and he slowly let the breath out. "It's okay. They need to get to know each other."

Squidge jumped on Chase and grabbed his neck, and Chase flipped over like a crocodile. When he got free, he pounced on Squidge and then ran off as though beckoning him to follow.

They all laughed softly, not wanting to interrupt their play. But their antics suddenly got a little tense as Chase grabbed Squidge by the neck and dragged him around the pen. Ben tensed, but Kier put a finger up to stop him separating them.

"Don't worry just yet. They're just asserting dominance and playing. No stink bombs have gone off, and despite the little bit of fluff in the air, they're just figuring each other out. There's no fur flying or broken skin."

"Ferrets play rough," Dane added as he slipped his arm through Ben's to give it a reassuring squeeze. Dane's hand was warm where it rested against his arm, and Ben let the tension leak from his body as they carried on watching the ferrets.

Squidge had the upper hand now, and they were both wrestling and making excited little dooking noises. Chase obviously missed having other ferrets to play with.

"Well, what do you think?" Kier asked.

The ferrets had started to explore together, Squidge sniffing at Ben's feet. Ben bent down, stroked Squidge's back, and picked him up. He was an adorable chunky white ferret with slightly yellow fur around his eyes. His paws seemed overly large, and Ben wouldn't be surprised if he was one of Jim Henson's puppets rather than an actual living creature.

Dane leaned into him and tickled Squidge's head. He wriggled in Ben's arms and went to chase Dane's fingers like a kitten. Chase raked at his jeans, and Ben grinned down at him and picked him up as well. "No need to get jealous. We love you too."

Dane laughed, head tipped back, and he shot Kier a conspiratorial look. "I think you've got your answer, darling."

"He's perfect," Ben said.

"What can I say? I'm the ferret whisperer." Dane couldn't argue with that. Not only had he found the perfect friend for Chase, but Kier also had the silver fox good looks of the dog trainer Cesar Millan from the TV show, *The Dog Whisperer*, only taller.

"Come on. Let's get all the paperwork sorted and pay the adoption fees," Dane said.

"Should we put him in a separate carrier? I have one in the car."

Kier shook his head. "I'm not sure you can split them up now." Squidge and Chase were straining towards each other as Ben held them, one in each hand. "Just keep an eye on them. There might be a few kerfuffles when Chase gets back to his own territory, but I have a good feeling about these two."

# Chapter Thirty-Six

*Dane*

IT WAS rare that Dane spent any one-on-one time with Jamie anymore. He missed his friend, but he understood. Jamie should put his boyfriend first, and he had Ben now, even if no one knew that he did. Ben was spending a rare night away with his old flatmates. It was odd without him, but Dane was happy Ben had other friends as well.

He and Jamie sat on the living room floor as the ferrets pranced, jumped, and dragged toys into weird hiding places. They were certainly getting along like a house on fire, though Speedy didn't seem to know quite who to run after when they got hyped up. Clever dog was sleeping on the sofa in Ben's spot while they all sat on the floor. Jamie tickled Squidge until he hopped and rolled onto his belly and then chased his fingers. Dane laughed, then yelped as Chase jumped over his legs and wiggled his butt in play.

"He's adorable," Jamie said about Squidge. Dane had forgotten it was their first meeting. "So… you and Ben got a ferret together?" Jamie turned to look at him, and he could feel his cheeks start to heat up. *Fuck.*

He shrugged, trying to go for nonchalance, unsure if he managed it. "Well, Ben did. You know ferrets like to be with other ferrets. They're like rats that way." He hoped bringing up rats would sidetrack him—no such luck.

"I know that, but it seems strange while he's still bunking at yours. Has he found his own place yet?"

Why wouldn't Jamie just shut up? "Why? I don't mind him here. Plus his money helps with the mortgage, and it's nice to have more than one animal in the house."

"Fuck. Okay, I'm just going to come out and say it. Are you in love with Ben?"

Dane was shocked at the question, though he probably shouldn't have been. A protest was on the tip of his tongue, but he couldn't get more than a splutter out. *Shit.*

"Don't get me wrong. Ben is a great guy, and if he were gay, I'd say you were perfect for each other, but he's not gay, and I don't want you to get hurt again." Jamie was so unobservant sometimes. The *again* shook him to the core, and in that second, as their gazes connected, Dane realised Jamie wasn't as unaware of the crush he used to have on him as he thought.

He wanted desperately to tell Jamie he was wrong and tell him all about his relationship with Ben, but he bit it back. He couldn't out Ben like that, especially not to one of his closest friends, one who also happened to be his boss, so he swallowed his protest. "I know, Jamie. Don't worry about him, he's safe from me. Plus, you know I've been shagging Sean. Ben is perfectly safe from me." The lie was sour on his tongue, but he hoped it would stop Jamie's questions.

Jamie gave him a friendly punch in the shoulder. "It's not just him I'm worried about, okay?"

"Let me put the terrors back and I'll grab my ukulele. I'm bloody rusty, so go easy on me."

Jamie laughed as he pulled himself up and grabbed his own uke off the coffee table. "You're rusty? When do you think I've had time to practice this last month? With the fire, the rats, and Liam? Hell, that last one is a full-time job on its own."

"Admit it. You love it."

Jamie played a few chords to Liam's favourite song. "I love him."

Dane's heart clenched—not because he still had feelings for Jamie, but because he wished he could say the same thing about Ben. Soon. He hoped.

They jammed for a few hours, both drinking lager and playing their favourite songs… rather badly. Dane didn't care. It was nice to play just for fun, and he was happily buzzed when Liam came to pick Jamie up.

They'd finally moved Ben's clothes into Dane's room, his few personal possessions had found homes throughout the house, and they'd started to ferret-proof the room. They'd left the futon so they'd have somewhere to sit, along with a few storage units, but everything else was gone. It wasn't quite ready for the ferrets yet, but it was getting there. Luckily, Jamie didn't have any reason to go into the bedrooms, and he hadn't seen how bare Ben's old room now was. If he'd been a bit more aware, he might have noticed just how integrated Ben was throughout the house, including the living room.

Dane had gone to bed and was snuggled under the covers feeling lonely without Ben. Even Speedy had abandoned him, preferring to sleep next to the ferrets' cage in the living room. He pressed his nose into Ben's pillow and took a deep breath of his scent. His eyes finally closed, but his mobile rang, interrupting the silence and making him jump. Dane blinked, pulled his face away from Ben's pillow, and reached for the phone. A smile spread across his face when he saw Ben's name flash up.

"Hey darling," he said into the phone.

"Hi. I didn't wake you, did I? Your voice sounds husky."

"Nah. I was just snuggled into your pillow." Ben groaned down the phone and Dane shivered and clutched the phone closer. "Smells like you," he admitted.

"You're killing me." There was a slightly awkward pause. "I wish I was there right next to you, holding you."

"Fuck, Ben," Dane groaned, eyes fluttering closed, cock stirring. "I miss you. Why did you stay at your friends' new place again?"

"Insanity. It's the only reason I can think of. Miss you too. Can't sleep without our legs tangled together anymore. Are the ferrets behaving?" They carried on talking quietly, both almost drifting off before starting a half-hearted attempt at another conversation. Finally they said their goodbyes.

That wasn't the kind of phone sex he'd expected. Phone love perhaps?

IT WAS a Friday and Dane's day off. He was knackered. They'd had an influx of dogs and puppies from a puppy farm, and it had been all hands on deck all week. Even though they worked tirelessly to save them, some were too sickly to be saved. Those cases took it out of him emotionally and physically. He still saw their bodies when he closed his eyes. It made him so mad that people did that to animals. He did what he could, but it was never enough.

This was his first day off since then, and he was determined to have a relaxing day doing nothing. He put the telly on, opened the ferret cage so Chase and Squidge could play, and promptly fell asleep. He woke a few hours later with a crick in his neck and a dry mouth. Speedy was still lying on the sofa next to him, but the ferrets were nowhere in sight. That wasn't worrying; they often found a corner to sleep in or snuggled into a blanket.

He got up slowly and stretched out the kinks, then peered under the furniture looking for small sleeping furry bodies. He frowned when he didn't spot them. "Chase, Squidge, wakey, wakey," he called, though he knew they wouldn't answer. Ferrets had awful recall, and if they were asleep, they slept like the dead. Literally. He looked in the cage and pulled out all the fleece blankets just in case they were curled up in one. Nothing.

Shit.

"Where are your brothers, Speedy?" he asked the dog, but Speedy just opened one eye and closed it again. Mild panic started to set in as he moved cushions off the sofa. Where the hell were they? He stood up and looked around the room. Then he realised he hadn't shut the door between the living room and upstairs. They could be anywhere.

A cold sweat covered his body as he pictured what trouble they could get into. "You better not be in the bathroom." There were too many holes they could squeeze into. He ran up the stairs and let out a sigh of relief when he saw the bathroom door was shut. When he came to his own bedroom, he saw the door was open just a crack. He pushed it open but didn't see anything. Why oh why were ferrets so small and bendy that they could practically fit anywhere?

Ben's dirty socks were beside the washing basket, and their bed was still rumpled from where they'd slept in each other's arms. If he were a ferret, where would he hide? Chase liked to sleep in wardrobes, so he opened the door further and rummaged in the shoes he kept at the bottom of it. Nothing. Dane crawled on the floor to the chest of draws and checked at the back of it.

"You little devils, where are you?" He said it loud enough, hoping they'd come out and investigate. No such luck. Ben was going to kill him if he'd lost them. What kind of vet was he if he couldn't look after two ferrets? If they'd gotten out of the house or under the floorboards—or something—he was never going to forgive himself.

His fingers itched to call Jamie to come help him look, but it was too obvious that he and Ben were sleeping in the same room, and Ben would be devastated if he went behind his back. He lay on his stomach and peered under the bed, but all he found were dust bunnies. "Chase, Squidge, come out now," he called to no avail.

Next he emptied the laundry on top of Ben's dirty socks and rifled through it. He didn't know how they could have climbed in there, but he was out of ideas. The image of emaciated dogs flashed through him, and panic bubbled up in his throat. He couldn't save *them*, and now he'd lost the ferrets.

Clothes were all over the floor, and he was sitting in the middle of it when Ben appeared in the doorway.

"This goes beyond sorting out darks and whites." He raised an eyebrow as Ben's head shot up in his direction. He hadn't even heard the door open. What if the ferrets snuck out while Ben was distracted greeting Speedy? His heart started to beat erratically, and Ben frowned when he didn't laugh at the joke.

"I lost the ferrets," he blurted out. To be fair, Ben's reaction wasn't as awful as he thought it would be.

"What do you mean?" He looked around the room at the mess.

"I didn't shut the living room door properly, then I fell asleep, and now they could be anywhere." He ran his hand through his hair, then sighed and started to shove the dirty clothes back into the basket. "What if they got outside?"

Ben pulled him to his feet and then into his arms. "I'm sure they couldn't have gotten outside, and you blocked up any holes downstairs. The bathroom door is closed, so they couldn't get to the pipes. I'm sure they're just asleep somewhere."

Why was Ben being so nice to him? He'd fucked up. "Why didn't I shut the door?"

Ben soothed the furrows on his forehead and pressed a kiss there. "Because you've been working overtime. You've had a shitty week." Dane started to protest, but Ben carried on. "You haven't told me what's happened, but I can tell it was bad."

Dane's chin quivered, and his eyes filled with tears. What was wrong with him? He was a vet; this was part of his job. It wasn't all fluffy puppies and cute kittens. He'd known that going in. "I couldn't save them." There had been so many. Ben didn't push for him to explain, just wrapped him in his arms and held on tight. Dane sighed and leaned against him. "I try not to bring work home, not the bad stuff anyway."

"You can't bottle it up. I'm here for you."

"How did you know something was wrong? I've worked late before."

Ben snorted and ran a soothing hand down Dane's back. "I know you. I can tell when you're sad. I didn't want to push you, and I wasn't sure you were allowed to talk about whatever was going on. Either way, I'm here for you. You're amazing, you know that?" Dane leaned backwards so he could look into Ben's eyes. He was so kind and thoughtful.

"You're saying that after I told you I lost our ferrets?" Dane said. Laughter spurted from between Ben's lips, and he stepped back to survey the room.

"They can't have got that far. You're just tired and worried. Let's look together." They looked in the wardrobe again, and Ben opened each drawer in the chest and looked behind and under furniture. "They may still be downstairs. Come on, take a hold of that side of the duvet, and we'll make the bed, then go check. I'm positive they're here somewhere."

They lifted the duvet upwards to smooth out the wrinkles and place it over the bed again. The quilt bunched up inside the cover, so Ben reached over to smooth out the lumps near the middle. He froze and bit at his lip to hide a grin.

"What?" He didn't say anything, just pulled the bedding back, and nestled there, right in the middle of the bed, were two ferrets curled up together so they couldn't tell where one ended and the other began.

"What the actual fuck?" Dane stared in disbelief while Ben chuckled and took a photo of them because they were too adorable lying there. "I've been calling and calling them. I looked everywhere."

"Not everywhere." Ben put his arm around him in consolation.

"I feel like a complete moron. I didn't even know they could climb that high." They sat on the bed, the ferrets between them, and looked at the two devils that had almost caused him a heart attack. Squidge yawned and stretched, then Chase uncurled himself and opened one eye. He spotted them both sitting there and went from dead sleep to hyperactive within one second. He jumped at Ben, then twisted and fell on Squidge, waking him fully. They wrestled, play fought, and dragged each other along the bed.

"They don't even care I was worried," Dane said as they played.

Ben reached over and patted his knee. "Don't take it to heart."

The ferrets tussled a little longer, then raced to the headboard, squeezed themselves into the gap between that and the mattress, and wiggled their way down between the bed and the wall. "I guess I know how they get on the bed now."

# Chapter Thirty-Seven

*Dane*

DANE SNUGGLED under the sheets, and his leg slipped between Ben's. They'd fallen asleep naked, and the scrape of the hairs on his legs tickling his skin sent delicious shivers down his spine. If he were more awake, he'd do more, but he enjoyed the blanket of sleep just keeping him under, and the smooth movement of Ben's breathing was quickly lulling him all the way back. Lazy mornings wrapped up in each other were his favourite.

Subconsciously he knew they'd slept in. The light was peeking from between the curtains, and Speedy had abandoned the end of their bed to sleep in his own bed in the corner of the room. They deserved the lie in.

The doorbell rang and almost broke the spell, but he was still too comfy, and Ben didn't stir. It rang again, and Speedy barked loudly and with enough volume that they both jumped awake, limbs so tangled they almost elbowed each other before stumbling out of bed.

"Times it?" Ben asked as he stumbled around for a pair of boxers. Dane had to bite back a smile as he pulled on a pair of Dane's. They were a little tight, the fabric straining over his thighs. Not that he was complaining. He enjoyed the view.

Dane turned around to look at the clock that was in Ben's direct line of vision—he was so adorable when he was sleepy. "It's ten thirty."

Ben cursed and flinched as the doorbell rang again. "We slept late. Who is that?" He yanked on last night's jeans and headed towards the door. Dane took his time, smiling as he slipped into Ben's boxers and pulled on his dressing gown. He wasn't going to feel guilty about sleeping in.

The door was already open when he followed Ben down the stairs. There was something in the way he was holding his shoulders, and the white skin around his knuckles as he gripped the edge of the front door that made the smile slip from his face. He stopped at Ben's side and pushed his hands into the pockets of his dressing gown so he didn't hug him or touch him in a way that was more than friendly.

"Is everything all right?"

There were three people on the doorstep. The older man and woman looked enough like Ben that Dane guessed this was his family, and the younger man was Ben's brother. Dane's stomach dropped, and he took a step further away from Ben in case it looked odd that they were standing too close, and he forced a smile when all three sets of eyes turned to him. Why hadn't he dressed properly? Ben's old boxershorts and his fluffy polka dot dressing gown were not the proper attire for meeting his secret boyfriend's family. He glanced down to make sure nothing was on show and tightened the knot on the belt around his waist.

He turned to Ben, who had at least put actual clothes on, even if they were from last night. The T-shirt was wrinkled but passable—oh God, was that a dry white stain on the hem? He prayed that no one would put two and two together.

"You must be Dane, Ben's landlord. I'm Ben's brother Lewis. Thought we'd surprise him with a visit before his birthday." Lewis was a larger, ruddier version of Ben. They had the same hair and eye colour and smile, though Ben wasn't smiling right then. Being called Ben's landlord left a sour taste in his mouth and he wondered exactly what Ben had told his family about him.

"Nice to meet you all. It's your birthday soon?" Dane asked because he couldn't ask what he really wanted to know. They'd known each other for years, but Ben had been on the outskirts of their friendship group until very recently.

"Not until next month." Ben shrugged his shoulders, but they were stiff, and the movement jarred. He was in shock, and the longer he kept them on the doorstep, the more awkward it was becoming.

"Your dad's out at sea next month, so we thought we'd plan a surprise visit," his mum said with a large smile. She either couldn't feel the tension or she was good at ignoring it. Ben was still frozen on the spot.

"Come in, come in. What a lovely surprise," Dane said. It was obvious to Dane that Ben was starting to panic. He subtly touched Ben's arm, and he flinched but moved forward to shake his dad and brother's hand and to hug his mum.

"Pleased to meet you. My name is Gloria, but everyone calls me Ria." Her handshake was gentle, and she kissed him on the cheek before Ben showed her into the living room.

Ben's dad stepped over the threshold and looked Dane up and down until he tensed. He wished he weren't wearing his fluffy polka dot dressing gown. He wanted to apologise for it, but he bit his inner cheek to stop himself. He didn't owe Jim an explanation, even if he was Ben's dad.

Eventually he held out a hand, and Dane shook it. "Jim, pleased to meet you." Jim put extra pressure into the shake, but Dane didn't let it show on his face. He wasn't a stranger to straight men thinking they needed to prove their masculinity.

"You should have told me you were coming. I would have planned things for us to do," Ben said, and Jim let Dane's hand go and followed his family into Dane's living room. Nerves fluttered in Dane's stomach as Ben's family looked around the room with interest. His mother peered at the photos on the fireplace. His dad and brother sat on the sofa, but their eyes were still roaming. What were they thinking? He tried looking around as if he were a stranger, but he didn't see anything that stood out, apart from the Pride flag that was draped over the back of one of the chairs. Otherwise, his house was very ordinary.

"If you'll excuse me, I should probably go and get dressed," he gave a nervous laugh and escaped upstairs before any of them said anything.

His heart was beating erratically when he stepped into the shower and let the hot spray warm his chilled skin. He took his time getting changed. Part of him hoped that Ben and his family had gone out by the time he'd dressed, dried his hair, and faffed about as much as he could.

He opened his bedroom door and jumped a mile when Ben was there. He pushed him back into his room and Dane went to argue, but Ben just pressed a finger to his lips. "Sorry, sorry. I've left them in the living room so I can get changed." He pulled at his T-shirt, and both of their gazes went to the flaky white stain on the front. "Shit," Ben closed his eyes and took a deep breath. "I did not expect this."

"It's nice they wanted to surprise you." Dane wasn't sure if he was trying to convince Ben or himself, but Ben grimaced and pulled Dane into his arms. Dane was stiff; it was difficult to relax into the hug while Ben's family were downstairs. It didn't feel right, as though he were lying. It shouldn't matter so much—they'd been lying to their friends for weeks about their relationship, but seeing Ben's family brought back all his insecurities and masses of guilt.

"You should hurry and get ready before your family think you've fallen down the loo." The joke fell flat to them both, but Ben nodded.

"We're all right, yeah? And they can't know—about us. Not yet anyway."

Dane ground his teeth and took a step backwards. It was impossible not to show his irritation. Was that why he'd come upstairs after him? To make sure he wasn't going to go down there and tell his family that they were fucking? "Don't worry, your secret is safe with me. Go, before they get suspicious." Ben frowned but did as he said. Dane let out a deep breath and sat on the edge of his bed. The bed that they'd both slept in that night. When he heard the shower, he forced himself to go back downstairs. He didn't want them to think anything was going on between them, so he pasted on a smile as he walked back into the living room.

"Would you all like another cup of tea?" He asked breezily as he walked towards the kitchen as if he was on a mission. They all nodded their heads, and he relaxed when he was on his own in the kitchen. He made Ben a cup as well, then cursed himself for not asking how they all took their tea and decided to place everything on a tray like his grandma used to, so they could all help themselves.

"Ooh, this is lovely, thank you," Ria said as she poured milk into her cup. Jim smirked at the setup, eyeing the floral milk jar and matching sugar bowl. Dane didn't use them often, but when there were more than two people drinking tea, it made sense.

"Thank you. My dad owns a farm. I get milk and eggs from him. Much better than what you can buy at the shop."

Lewis grabbed his cup and piled in sugar and a generous amount of milk, then knelt in front of the ferrets' cage to watch them sleep in their hammock.

"Lazy little buggers, aren't they?"

"They're lazy until they're not," Dane said, thankful to have something to talk about. He told them about almost losing them the night before, though he left out how Ben had comforted him and how they'd tumbled into bed early that night.

"I don't know what Ben's fascination is with them," Jim cut in. "You must think they're weird pets for a grown man." Dane wished Ben would hurry up and get changed so he could get out of there. If he thought the ferrets were weird, he'd probably hate Jamie and Liam's house, with all the pet rats they had.

"I'm a vet, so I love animals. Ferrets are quite popular round here because of all the farmland. They're used for working. Ours—I mean Ben's ferrets are just pets, but they are wonderful social animals. They get on with my dog well too." Speedy looked up from his bed in the corner of the room and lay his head back down again.

Jim grumbled into his tea but didn't argue the point any more.

Ben came back into the living room freshly showered, his short hair still wet, and wearing clean clothes with no dubious stains on them. His smile was as forced as Dane's, and his eyes had a look similar to some scared animals he'd treated. It made him feel guilty for how he'd treated him upstairs, but his feelings were no less genuine than Ben's.

"Well, I need to take Speedy for a walk, so I'll leave you all to catch up. It was lovely meeting you all," Dane said. He needed to get out of there, and once he'd said the W word, Speedy went crazy and jumped at his feet in excitement.

"You're not going to come to lunch with us?" Ben asked, and Dane shook his head. The last thing he wanted to do was sit through an awkward meal with Ben's family pretending he wasn't in a relationship with their son.

"No. I need to take the dog out, and then I promised my dad I'd pop around to look at one of his goats. She has a limp, and he's concerned." It wasn't entirely a lie, but his dad hadn't been too concerned and was happy just to keep an eye on it himself.

"But you'll come for dinner tonight?" Ria asked. "It would be nice to get to know one of Ben's friends." At least he was a friend now and not just a landlord, though if he could have thought of an excuse to get out of it, he would have.

"I'd love to," he said instead. "Thanks for inviting me. I'll see you all tonight." He nodded, and with one last look at Ben, he let Speedy drag him towards the front door.

# Chapter Thirty-Eight

*Ben*

BEN'S PARENTS were napping in their hotel room after lunch, but he didn't get the same reprieve from Lewis. Ben managed to get the whole gang together for an impromptu walk over Chasewater, which at least took some of the heat off him. He hated the tension between him and Dane, but there was nothing he could do until they left.

Ben put both ferrets in their harnesses and then placed them in their carrier so they would be safe in the car for the short ride to the Chase. Dane was in his room getting changed, and Ben frowned as Lewis walked around the living room peering at every photo and picking up every knickknack as if he had every right.

"Be careful with that, will you?" Ben snapped. Lewis looked at him and put the ornament back on the mantlepiece.

"What is your problem? I'm just looking. Though to be honest, I thought you'd be shacked up with Donna by now, not living with some gay guy."

Ben ground his teeth, anger and shame mixing inside him until he just wanted to shove Lewis out the door until he disappeared. He was a huge reminder that his family wouldn't understand his relationship with Dane.

"He's not *some gay guy*. He's a friend. I'm lucky he's letting me rent his spare room from him."

"Well, what about Donna? Mum hasn't stopped talking about her." Lewis sounded bitter.

"We broke up. We were going in opposite directions." It was hard to explain why someone was so wrong for him when they looked so right on paper without outing himself. "Look, Dane will be down in a minute. Try not to offend him or any of our friends, all right?"

Lewis rolled his eyes. "Ye of little faith. I do know how to talk to people. Though, it's a bit weird, isn't it?"

"What?" Ben kept an eye on the door for Dane.

"You being besties with a group of gay guys. Are you their fag hag or something?" He laughed at his own joke, not realising or not caring that Ben hadn't joined in. Perhaps he would have once. He'd have been so desperate to fit in that he would mimic everything, even the things that made him unhappy. But he didn't need to do that anymore. He fit in with Dane and their friends. And it wasn't because of his relationship with Dane.

"Are you guys ready?" Dane said as he walked through the door, Speedy at his heels, already on his lead. Dane's smile was overly bright, and his actions overly camp. Ben wished he could hug him, reassure him that everything was okay, but he didn't know how to do it with Lewis right there.

He smiled at him and hoped Dane could see how much he cared in his eyes. Dane gave him a minute nod, and he relaxed slightly. "Let's head to Chasewater and meet the others, then."

The best thing to do while Lewis was there was keep him as busy and distracted as possible, and then when the pubs were open, ply him with enough beer to keep him merry. He wasn't a bad guy, he was just set in his ways and didn't see many people who were different to him. Ben didn't think he was homophobic, but he'd say things without realising it because that's what their dad was like and that's what his friends were like.

He hadn't gone to uni or moved away like Ben had, so his small-town mentality hadn't moved on with the times. The small fishing villages they grew up in were a lot different to Lockstone, which was more progressive in lots of ways.

Jamie and Liam were holding hands waiting in the car park for them. Markus and Cal were a few feet away on the small playground that was nestled between the car park and the lake. And Liam's best friend Selena and her girlfriend Dawn were also there. Ben wasn't sure if that was a good thing or not, because Lewis was sure to hit on one or both. He prayed that his brother would behave himself, but he didn't think God would listen.

Selena and Dawn gave him a tight hug. "Hi Ben," Selena said. "It's so good to see you. We need to have a monopoly rematch."

Ben laughed but shook his head. Selena adored board games, and they all often got together to play, but she was a shark, and he had no intention of being bankrupted by her yet again.

"I told you, babe. You need to let someone else win once in a while." Dawn winked. Lewis leered behind their backs, but Ben pretended he hadn't seen him do it. Ben had always thought he'd been shit with women, but Lewis didn't know how to talk to a woman without coming on to them.

"Everyone, this is my brother Lewis. Lewis this is Selena, Dawn, Jamie, Liam. That's Markus over there with Cal, and his son Arthur."

Lewis shook everyone's hands, and Ben relaxed when he didn't say anything insulting. He even shook Arthur's hand, and Arthur gave him a wide smile. So far so good. He'd introduced everyone to his brother, and Lewis hadn't offended anyone.

Dane got the ferrets out of their carrier pod and attached the leads to their harnesses. As soon as he put them on the ground, they ran circles around Dane's legs until he almost toppled over. They tangled their leads around each other and sniffed at the grass. "Hold one of these devils, will you?" Dane said, scooping them up and holding one out to him.

He laughed and held Squidge to his chest. "Let's head to the water." They all headed towards the dam. Dane took Speedy off the lead and gave Arthur a tennis ball.

"So how long are you in town, Lewis?" Markus asked.

"Just until tomorrow. It's just a flying visit, but I'm back at work on Monday. Hey, Ben, did I tell you I got a new job as a bar manager?"

Ben's mouth dropped open in shock. "No, you didn't tell me that. Dad must have had a heart attack." Lewis laughed in agreement, and Ben explained for everyone. "He and Dad are—were both fishermen. Never thought you'd get off the boats."

He shrugged. "I worked in bars in my last year of college. I like to drink. It's the perfect combination." Ben wasn't sure it was as perfect as he made out, but he kept his thoughts quiet. Markus asked him something, and Lewis carried on talking, so Ben slowed his walk until he and Dane were at the back of the group.

"I am sorry about them all turning up like this."

Dane shrugged, and Ben had a feeling that he'd said the wrong thing. "I think Lewis is getting along great with Markus. He always was more of a bloke's bloke. Lewis probably doesn't even realise he and Cal are together."

"God, I just hope he doesn't say something offensive," Ben said. The tension between them lessened slightly, and Ben hoped everything was okay between them.

"I'm sure Markus won't hold it against you if he does," Dane said. Their hands brushed as the ferrets pulled on their leads. It would be the most natural thing in the world to take hold of Dane's hand, and he desperately wanted to. He glanced ahead. Jamie and Liam were holding hands and Lewis and Markus were chatting while Cal and Arthur were ahead with Speedy. No one would see. He straightened out his pinkie and brushed the back of Dane's hand with it.

Dane jerked away and kept his head facing forward. Perhaps the tension wasn't completely gone. Maybe one day soon, he'd be brave enough to hold his hand for everyone to see.

# Chapter Thirty-Nine

*Ben*

BEN UNLOCKED the front door and instantly cheered up when Speedy ran over to greet him. He looked up, and Dane was sitting on the sofa where his parents had sat hours earlier. He didn't look up, and Ben's stomach lurched. "Hey," he said.

Dane did turn to him then, but there was tension in his eyes, and his smile was forced. "Lewis get to the hotel all right?" He glanced at the door as though he were expecting him to walk through.

"Yeah, I just dropped him off. He's going to clean up, and I'll meet him with Mum and Dad later for dinner. You're still coming to dinner, right? I thought we'd go to that little Indian restaurant that Jamie and Liam rave about."

"I'll go if you still want me to go. Otherwise I can make myself scarce and you can make up some excuse." Ben sat down next to him, and Dane tensed. He grabbed his hands and threaded their fingers. Dane's hands felt cold and clammy. He hated that Dane was so uncomfortable. Especially when it was his fault.

"Of course I want you there." It was the only thing he *did* want. His family weren't horrible, his parents had never hit him as a kid, but he'd never felt like he could be himself. He always felt like he had to be what they expected, and it had got to the point that he didn't know if what he was doing was because he wanted to do it or because they expected it of him. That's when he knew he had to move before he suffocated on their expectations. All those old feelings came back with a vengeance when he saw them standing on the doorstep. He needed to keep them happy until they went home Sunday afternoon, and then they could get back to normal.

"They're going home tomorrow, and then we can get back to normal," he promised, pressing his leg closer to Dane's, his warmth spreading to him. Dane moved his leg and pulled his hand away, and ice set into his veins. "What's wrong? I know my brother can be a bit much."

"That's not it. You said when they leave, we can get back to normal. I'm presuming that means hiding this from your family and our friends even longer?"

"That seemed to be all right yesterday." He knew it was the wrong thing to say before he'd even said it, but it didn't make it any less true.

"Perhaps this visit has pulled the wool from my eyes," Dane said as he stared at his hands. "I didn't let myself think of what came next with us. I didn't want to jinx us by asking you to come out, but now this has happened, I wonder if you'll ever be ready."

"It's just…. They're old-fashioned and they have all these ideas for my future. They'd be so disappointed." Ben had worked so hard all his life at not disappointing them. The only things he'd ever really done for himself were going to university then taking the job offer in Lockstone. Everything else he'd done because it was expected of him. Until Dane.

"And mine aren't? Our families aren't that different—farmers, fishermen. They might be shocked, but I bet they'd get over it. If you can't tell them yet, then what about our friends? It's not like they'll judge us or go running to your family."

Ben's throat constricted, and he pulled at the neck of his T-shirt and sucked more air into his lungs. It didn't stop his vision blurring. How could they tell their friends when he was so confused himself? Everyone would ask questions, and he wasn't sure he could answer them. He was coming to terms with having a relationship with a man, and he still couldn't make up his mind if he was demisexual or not.

He wanted to be with Dane. It was the only thing he was certain of, but the idea of disappointing his family, of trying to explain to his friends something he didn't understand, was too much. "I need more time. I need to get everything straight in my head first."

"Straight." Dane snorted and stood up. "Yeah, sure. Text me the details about tonight, and I'll meet you there. I need to head into work for a few hours right now." Dane grabbed his wallet and keys, whistled for Speedy, and left him there alone.

Ben had a nasty suspicion that even when his parents and Lewis left, things wouldn't go back to normal like he wanted them to. He crossed his fingers and prayed, but everything was different now their bubble had been burst.

BEN TEXTED Dane the time to get to the restaurant, but he didn't hear back, so he could only hope that he'd turn up. No matter how awkward the meal might be, he wanted Dane to be there. Why had his family turned up just when things were going well?

The Indian restaurant didn't look like much from the outside, but the food was out of this world and it was family run. He could tell that his dad didn't think much of it just from the minute lip curl he gave as they walked through the door.

It wasn't as though his dad was a snob. He was happier with pub grub than any fancy restaurant, and Ben knew that he enjoyed Indian food, he just enjoyed finding fault with Ben more. He'd almost forgotten that about him in the few years he'd been in Lockstone.

When the door opened a few minutes later, Ben looked towards the door, expecting to see Dane. He did *not* expect to see Donna. His mouth dropped open and his heart jumped into his throat as his mother and father stood up and ushered her over. "Donna! So good of you to join us." His mum pulled her into a hug, and Ben just watched like a car crash he couldn't look away from.

She finally turned to face him, and he stood, his chair squeaking across the floor. He wiped his sweaty palm along his jeans. "Donna. I didn't know you were coming tonight."

She frowned, then bit at her lip. "Your mum rang me. Shit, have I messed things up? I presumed you knew… I can… go if you'd rather?" He looked at his parents and wanted to scream at them for doing this. But he couldn't ask her to leave; that would be mean and look awful.

"Of course not. Take a seat. I'll explain everything to Dane later."

"Do they know about Dane?" Donna whispered, and he shook his head with a forced smile on his face. "Tell me that they know we aren't together anymore."

"I've been busy. I never got around to talking to them." Donna glared at him, then turned to smile at his family. Why hadn't he told them he and Donna had split up? He could have told them that without mentioning Dane, but he'd allowed them to carry on obliviously, happy that he was in a relationship they approved of. And it was too late now.

He motioned to the seat he'd saved for Dane, then realised they'd need a bigger table once Dane got there. He stood and motioned to the waiter. "Excuse me, could we move to a bigger table. We're waiting on an extra person."

"Of course, sir," the waiter said. He was just setting another table for them when Dane walked in. He saw Ben, then Donna sitting with his family, and he visibly flinched.

Ben's stomach lurched, and he wove between tables to get to him. "It's not what it looks like. I had no clue she'd be here." The pain in his eyes almost took Ben's breath away, and Ben wanted nothing more than to pull him into his arms and kiss the hurt away. He did neither of those things.

"I get it. I guess you never told them you and Donna broke up, let alone anything about me. But it's fine. I only came to give my apologies and say I can't stay. I forgot that the band is playing tonight, so I can't stay for dinner." He pushed past Ben, straightened his shoulders, and glided over to the table like he had all the confidence in the world.

"Hello, everybody, I just wanted to say I completely forgot I had a gig tonight, so I won't be joining you. I hope you enjoy your meals. Donna, it's good to see you again." With that, Dane twirled around and, without a glance Ben's way, was gone. Shit.

Ben wanted to follow him, but his dad said something about not having to move tables now, and Donna sat next to them awkwardly. She stared at him, then the door, but he didn't understand what she was trying to say. So he did what he always did; he sat down and smiled while he screamed on the inside.

Dinner was awkward at best, though his parents ignored his agitation as they plied all their attention on Donna. Ben glanced at his watch again. They'd finished their meal; he'd forced down a chicken balti, and now his mum and dad were drinking Irish coffees and talking to Donna. Only Lewis looked as excited to be there as he was. They shared a glance, which reminded Ben of numerous dinners as children when their parents had lingered and all they wanted to do was be outside.

"Your father and I are exhausted from the drive. We're going to head back to the hotel so we're fresh for tomorrow. You youngsters should all go out. The night is young. Your friend is playing in a band, isn't he?"

Ben didn't want to walk into the Duck with Donna and Lewis. He just wanted to find Dane and make sure they were good.

"He is. Good idea," Ben waffled as he asked for the bill and paid for their meal. His father was adamant that he drive them the short distance to the pub, and Ben was sure he'd only done that so he couldn't get out of it.

They got out of the car in the small car park at the front of the Drunken Duck, and they all watched them drive off. Ben turned to Lewis and said, "Go ahead and get the pints in. I need to speak with Donna first." Lewis winked at them and slapped him on the back.

Ben took in a deep breath and turned to Donna. She looked as awkward as he felt. "Can we chat for a second?" She nodded and they moved to a quieter part of the car park.

"I'm sorry about tonight," she said before he could say anything. "Your mum is a force to be reckoned with, and before I even knew what I was doing, I'd agreed. I wouldn't have if I'd known you'd not told them we weren't together." She raised an eyebrow at him and his cheeks started to burn. It had been easier to let his parents believe they were still together.

"No need to be sorry. *I* should be sorry. I didn't tell them about us, and I know what she's like. I'm sorry that they dragged you into it. They really like you." He wished they would like Dane, but he knew without a shadow of a doubt that if he told them about their relationship, they'd go ballistic.

"I like them too, but if I wanted to get cosy with someone's family, I'd find an actual boyfriend." She gave a small smile.

"I get it. I really *am* sorry to drag you into my drama."

"That's okay. I dragged you into plenty of mine. Now you need to find Dane."

Ben forced a smile. All he wanted to do was find Dane and make sure he was all right, but he nodded and they walked into the pub together.

The Ratpack Rangers were already playing, and Lewis just bought their drinks and made his way back to them. Ben automatically gravitated towards the booth that was always reserved in the corner, but then realised he didn't really have the right to sit there with his brother and pretend ex.

Liam had already spotted them, and he waved them over, oblivious to the tension. They stood around the end of the booth, but none of them sat down, knowing that the seats were saved for Dane, Jamie, and Markus. They all chatted between songs, but Ben couldn't stop staring at Dane.

# Chapter Forty

*Dane*

IT WAS surprisingly easy to convince the guys to go to the Duck and play an impromptu gig. They didn't ask why, though Dane was sure Markus knew something was wrong. His smile was too wide, and he drank too much, but he needed the courage. He couldn't stop seeing Donna sitting at that table surrounded by Ben's family. She fit in so well. Even Ben's dad was smiling. He hated her, even though, deep down, he knew Ben didn't want her. It would be easier for him if he did; his family would love it.

His chest was heavy, and his hands shook as he gripped the microphone. His ukulele hung around his chest, and he sang as Jamie and Markus played. By the time he joined in at the chorus, he'd got the shaking under control and he was sure that no one watching them could tell how much he was hurting inside.

Dane was almost back to normal when he saw Ben's head at the back of the bar. The joy he felt was instantly snuffed out when he saw Donna next to him. Ben's brother was there too, but he couldn't stop watching as Ben moved them all closer to their booth.

His fingers fumbled with the chords, and Jamie shot him a worried glance. So he smiled and forced himself to look at his hands and concentrate on the music, though it was harder than it usually was.

When they finally finished their set, he put his uke back in its case and stashed it in the back room. Jamie threaded his arm through his, and they wound their way through the crowds to get to their seats. "You all right?"

Dane nodded. "Of course." He was lying through his teeth, but Jamie bought it and was soon distracted when Liam pulled him into the booth for a kiss. Dane didn't want to look at Ben, but he knew it would look odd, so he forced himself to glance at him and smiled at him and Donna.

"Hi Lewis, nice to see you again." It was easier to concentrate on Ben's brother than on Ben himself.

"You too. You guys were pretty cool. I didn't expect a ukulele to sound like that."

"Thanks. We just do it for a laugh. People seem to like it." He could see Ben staring at him from the corner of his eye, and his skin tingled with the need to look at him, but he refused to give in. Donna said something about enjoying it too, but luckily Jamie came up for air and initiated her in conversation.

Markus started to talk to Lewis, and they sat in the booth together. Ben stepped closer to Dane, but he refused to acknowledge him. Instead he rested his hip against the table and leaned in as though he were listening to both conversations, when in reality he had no idea what they were saying.

Ben sighed but stood next to him. Dane felt something touch the back of his hand and flinched away, rubbing it on his jeans. When the touch came again, he glanced down and realised that Ben's little finger had brushed the back of his hand. He frowned and shoved it in his pocket so Ben couldn't reach. Was it petty? Maybe. But he couldn't stop himself. He wanted Ben to feel some semblance of the pain he felt.

What the hell was Ben doing, anyway? He never usually wanted to touch in public. Dane couldn't do this here. His eyes started to burn, and he blinked until he was sure no tears would fall. The secrets were tearing him apart, and he couldn't lie to their friends anymore. He wondered what Ben would say if he knew Markus and Cal knew about them? He'd freak out, even though no one here would judge him. Perhaps his parents and brother would, but none of their friends.

"Can I talk to you?" Ben whispered next to his ear. Dane jumped. He hadn't seen Ben move and hadn't been expecting it.

"Not now, darling. That would be rude to your *guests*." Ben sighed but moved back enough that Dane could finally breathe. "Anyone want another?" He held up his empty pint glass, and Jamie and Markus nodded.

"I'll help you carry," Ben said.

Dane shot him an irritated look. "I'm perfectly fine getting our drinks." But Ben wasn't deterred and followed him. Dane stood in the queue at the bar and clenched his teeth while he watched the barmaids go back and forth.

"I'm really sorry about all this."

"I know." And he did. But that didn't stop his heart from hurting because Ben hadn't even told his parents he wasn't with Donna anymore. He'd let them go on thinking they were a couple—when they'd never been one in the first place.

"My parents called Donna."

"That's not the point, Ben, and you know it. You never told them you weren't with her anymore. You let them think you were still with Donna because that was easier for you. While we were together, they were blissfully unaware and happy that their eldest son had a great girlfriend they could brag about to all their friends." The words tumbled out of his mouth with one breath, and he had to take a moment to calm down and collect himself. "Look, I don't want to talk about this now. This isn't the time or the place. It's blatantly obvious you aren't going to tell your folks about us any time soon, so let's wait for them to leave." He was probably overreacting, but he couldn't stop. His feelings were hurt, and Ben was at fault. It was the perfect opportunity for Ben to tell his parents about them, but he hadn't, and now Dane had to pretend it didn't kill him. Would he ever be ready? They'd hid from their friends, and Dane had dealt with it, understood it, but this fiasco made him realise Ben might never be ready to come out. There was no way Dane could live like that.

"All right… we'll talk at home?" Ben sounded so hopeful.

"Sure." It's not like they could talk in the middle of a busy pub. Dane stepped closer to the bar as people moved away, and Ben stayed silent at his side. He ordered their drinks and made their way back to their table.

Donna was still talking to Jamie and Liam, but she turned to smile at Ben when they got to the table. Dane took a large gulp of his pint and wished he'd got something stronger. Ben stayed by his side, but instead of being reassured, Dane became more and more frustrated.

He put his half-empty pint glass on the table and stepped back. Ben jumped beside him and looked at him questioningly. "Going for a piss," he mumbled and walked off towards the toilets.

When he made it to the empty corridor opposite the toilets, he leaned against the wall and took a deep breath. His limbs were aching from holding himself so tightly, from pretending everything was fine. He closed his eyes just for a second. A familiar hand pressed against his arm and he jumped, eyes flying open. *Ben*. Of course. "Why are you following me? I just wanted a few minutes alone." Ben looked as though Dane had punched him, and he felt a pang of guilt before he squashed it. He bypassed the toilet and walked outside towards the smoking area. He needed some air; he didn't care if it was fresh or not.

There were a few women in the corner smoking, so Dane stood in the opposite corner, which was closest to the car park and cordoned off by a wooden fence. He'd forgotten about the fence; it made it impossible to get away.

"I'm worried about you," Ben said. Dane had no doubt that what he'd said was true, but it made him angrier. Didn't he realise how hard it was for him to not only pretend they were just friends to his family, but then to walk in on them all with Donna sitting with them?

He ached with the pain of hiding their relationship. It didn't matter that he'd been fine with it yesterday—today he'd seen their future if they carried on like they were, and he didn't like it. He wanted to hold Ben's hand as they walked down the street, he wanted to kiss him before they played a gig. He wanted to be acknowledged. He loved Ben with everything he was, but it would break him to carry on as they were for months or years down the line.

"You don't need to be worried; I just need a minute to myself." *Leave, please*, he added silently. His throat ached with unshed tears, and the last thing he wanted to do was cry. It was ridiculous to feel like this. It felt like he'd lost Ben already.

Ben didn't step away. He looked around, and there were still only the two smokers outside and they weren't paying them any attention, so he rubbed Dane's arm and pulled him into a hug. Dane knew he shouldn't, but he was weak, and Ben's warm arms felt so good around him, even if he knew he'd never be this affectionate in front of their friends.

"I know this is all really shitty, but they'll be gone tomorrow," Ben promised. But what about the day after? Or the week, month, year after? Would Ben ever find the courage to tell his family about them? Dane had been willing to wait before all this happened, but now he couldn't see Ben ever coming out, and as much as he wanted to be with him, he couldn't hide forever.

He wasn't sure who initiated the kiss, but their lips were drawn together. Dane clung to him like he was drowning. He would be strong later, but right in that moment, he needed Ben.

His hands slipped under Ben's T-shirt and raked the skin of his back. He didn't worry about how hard he was being; he wanted Ben to feel it. From the sounds Ben was making in his throat as they kissed, it didn't seem as though he hated it.

Their tongues slid against each other as Ben thrust into his mouth. Ben was always a laidback guy, but he kissed with an assertiveness that made Dane dizzy.

Ben pushed him against the waist-high fence and ground their hips together, and his need clouded his mind until he forgot where they were. Dane absently heard the rumble of a car and saw the harsh beam of headlights through his closed eyes.

A loud angry honk of a horn pulled them apart, but it was Ben's "Oh, God" that had Dane worried.

# Chapter Forty-One

*Ben*

"OH GOD," Ben said as he stumbled away from Dane and looked towards the honking car. They were directly in the beam of their headlights, and he squinted his eyes as he stared towards them. He didn't need to see them to know who was in that car. His stomach dropped and the alcohol he'd consumed threatened to come back up. What were the odds of this happening? A cold sweat formed over his skin, and he leaned his hands on the low fence and clutched the rickety wood. He needed something to hold on to because his legs were shaking. The bright light was blinding, but he could picture the looks on the faces of his parents as they sat in the car watching him kiss a man.

The engine stopped, and the lights went off, leaving white spots floating in front of his eyes. Ben couldn't speak; his pulse was in his throat and no words would come out. It felt like an eternity that they stood there in limbo, but he knew it could only be seconds. His dad was behind the wheel, and his face was furious. He rolled down the window and stuck his head out. "What the hell do you think you're doing?"

Ben winced, his father used to say that to him growing up, but never with so much venom. He looked at his mother, hoping it would give him inspiration for what to say, but her face was pale, eyes wide with shock. She looked like he'd killed her puppy.

Dane shifted next to him and placed a hand on his lower back, but Ben flinched and stepped away. He couldn't deal with his touch right then. If anyone was nice to him, he would break down. "Don't," he said to Dane, then to his parents, "It's not what it looks like." It was the wrong thing to say—he knew that as soon as the words left his lips—but he didn't know what else to say or how to make Dane and his parents happy. The familiar panic settled like a dead weight in his stomach and slowly rose until his throat started to close.

He wheezed as he sucked in air and tried to calm his breathing.

He took a step away from Dane, and the gap felt momentous. But he needed the space to think, and he couldn't do it with Dane crowding him and his parents looking at him like he was scum.

His mum got out of the car and took a step towards them, but her eyes went to Dane and she scowled. She leaned against the front of the car. "Tell me I didn't see what I think I saw." She turned back to him, her face twisted. "What am I meant to say to Aunt Maureen and all the cousins? We've done nothing but talk about you and your lovely girlfriend."

"Maybe you shouldn't have bragged to the family, then. You only met her once, and we were just friends." Ben swallowed painfully. "She came with me to stop all the comments I usually get. *Are you still single? I know someone you'd love. Let me set you up. Henry's got a girlfriend. William is going to propose.* I couldn't take it anymore." He didn't know what to say that would appease everyone, so he let the words tumble out. "Truth be told, I would have preferred it if Dane were with me." He licked his lips, and he could still taste Dane there.

"What are you talking about? You're not gay. You can't be. I would have known." His mother was pale in the semidarkness.

"I'm sorry." That's what you say when someone is angry and upset with you, isn't it? "It's not—I mean I'm sorry." Dane seemed to fold in on himself, and Ben wanted to say more, tell them that he loved Dane, but when he turned towards Dane, his dad got out of the car and strode towards them. He didn't stop at the front of the car like his mum, but at the fence, so close he could touch—or punch if he wanted.

They were gaining an audience, and that hiked up his anxiety until his heartbeat was loud and erratic in his ears. "Can we go somewhere private and talk about this?" He was scared to look behind him and see who was there.

His dad shook his head. "So, you're a fucking queer now?" He said *queer* like it was a dirty word. Ben had always rather liked the sound of the word, especially when Dane and Jamie said it.

Ben clambered over the fence to put him closer to his mum and dad.

"It's not what it looks like. I'm not gay... I'm dem... it's not some... we're not. Shit." He didn't know how to explain that Dane was more than a passing phase, more than an experiment he'd get over. And if he tried to explain he was demisexual they wouldn't understand one bit. There was nothing he could say that would make it easier for them, not unless he lied and pretended Dane meant nothing to him, and he couldn't do that. He ran his hand through his hair nervously.

How did he explain that he was in love with Dane because he was a good person and it had nothing to do with him being a man? His parents were old-fashioned, set in their ways. They'd never listened to him before, so why would they start now?

This was all a fucking mess. He closed his eyes and took in a deep breath, hoping to calm himself down, but it didn't work. Shit. When he opened his eyes again, his parents were still scowling.

"Mum," He pleaded, though he wasn't entirely sure what he was pleading for or how she could or would help.

"How could you do that to Donna?" she asked.

Ben ground his teeth together. "This has nothing to do with her. We're not even together. We're just friends. We've always been just friends. What are you even doing here, anyway? I thought you'd gone back to the hotel."

"Your brother left his phone and hotel key in the car. We thought we'd bring them back for him." His dad's gaze shifted to over his shoulder, and Ben turned and saw Lewis there... with Markus, Jamie, and Donna. Shit. When had that happened?

"Is that why you broke up with Donna?" Why was his mother so obsessed with her?

"It's got nothing to do with Donna. I just told you, we were only friends. Can we please get out of this shit show and talk privately?" He didn't know what he was going to say, and he was terrified. His parents had caught him kissing Dane. There was no way he could explain that away, and now all their friends were watching it all play out.

He wanted to turn to Dane, but he wouldn't let himself. He didn't think he'd have the strength to talk to them if he did. When he'd thought about coming out, he pictured him and Dane telling their friends. He'd never let himself imagine telling his parents. Never in his wildest dreams did he expect this.

"Get back in the car. We'll go back to your hotel. We'll talk about this." He just wanted to get off this godforsaken car park.

"Nothing to talk about. It's wrong." His dad walked back to the car, but his mum hesitated. He had a moment of hope that she was hesitating for him, but her eyes went to someone behind him. He was afraid to see who was there. Then his mother turned around and opened the passenger door. His dad turned on the headlights, blinding them all, and then they drove off.

He was frozen to the spot, his eyes where their car had been. Nausea churned in his stomach, and he jumped when a hand clapped down on his shoulder. Lewis looked at him with curiosity mixed with sympathy. When had he got there? At least he wasn't looking at him with disgust like his parents had.

That touch unlocked something within him, and he twisted around to look for Dane. He needed him, needed his arms around him.

"Where's Dane?"

"Jamie and Markus ushered him away. You've got some explaining to do." Ben didn't want to explain anything. He wanted Dane.

HE HADN'T seen Dane or any of their friends leave through the car park, so he turned around, hoping they would be inside in their usual booth. "I need to find Dane." He needed to explain, and then they'd be okay.

He tried ringing him, but he didn't answer. He sent a text and got no reply.

Lewis started to follow him, though thankfully Donna stayed where she was. "What are you doing?" Ben snapped.

Lewis laughed and opened his arms wide as they walked. "I'm coming with you. Not like I've got anywhere else to go. Mum and Dad never did give me my phone or hotel key."

Ben rolled his eyes but let Lewis come with him. He didn't have the will to fight with someone else. Lewis fell in beside him and was quiet for the thirty seconds it took to get to the door.

"Are you going to tell me what's been going on? I know we're not exactly close, but I'm not as much of an arsehole as you think I am."

Ben sighed in frustration and turned back to Lewis. "I don't think you're an arsehole. We just don't have much in common." Their dad had always played one off against the other, so they'd never really had a chance. "I've been seeing Dane. I *am* seeing Dane. No one knew because I've forced him to keep it a secret." He looked back towards the door, hoping that Dane would appear. "I was worried what Mum and Dad would think. You too." He was worried about what everyone else would think apart from the one person who really mattered.

It wasn't the best place for this conversation. Someone stumbled between them as they walked through the short corridor that connected the toilets to the main bar area. He opened the toilet door, and the waft of piss and stale beer was thick in the air. Classy.

"I'm not gonna lie. It's a bit of a shock finding out you like dick." Ben winced. Did he have to be so crude? It wasn't about dick at all. Dane just happened to have one. "He's a nice enough guy, but I don't see what you see in him or *any* guy. I'm not been homophobic or some shit."

"I don't care what you think." They both knew it was a lie, but nothing mattered but finding Dane and explaining right then. He needed Dane to know that he loved him and wanted him. That was more important than finding excuses for Lewis. He pushed past him, back into the busy pub, and wound his way through the crowd to what he'd come to think of as their booth. But no one was there.

Ben looked around wildly, but everyone was gone. Tigger stood behind the bar, and he pushed his way to the front. "Tig, have you seen Dane?"

In an instant Tigger's face went from the usual happy-go-lucky smirk to serious. It was obvious that he knew what had happened outside. "No idea, man."

"Please, he's not answering my calls."

Tigger leaned his elbows on the bar and shook his head. "Perhaps you need to give him some space."

That was the last thing Ben wanted to do. He was afraid if he gave him space now they'd never bridge the gap. "Did he tell you where he went?" Panic set in, and he looked behind Tigger's shoulder to the door behind him.

"Just go home, Ben." That didn't sound like a bad idea. Perhaps Dane was there. He nodded and pushed away from the bar. Lewis met him at the main door, and he pushed it open for him.

He shivered as the cool air hit him, but he didn't stop as he walked the short distance back to Dane's. He prayed he'd find him there or he'd catch up with him before he got there.

"You can't come with me. I need to speak to Dane," Ben said, looking sideways at Lewis.

Lewis shook his head but didn't stop walking. "If he's at your house I'll use your phone to call a taxi to the hotel. If not, I'll stay with you for a bit."

Ben wasn't used to this supportive brother. It was kind of nice. The house was in darkness when he walked up the driveway. He opened the door, and Speedy came running and jumped at his knees. He bent down and stroked him. "Where's your dad, huh?" He turned on the lights and walked into the living room. A part of him was hoping Dane would be sitting there in the dark, but his luck had finally run out.

He pulled out his phone and rang Dane, but he wasn't surprised when he didn't answer.

He flopped down on the sofa, head in his hands as he played out everything that had happened.

"So... you really like him more than any of your exes?" Lewis nudged his foot until he looked up.

"More than like." He didn't want to tell Lewis that he loved Dane. Dane deserved to hear it first.

"Yeah, I'm starting to realise that. You're not even worried about what Mum and Dad are thinking right now. You're more worried about Dane. That says a lot."

"I should have put him above them in the first place." Ben texted him again, suddenly terrified that no matter what he said to Dane, he would think this was all too much.

"Is he good in bed?" Lewis leered at him, which was uncomfortable, made even worse because they were brothers.

Ben thought about everything he and Dane had done and how mind-blowing it was. Then he thought about everything he'd been too scared to do and hoped they'd get to do it. He didn't want to lose Dane because he was a coward.

# Chapter Forty-Two

*Dane*

SICKNESS CHURNED in Dane's stomach as he sat with Jamie and Liam on Tigger's sofa in the small flat above the bar. As they sat in the unfamiliar living room, his whole relationship with Ben tumbled from his lips. It was a relief to finally tell his best friend. It had been difficult keeping his feelings for Ben a secret, but he hadn't wanted to reveal their relationship this way. He'd honestly believed that they were going to work out, that they'd come out to their friends and then Ben would come out to his family. He hadn't expected this—or hadn't wanted it.

"This is why gay guys should stay away from sexually confused men," Dane said with a bitter laugh. He shuddered at the memory of Ben's face when he realised his parents had caught them kissing. He'd pulled away from Dane like he had the plague and then hadn't looked at him the whole time they were in the car park.

Jamie and Liam had managed to usher him away without Ben even realising. There was a bitter taste in his mouth that wouldn't go away. He looked around Tigger's living room, inspecting every inch he could see so he wouldn't have to think about Ben and their so-called relationship.

The room was small, comfortable, and cluttered with music memorabilia. A record player, shelves of vinyl, and guitars stood against the wall. It was very punk rock and gave him an insight into the bar owner that he'd never really seen before. Despite knowing he loved music, Dane hadn't realised he played any instruments, but it was obvious from the guitars and amps in the room that they were more than just for show.

There was a bottle of whisky on a unit next to the old record player in the corner, and Liam found a glass and poured a generous amount in it. He waved the glass in front of Dane's face, and Dane automatically reached for it. He stared at the amber liquid, brain fried.

"Drink it," Liam demanded.

Dane was too exhausted to think for himself, so he did as Liam asked. The alcohol burned on the way down but did nothing to numb the pain in his heart. Ben's response to his parents kept replaying on a loop through his mind.

He saw how Ben's expression had changed once he realised it was his mum and dad in that car. He'd known Ben wanted to keep their relationship a secret because he wasn't ready to tell anyone, but he hadn't expected him to reject him like that. He was the one who had initiated that kiss. And Dane had loved it. Ben had never been so dominant before, and he'd loved how he'd taken charge.

"You and Ben." Jamie sounded shell-shocked.

"Not anymore. Did you see how he pulled away from me? He wouldn't even look at me. He's more concerned with what his parents think." Dane shivered and the hairs on his arms stood on end. His phone rang. *Ben.* He desperately wanted to answer it, to make sure Ben was all right. Coming out was never easy, and even though Dane was hurt at being pushed aside, it must have been a shock for Ben.

Shit, was he being unreasonable? How could he feel anger and guilt in equal measures? He didn't answer the call. He was afraid of what Ben would tell him.

"Am I being unreasonable?" Dane asked out loud this time. He ran a hand through his hair. "Ben was so shocked when they caught us, and I wanted to comfort him, but he kept pushing me away. Wouldn't even stand next to me. Wouldn't even look at me." He blinked away the tears as they formed in his eyes.

"I don't know, man. He's got a lot to process, even without his folks finding out like that. Doesn't mean he should treat you like shit, though," Liam said.

Jamie still seemed shocked. "I should have realised something was going on when I came to your house last week. You got a ferret together. I've worked with him for years, and I didn't have a clue he swung our way. I knew you had a crush, but I was completely oblivious to Ben." Jamie said.

Dane gave a dry laugh. "I'm not sure he does swing our way, not really." Had he deluded himself all this time? Was Ben just experimenting? Now his family had burst their bubble, had he realised it just wasn't worth the hassle? Ben hated confrontation and was a people pleaser.

What if he wanted to please his parents so much that he wanted nothing to do with Dane anymore?

He groaned and leaned his head back on the chair. What had he done? Why had he given in? He should have been stronger, should have stayed friends, at least until Ben wasn't as confused, but he was weak and hadn't been able to stop himself—especially after that kiss at Pride and then again when Ben initiated that second kiss.

Jamie's phone rang next, and they all flinched. "It's Ben. Want me to answer?" Jamie looked towards Dane, but he shook his head. He couldn't face him. He was too afraid of what he would hear.

"Ben was raised to be the good son. What if he does what his dad wants? What if he decides he doesn't want me anymore." He bit his lip and looked at Jamie as though he might have the answers.

"That doesn't sound like Ben. If he was with you—even in secret, then it's because he wants you. I don't think his dad has got much say in it, even if he does desperately want his approval. Maybe you should answer the phone to him."

Dane shook his head. He wanted to comfort Ben, but Ben had decisions to make on his own, and Dane wouldn't hide anymore.

"My gaydar didn't go off for Ben at all. I don't get it. I mean gay guys talk about turning straight guys, but it's just a myth. I don't know anyone that's actually done it," Liam said as he sat on the arm of the chair next to Jamie. "Sorry, that wasn't exactly helpful. I'm sure he was just shocked that his parents caught you in a compromising position."

"Either way he hadn't told them he wasn't in a relationship with Donna anymore, not until they caught us together. He could have at least told them that. And he's not straight. Confused. Possibly—probably—demisexual." There, the anger was coming back slightly. "Why keep on pretending he was still with Donna? You're right. I had a major crush on him, but I didn't think it would lead anywhere. We just became really good friends after he moved in, and it progressed from there."

Liam cocked his head to the side. "Huh. Never would have thought it. Though looking back, he never seemed that interested in women."

"He dated Donna," Jamie interrupted.

Dane scowled. "Haven't you been listening to anything I just said? He wasn't dating her. They used each other to stop their families pressuring them or trying to set them up. It was purely platonic."

"Ben was probably just shocked. It's not exactly the way anyone wants to come out."

Dane rolled his eyes. "I know that, but we spent the whole day lying and pretending, and he wanted to just get through the weekend and then for us to get back to normal. I realised his normal was us sneaking around, and he had no intention of coming out any time soon, even to you guys. I thought I was fine with it, and I get he has stuff to process, but I didn't see him working through anything, and I can't live like that. This whole thing with his parents just made it more obvious."

# Chapter Forty-Three

*Ben*

DANE DIDN'T come home. Ben spent the night on the sofa waiting and hoping, but he didn't show, not even to let Speedy out. He let Lewis sleep on the futon in his old room, the only thing left to move out before they turned it into a room for the ferrets. Ben prayed that Dane wouldn't ask him to leave and they would still go ahead. He'd hoped Dane would turn up in the middle of the night, so he waited up, but even if he hadn't, he would have stayed on the sofa. It seemed wrong to sleep in Dane's bed without him there.

His body ached and he rubbed at his tired eyes when he eventually got up early the next morning. Dane still hadn't come home and none of their friends were answering their phones. He presumed he was at Jamie and Liam's, but he didn't know for sure.

Lewis came downstairs showered and dressed in some of Ben's clothes. He took one look at the state of Ben still in yesterday's clothes and ordered him upstairs to clean up. But the shower did nothing for his nerves or the crick in his neck. He didn't know how to fix this.

*Shit*. That was a lie. He did know how to fix this. He had to stop being a coward and man up. So he took a deep breath and tried to centre himself. He thought about what he would want if he didn't have to be afraid of what others thought. There was no contest. Dane was everything to him, and he should have shown that last night. He'd let worry, shame, and confusion become more important than Dane.

It threw him for a loop when his family turned up. And when they'd gone behind his back and invited Donna, all his old insecurities came back full force. But instead of turning to Dane, he'd pushed him away, and now he wasn't sure if Dane would ever forgive him. This wasn't how he wanted to tell their friends or his family.

Lewis had made him a cup of tea when he got back downstairs. He took it with a quick thanks.

"Dane didn't come back, then?" Lewis asked.

"No, and no one is answering their phones."

"It seems like they've all taken his side."

Ben glared at him and crossed his arms. "Don't be a dick. I fucked up last night. He deserves to have them all on his side. I just wish someone would answer their phone."

"Do you know where he stayed last night?"

"I have an idea."

"You should probably start knocking on doors, then, if you want to make it up to him. Do you?"

"Of course I want to make it up to him, I was out of order last night."

"Then stop waiting for him to come to you."

Ben blinked and looked at his younger brother. He'd always thought Lewis was kind of shallow, and they'd never really hung out or become friends despite there only being eighteen months between them. He'd expected him to be like their parents. Never in a million years did he think Lewis would give him advice—and good advice, at that.

"You're not just a pretty face, are you?" Ben gave a weak smile and Lewis grinned widely.

"What are you going to do?"

Ben bit his lip, thoughts racing. "You're right. I need to do something." He walked over to the window and pulled back the curtains. Markus's car was outside of Cal's. It hadn't been there the night before. Ben turned to Lewis. "Mum and Dad wanted me to show them where I worked this morning. Before all this went down. Think you can persuade them to come?" Lewis didn't look so sure.

"What are you going to do?"

"It depends on Dane. Can you do it?"

"I can try."

"I don't care how you do it, but get them there. I'll call you a taxi to take you to the hotel." Lewis didn't argue anymore. "Get them there around ten. I'll text you if the time differs, so pick up your goddamn phone." If only he hadn't forgotten his phone, then their parents wouldn't have come back to the pub.

"Let's do it, then. I'll get them there and you can do the rest."

Ben nodded, grateful that Lewis didn't ask too many questions, because he wasn't sure exactly how this would work. He called Lewis a taxi, and when his brother was gone, he hopped over the small wall between his house and Cal's and knocked the door.

Markus answered and didn't look surprised to see him. "He's not here," he said.

"I know, I just need to speak to him. To apologise."

Markus snorted and crossed his arms. "I knew you were going to break his heart."

Ben's eyes widened when he realised that Markus must have known and that Dane must have told him. "I'm trying not to. It's just not how I wanted to come out to you guys and especially my family. You saw them. They're not exactly accepting."

"Were you going to come out at all?"

"I was trying to sort everything out in my head so I had a good argument for when you guys made some comment about me being straight and then to my parents when they tried to tell me how wrong it was." Markus didn't answer that, and Ben sighed and ran his hand through his slightly damp hair. "Look. I really need to speak to Dane and explain my behaviour, but mostly to tell him I'm in love with him—deeply, desperately." He hadn't wanted to tell Markus that, but he could tell that Dane's friend needed to hear it.

"Is there any way you could get him to Chasewater so I can talk to him? He's not answering any of my calls, and I'm worried he won't come home if I stay. I just need to explain everything like I should have last night."

Markus stared at him until he was uncomfortable, and Ben found himself shifting awkwardly. But he eventually nodded slowly, and Ben let out a sigh of relief.

"I'll see what I can do."

"About nine-thirty? Text me if you have trouble." Markus shrugged. "Thanks. And Markus, I really do love him, okay?"

Markus didn't reply, and Ben jumped back over the wall into Dane's front garden. He had a little bit of time to let Speedy out and play with the ferrets, so he tried to figure out exactly what he was going to say while he did it.

BEN WAS pacing back and forth across the small dirt track that led to Lockstone pond—the pond where he'd found Chase. There was no one else about, not even the people he wanted there. He checked his phone—9:15 a.m. No texts or missed calls. He took a deep breath and tried to steady his nerves. He hoped he was doing the right thing. It could blow up in his face, but he had to try. He wondered if this was good idea, but before he let panic take over, he spotted Dane and their friends in the distance. He stopped pacing and watched. His palms were sweating, and his mouth was dry. He could tell when Dane saw him because he stopped walking and took a few steps back. Markus bent into him and said something, but Dane shook his head and turned around.

The nerves in Ben's stomach made way for panic. He couldn't let Dane leave. Before he could think too much about it, Ben walked over to the group, his eyes only on Dane—he was pale and had large bags under his eyes. "Dane," he blurted.

Dane's whole body tensed, but he didn't look at him. Was this how he'd felt last night when Ben refused to look his way? Dane shoved Markus until he let go of him.

"What the hell is this? You tricked me?" He glared at their friends and started to stride off in the opposite direction.

"It's not their fault. I asked Markus to bring you. I wanted to apologise. To explain."

Dane was deflated. "You don't need to say anything." He laughed, but it wasn't a happy sound. "I was a fool to think you'd choose me, that anyone would choose me."

His words broke Ben's heart. He hated that Dane didn't think he was good enough, that he didn't think anyone would put him first. He'd played right into that theory, and now he had to prove to Dane that he was wrong, that he was worth it and that Ben would always choose him.

Ben moved in front of him and gripped his arms until Dane looked up. His mouth was drawn and even now he looked over Ben's shoulder rather than into his eyes. Ben let go of one of his arms and traced a finger along his jaw until their eyes connected. Their friends faded into the background, and it was just the two of them.

"I'm sorry for how I treated you last night. If I could go back in time, I'd stand proud beside you and introduce you as my boyfriend, no matter what my parents thought. It's not an excuse, but I was scared." His mouth twisted into a sad smile that matched Dane's bitter laugh. "I'm always scared, because whatever I do is never good enough for them. I think a lot about what they think—about what others think, and

I let it rule me. I wanted to come out to our friends." He glanced at them for a second and carried on. "But as per usual, I was scared, afraid they wouldn't think I was good enough for you, afraid that the best friends I've made in my life wouldn't want me to be part of their group anymore. I was terrified everyone would judge me for saying I was straight for so long. Whatever way you look at it, I was afraid, ashamed, and basically fucked up."

Dane was still tense, but at least he was looking at him and he hadn't moved away. It gave Ben enough courage to carry on. He licked at his dry lips. "I'm more afraid of losing you than any of those other things."

"I'm not sure I can do this." Those words were worse than anything his parents had said.

"Don't say that—" Ben reached for Dane, but then there was another voice behind him. Shit, they were early. He'd hoped to speak with Dane privately first. Dane's eyes widened as he looked over Ben's shoulder.

"What the hell is this? Why did you bring us here, Lewis?" Dane flinched and went to step away from him, but Ben refused to let him go, not this time. He had to show him that he was serious.

"I wanted a do-over of last night," he said to Dane, eyes pleading for him to give him a chance. "I handled it all wrong, and I'm sorry. Trust me."

Dane still looked like he wanted to run away, but he didn't move again, and Ben squeezed his arm in assurance.

His parents were practically stewing behind him, but Dane was more important. Ben turned around, pulled his shoulders back, and stood to his full height. His dad looked smaller today—still as angry and as bigoted as ever, but Ben didn't feel drowned by his expectations any longer. It was time to stand up for what he believed in.

"I asked Lewis to bring you."

"So we could watch you fondle your boyfriend?" His dad's hands fisted at his sides. "Is this why you moved away? So, you could fuck men in private?" He took a step towards them, but this time Ben didn't move away or push Dane away.

"We thought you'd finally sorted your life out when you brought Donna home to meet us," his mum said. Then she turned to look at Dane, eyes narrowing. "She's such a nice girl. Why are you ruining that for him?"

Dane tensed next to him, and Ben pulled him into his side and stroked a comforting hand down his side until it rested on the swell of his hip.

"I tried my whole life to be what you wanted, to do things I knew would please you. It was never enough. I moved here because it was suffocating, and I was losing myself."

His mum wiped at eyes that hadn't even shed a tear, but it didn't make him want to back down this time. "I moved here, and this group of guys became my friends. They didn't judge me, didn't push me into finding a girlfriend. They just let me hang out with them." He pulled Dane in tighter to his side. "I can't tell you when I fell in love with Dane because it happened gradually." He could feel Dane's shock, and he turned to him, their faces so close, and pressed a quick kiss to his mouth. Only his dad cursing in the background ruined it. "I love you, okay?"

Dane nodded his head slowly, and Ben smiled, finally feeling strong enough. "I should have said this last night, but I let all my old hang-ups get the better of me. I'm redoing it all. You can think what you want. You can disown me. I'm in a relationship with Dane, who happens to be a man, and I'm proud to be with him." Then he turned to Dane. "Do you forgive me?"

Dane's face was so serious, and Ben had a moment of worry that he would say no, that none of this drama was worth it. But he nodded his head, and Ben let out a breath and pulled him into his arms.

"You can't do this," his mum said behind them. "What will our friends say?"

Ben slowly turned back to them. "I. Don't. Care." It was liberating to say and even better to feel it. For once in his life, he was living the life he wanted and not the one expected of him.

"You can't be serious," his dad said. Ben wasn't sure how else to tell them. He'd told his boyfriend he loved him, that he'd chosen him. What was not serious about that?

Lewis gave a loud continuous fake cough until they all turned to look at him. He gave a sheepish smirk. "Is now the right time to tell you that my girlfriend is pregnant?"

Their mum's mouth dropped even further, and her cheeks turned red. "The stripper?"

"She's not a stripper, she's a pole dancer. She teaches classes to hen-dos and parties." Lewis grinned. "She's very bendy."

Ben was as shocked as his parents were, but not for the same reason. Lewis hadn't mentioned a girlfriend all weekend. "Sorry to take your thunder." He sent Ben a wink. "I've been trying to figure out how to tell them without getting their knickers in a twist."

"This is why you gave up fishing?" their father said.

Lewis shrugged. "We're both making changes for the baby."

Ben pressed a kiss to Dane's cheek and then walked over to his brother. "Congratulations." Lewis's grin got wider, and he grabbed Ben into a tight hug.

"Thank you. You'll have to come and meet Tasha and the baby. He or she will need his uncle." Lewis looked over at Dane. "Uncles."

Ben hugged him again. "We will, and thanks for taking the heat off us," he whispered.

"No problem. They'll come around once they realise baby equals grandchild."

Ben took a step towards his parents, and for the first time in his life, he didn't feel small. He wanted to keep them in his life but not at the expense of Dane. "I love you both—you're my parents—but don't ask me to choose between you and him. You won't like the outcome." Dane moved to stand by him, and instead of rejecting him, this time Ben took his hand and squeezed.

# Chapter Forty-Four

*Dane*

DANE RODE home with Ben, but he was in shock. What just happened? He was restless in the car, and the air was thick with energy that threatened to take his breath away. They didn't talk, and though there was tension, it wasn't the bad kind. Ben squeezed his leg and gave him a sweet smile, but he continued to concentrate on the road.

Nerves fluttered in Dane's stomach, and he started to shake as he opened their front door. Speedy jumped at his legs, and he couldn't even reach down to stroke him. Ben locked the door behind them, fed the dog, then swept Dane into his arms until the shakes turned to shudders and he finally melted into Ben's embrace.

"Shit, Ben," he said into his neck. "I love you too, you bastard." He hadn't said it when Ben had, but he'd felt it.

"I'm so incredibly proud to call myself your boyfriend. Never think you're not good enough. I'm so thankful you've forgiven me and I'm so sorry about my parents and how I treated you."

Dane trailed his hand through Ben's messy hair until he cupped the back of his head. "It's okay. It's all okay now." No one had ever done anything like that for him before. It was painful watching Ben's parents reject him—not once, but twice. He would be forever grateful that Ben turned to him for comfort.

Ben rubbed their cheeks together, and the sweet scrape of stubble sent goosebumps down his arms. He'd thought he'd lost this. He steered Ben's mouth to his and nibbled at his lips before Ben took control and swiped his tongue inside Dane's mouth. Dane whimpered, and his knees shook so much that Ben had to grip him around the waist to keep him upright.

When they finally pulled apart, Dane could feel Ben's erection brushing against him. He could barely think as their cocks found friction with each other.

"I want you," Ben said. Dane's eyes widened, and his cock jerked inside his jeans. Jesus. "I've wanted you for ages, but story of my life, I was afraid. Not of you, but of me. That I'd do something wrong, I wouldn't be good enough, or my reaction would be wrong some way."

"You don't need to be afraid." Dane's heart broke for Ben. He had spent his whole life being told by his parents that he wasn't good enough. At least Dane had his dad and brother. They didn't always see eye to eye, but they respected each other's wishes. "Whatever you do, whatever we do together, I'm going to love it as long as you want it. Anything you don't want to do, we won't do, all right?" He pressed the palm of his hand against Ben's cheek, and Ben turned into it and kissed the soft skin there.

"I want you in ways I've never wanted anyone. I feel empty inside, which is ridiculous, because you've never even been in me." His voice became low, his words husky, and Dane almost came at his words when he realised what they meant. He'd tried not to think too much about being inside him.

"Take me to bed, Dane," Ben whispered in his ear. Dane looked at Ben's face, the harsh line of his mouth as he sucked in air through his nose, his blown pupils, and the look of desire that was only for him.

He took a step towards the stairs and held out his hand. Ben's fingers were warm in his and he couldn't wait to feel them elsewhere. When Ben stepped over the threshold and into what Dane now thought of as their room, he pushed him back against the wall until their chests were flush.

Ben gasped and tilted his head backwards, hitting the wall. He thrust his hips into Dane's, denim scraping denim. Dane might be the one who had Ben pinned against the wall, but it was Ben who gripped his hips and found a rhythm for them both. Dane arched his back and pressed into him while Ben's gaze roamed down his chest to where their groins thrust against each other.

Watching Ben watch them was one of the hottest things he'd ever witnessed—until Ben deftly undid Dane's jeans and pulled his cock out. He gave it a few strong pulls, and then he was undoing his own jeans, pulling his cock out.

Ben was beautiful. Dane couldn't do anything but let him work his magic as Ben grabbed his hips and pulled him close again, thrusting against him as he had before. But this time, hot hard flesh rubbed against hot hard flesh. It was downright dirty and way beyond anything Dane thought Ben would do, but he loved it, loved that Ben felt comfortable taking what he wanted.

Their cocks glided slickly together, precome making each thrust smooth and wet. Dane was so hard he hurt. He was desperate to come and desperate to prolong what they were doing. Ben's breath came in gasps against his ear, and he shivered when he pressed long wet kisses along his jaw until he reached Dane's mouth.

Ben's tongue pushed in without hesitation and curled against his own. There was a clash of teeth, small bites against lips, and still it continued. Dane grabbed Ben's head and held on tightly, but he didn't take over the direction of their explosive kiss.

"Bed," Ben said into his mouth. He pulled away, and Dane would have fallen if his hand hadn't shot out to steady him. They both grinned, and the humour cooled them off enough that Dane wasn't going to shoot just from breathing.

All inhibitions disappeared as Ben pulled his T-shirt over his head. Dane sighed as, inch by inch, his skin was revealed. He'd seen it before—they'd slept in this bed together for months and they'd done other things—but this was different. Then Ben turned to look at Dane and he realised he was still fully dressed, with just his cock poking out of his fly.

He toed off his trainers, pushed his jeans and boxers down over his hips, and kicked them away. Ben had completely forgotten what he was doing in favour of watching Dane. Dane played with the hem of his T-shirt, teasing the head of his dick until Ben growled, and then he pulled it over his head until he was naked.

Ben needed to be naked too. Dane stepped right into him and pushed his jeans down until he stepped out of them. Then they were in each other's arms as they toppled to the bed. They wrestled until Ben was straddling him, Dane's cock gliding between his arse cheeks, teasing.

He leaned over and kissed Dane until he was breathless. Ben was like a starving man, touching everywhere, kissing like his life depended on it. Dane loved each shaking touch, each bite of his fingernails as they explored his skin. His eyes were wild, and Dane could barely comprehend that he was the object of that desire.

A pool of precome dripped from the slit in his cock, and Ben wiped it with his thumb, making Dane hiss and thrust up into his touch. Ben laughed when he didn't get far, his weight pushing him into the mattress.

"Tease," Dane accused.

Ben smiled and smeared the precome on his thumb over Dane's six-pack. He watched his hands intently, and then his eyes rolled up and caught Dane's in a molten look.

"I used to think sex was too much hassle, too messy. Much easier to orgasm alone." Ben shifted until he was lying over Dane, his weight pressing him into the bed and their cocks nestled together.

He licked at Dane's lips then thrust his tongue inside his mouth to explore the dark depths, each dip of his tongue deepening the kiss until Dane thought he would devour him whole. He grabbed Ben's shoulders and held tight until Ben pulled his mouth away, breathing heavily. Dane wasn't much better off.

Ben's lips were glistening from their kiss, his mouth swollen. He wiped at the moisture with his hand, looked at the heel of his hand, and rolled his eyes back up to Dane.

"Used to think kissing was too—empty, messy."

"And now?" Dane's voice was breathless and shaky.

Ben cocked his head to one side, licked his lips, then licked his hand where he'd wiped away the remnants of their kiss. Then he leaned forward to kiss him again, making sure it was deep and wet. Jesus.

"Still messy. But I like it because it's you. Definitely not empty." To prove it, he kissed him again.

Dane's heart was full as Ben explored him. Each touch was fire to the flame, and his cock was heavy and hard. He wanted Ben so desperately that he was sure he was going to come if Ben carried on like he was. While Ben was distracted, Dane pushed him onto his back, and with a smirk and the wiggle of his eyebrows, he said, "My turn now, darling." He drew out the *darling* and Ben whimpered, hands fisting the sheets beneath them.

It was intimidating to be someone's first, especially when they'd never found pleasure in the physical act before, but Ben's forceful and thorough exploration of Dane's body had settled any nerves he had about Ben not wanting this.

Dane knelt over him and placed a hand over Ben's heart, enjoying the gallop he could feel against his palm. He was breathing so hard that

Dane thought he might come… and that would send Dane over the edge. He was close, and they hadn't even gotten to third base yet.

He crawled down Ben's gorgeous body, pressed small biting kisses to his pecs, and swirled his tongue around each of his nipples until they turned to tight buds. Ben arched up off the bed and grabbed the back of Dane's head to hold him there.

"Oh, fuck."

"Like that, do you?" Dane said, his mouth still pressed against his nipple. Ben shuddered and fell back onto the bed, shock showing in his pale grey eyes. He kissed his way down the middle of Ben's abs, felt the muscles clench under his tongue, then laved at his belly button.

Ben's straining cock bounced under his chin, leaving a wet trail that made Dane's mouth water. He took his time teasing him, making him feel. Then he curled his fingers around the base of Ben's cock and rubbed his cheek against it.

He knew what the soft scrape of stubble was like and wanted to drive Ben mad with the sensation. As much as he wanted to swallow him down, he wanted to draw out the experience. He pushed Ben's cock against his stomach and licked at his balls.

Ben gave a strangled gasp, and his legs fell further open, giving him more room. Then Dane sucked a ball into his mouth and ran his tongue along the furred sack while he massaged the other with his fingers. Ben became restless, his legs moving again and his breath harsh.

When he was sure Ben was going out of his mind, he pulled back and licked the sensitive strip of skin behind his balls to his hole. Ben's body tensed and Dane wondered if he'd gone too far, but just as he was about to pull away, Ben's body turned to liquid and melted against him.

Dane ran his tongue around Ben's tight hole. "What are you doing? You can't…." Dane lifted his gaze, and saw Ben pushing himself up on his elbows. His eyes were black with desire, and though his words were shocked, he was still shoving his arse against Dane's mouth as if he had no control.

Dane smiled against him, enjoying the musky sweet taste of him. He held on to Ben's thighs, pointed his tongue, and pushed into Ben as hard as he could. Ben groaned and let out a strangled cry, and when the tight ring of muscle began to flutter against him, Dane pulled away and reached for the lube in the bedside drawer.

He didn't want to shock Ben out of this state of bliss, so he poured some onto his fingers to warm it up, and only when his fingers were warm did he run them along his crease. He pushed one of Ben's knees further to his chest and knelt up so he had more room to see what he was doing.

He quickly glanced at Ben's face to make sure he wanted this. Ben was watching him, eyes burning with heat, mouth parted, sucking in air. So he pressed against Ben's hole, testing, teasing, and slowly pressed inside, all the time watching the expressions wash over Ben's face.

"This okay?" he said through gritted teeth.

Ben nodded his head slowly, as if the pleasure was unexpected, and perhaps it was. Ben's channel sucked Dane's finger into its tight depth, and he couldn't stop imagining it around his cock. And when Ben's erection hadn't dimmed at the small intrusion, Dane moved his finger and pushed further into him.

# Chapter Forty-Five

*Ben*

BEN'S HEART raced so fast he thought it was going to break through his chest. He lay on the bed, sheets wrinkled beneath him, his body on fire and so sensitive he could feel each crease. As Dane moved his finger inside of him, his whole body came alive.

Electricity shot through each nerve ending as Dane did something with his finger that made him see stars. Was this what people felt when they had sex? Was this why everyone seemed so obsessed with it? In his entire life, he'd never been so turned on.

Dane's finger left his body and he whimpered, hating being so empty, but Dane was back quickly, and the pressure was more as he pressed two fingers into him. Ben's cock was harder than it had ever been, and his balls were drawn up tight. Dane's fingers shifted inside him and he almost came, but he didn't want this to end too soon. He was afraid he would never feel like this again, that it would be a fluke or a one-off deal no matter what his feelings for Dane were.

Warmth spread down his limbs, and he pulled his knee into his chest and spread his other leg wide to give Dane room. He should be embarrassed by his behaviour, but he loved how Dane couldn't stop watching his fingers disappear inside him. It made Ben's cock jerk, and he had to grip it to stave off his orgasm.

"Please," he gasped. Dane looked up and, seeing the state he was in, took pity and leaned over. Fingers still in place, he kissed him. "So close." His words were swallowed by the kiss, but it didn't matter. Dane knew what he'd said.

Dane pulled back with a gasp, mouth glistening with their combined saliva, and he then reached into the bedside cabinet and grabbed a condom. Ben watched Dane rip the packet open and roll it over his dick. His own cock swelled at the sight and his hole twitched eagerly.

Dane poured more lube into his hands and coated the condom. Then he moved in between Ben's legs. He stroked Ben's thighs and soothed the tense muscles until his breathing calmed. Sweat dripped down his forehead, and he trembled at Dane's feather-light touches.

"Ready?" Dane asked. Ben nodded, expecting him to push right in. Nerves raced in his belly, but they were nerves of the unknown, not like anything he'd ever felt in the past, and they coiled with excitement until he didn't know what he was feeling. It didn't matter; he ached with need, and even if there was pain, he wanted Dane inside of him.

Dane ran his fingers down Ben's crease and teased his loosened hole until Ben was moving his hips, trying to find his fingers. He grinned when Ben cursed, and with one final heated glance, he grabbed his cock to steady it and slowly pushed forward.

Ben gasped and the air left his lungs as Dane's impossibly long cock breached him. It wasn't pain exactly, but the stretch was uncomfortable and new, and the feeling of fullness was both what he'd been aching for and strange at the same time.

Dane pushed into him slowly, and when Ben felt his balls against his arse, he stilled for a few seconds, allowing him to get used to it. His cock was still hard, though the worry that he'd come straight away had gone. He clenched his muscles around Dane, getting a feel for it. Dane groaned above him, his eyes closing tight. He bit at his lip, and his fingers dug into Ben's hips. He kept so still he was like a statue above him. Ben appreciated it, but he needed to move.

Ben shuddered, then rotated his hips. It didn't hurt, and he was getting used to the feel of Dane inside him. He moved the heel of one foot until it pressed into Dane's lower back, urging him forward. He wanted this—the attraction and arousal he felt for Dane wasn't disappearing, and now he needed more, so much more.

Dane's eyes shot open and found his. "More," Ben said, and Dane took him at his word. He hooked Ben's free leg over his arm, then pulled out until the head of his cock barely touched Ben's hole. He hated the emptiness, but before he could protest, Dane snapped his hips forward and filled him completely. Then he leaned over him so he could kiss him.

This position was sharper, and each thrust of Dane's hips had Ben seeing fireworks. His skin tingled all over, and he lost all ability to use his limbs. His nails scraped along Dane's shoulders as he thrust, slippery against his sweat-slicked skin. Then his hands fell useless to his sides as Dane sat up, hips pummelling into him.

"Look at us," Dane gasped, and Ben watched him as he watched himself slide into Ben's body. His stomach muscles tightened. There was something forbidden about Dane watching them like that, but it turned him on until he could barely see straight.

Dane gripped his cock, and Ben let out a cry as sensation overload almost threatened to send him over the edge. His orgasm had been simmering since their car journey, and now it was burning bright. Dane cupped his balls with his free hand, one finger at his rim, and Ben gasped and curled up on his elbow to watch Dane pummel into him.

It was a shock when he came. He'd been on the brink of overwhelming pleasure, and suddenly he was soaring over the edge in ecstasy. He fell back onto the bed, and Dane collapsed over him, pushing into him desperately, all rhythm gone. He pressed his face into Ben's neck, and Ben wrapped both legs around his hips.

Dane came on a strangled cry, and Ben shivered as he swelled inside him, pleasure racing up his spine. He wondered what it would be like without a condom, and his cock tried to take interest but couldn't.

Dane's body melted against his, and with each gasp of air, Ben felt his tongue against his neck. His arms and legs were heavy, his hips hurt, and his arse ached in the best possible way as Dane slowly pulled out of him. Ben wrapped his arms around Dane and held on tight, never wanting to let go.

"Never thought it could be like that," he mumbled into Dane's damp hair. He could feel Dane's smile, and it made him ridiculously happy.

He lifted his head up and pressed a kiss to Ben's chin. "It's because you love me, darling," he said with a grin.

"Yeah, it is," Ben said back.

# Chapter Forty-Six

*Ben*
*Epilogue*

DEVON WAS cold in winter, but there was something about the sea breeze and the sand that drew him in no matter what the weather. The sea was rough, waves crashed against the sand, and the sky was bright blue as the wind whipped against their faces. It was beautiful. And Ben was glad he got to share this with Dane.

They were wearing gloves and managing to hold hands as they walked along the beach. There was sand in his boots and his nose was frozen, but he'd never been happier.

Speedy ran ahead of them with a tennis ball in his mouth, and they each held a lead with one ferret on the end. Chase and Squidge hadn't liked the sand at first, but they soon realised how fun it could be. Now they were dancing and digging like they were sandworms. They were absolutely covered, and it would take them forever to get the sand out, but Ben loved watching them have so much fun.

This was their first time in Devon as a couple, and although his parents hadn't come around, his brother and his girlfriend were fantastic. So were Dane's dad and brother. He had more family now than he'd ever had before, and he was glad Lewis and Tasha were part of that. They'd had their baby a month earlier, and Ben and Dane had come out for a visit. Ben got a kick out of Dane's smile whenever Lewis called him uncle, and he looked so sweet holding the baby.

He also looked sweet holding a ferret covered in sand. "He's trying to eat the sand now." Dane rolled his eyes and tucked Chase under his arm.

Chase gave Ben a disgruntled look but lay in comfort until Squidge started to rake at Ben's legs to be picked up. "You little copycat." Ben pressed a kiss onto his sandy head, and they carried on walking.

"There's always one thing I've wondered about you," Ben said, a teasing smile on his lips.

"Oh, yeah? What's that?"

"Why is your nickname Dane? It's not the usual shortening of Daniel."

Dane gave him a sideways look and burst out laughing. "That's what you wanted to ask me?"

"It keeps me up at night."

"You're an odd man, Bentley Clifford." Ben winced at hearing his full name. Most people presumed his full name was Benjamin, and he preferred it that way. "But to answer your very important question—there were four Daniels in my class at primary school. It was getting confusing. We had a Dan, Danny, and Daniel, and I ended up with Dane, which I thought was much more exotic."

"It suits you."

Dane beamed at him. "I thought so."

They walked further up the beach, and Ben could just make out Lewis carrying Conner in some contraption against his chest while holding hands with Tasha. They were incredibly sweet together, and Ben was happy he was getting to know his brother without their parents putting pressure on them. They still hadn't come around to Lewis and Tasha's relationship either, so at least Ben knew he wasn't special in that respect.

"I got something for you," Dane said as he reached into his pocket.

"Oh?"

Dane pulled out a sleeveless T-shirt with white, black, grey, and purple stripes on. "I saw this at one of the grockle shops in Paignton. I thought you could wear it for Pride this year."

Ben thought back to his first Pride and remembered how gorgeous Dane had looked in his rainbow pride T-shirt. "I love it. Thank you." He leaned over and kissed Dane on the mouth. That T-shirt confirmed their relationship in a way nothing else could. Not only did Dane accept his sexuality, he saw a future where they'd both wear their rainbow T-shirts for Pride, and Ben couldn't wait.

Contentment ran through him as they slowly made their way to Lewis and his family. *Their* family. Ben stopped before they reached them and pulled Dane to him. "I have another question," he said, huddling in close. The ferrets wriggled in their arms, and Chase leaned over to lick his nose, which made them both laugh.

"And what's that?" Dane asked as he kissed the ferret on the head.

"Want to get another ferret with me?"

Dane froze, his eyes wide. He didn't move a muscle, though Chase kept leaning backwards and licked at his chin.

"You're asking me this now, on a freezing cold beach, with a ferret biting my chin?"

Ben stepped in and pulled him as close as their big puffy coats would allow. The ferrets moved like boneless balls of fluff between them.

"It seemed like the perfect moment." He cupped the side of Dane's face with his gloved hand and leaned over to kiss him. Their lips were cold from the wind, but they soon warmed up. Squidge moved restlessly in his other hand, and Ben felt a sharp pain in his earlobe.

"Ouch!" He pulled away from their kiss and, as Dane started to laugh, realised Squidge had clamped down on his ear, vying for his attention.

"You're right. This moment is pretty damn perfect." Dane beamed at him and took the ferret out of his arms. Lewis and Tasha reached them, baby Conner was asleep, and all Ben could see was the top of his woolly hat.

Dane handed the ferrets off to Tasha and wrapped his arms around Ben.

"Yes. Let's give in to Ferret Math and expand our family," he said as Ben kissed him again. He heard the catcalls, but Dane's mouth was too distracting.

"Poor Speedy is going to be inundated with small furry carpet sharks."

Speedy jumped at their legs, barking, and pushed his ball at their feet. Yeah, it *was* pretty damn perfect.

ANDI LEE lives in the UK, close enough to Birmingham city to be considered a 'Brummie,' but far enough away to enjoy the Staffordshire countryside. She enjoys writing in many different genres as long as they contain a large dose of cute guys falling in love. She's a sucker for a happy ending.

When she's not writing, she enjoys making junk journals and also jewelry out of polymer clay and resin. She has kept pet rats on and off for twenty years, and she fell in love with her first ferret when she found him on her way to work one day. Years later she happened to find another ferret on her thirty-first birthday. He was the best present she ever received. She is now owned by a small but fierce ferret called Oona.

You can find her at www.andileewrites.com
Twitter: @andileewrites
Instagram: andileewrites

AN ANIMAL LARK NOVEL

*mischief*
# MAKER
## ANDI LEE

An Animal Lark Novel

What to expect when your pet rat is expecting, or how to fall in love at a pet show.

Jamie Hewett rescues and breeds prize-winning fancy rats. While he's surrounded by supportive, animal-loving friends, his ex-boyfriend has never been one of them. One embarrassing breakup later, he definitely isn't looking for love again, but perhaps a rebound relationship might ease his broken heart.

Liam Donnelly's quirky dating life is the subject of a popular vlog, and his viewers have interesting ideas on where he might find romance. When they suggest he take Mabel, his new rat, to a pet show, he's up for the adventure.

Although they can't deny their growing interest in each other, neither Jamie nor Liam believes in love at first sight. They've both had bad luck with men, and Jamie isn't pleased that Liam makes a living as a serial dater. On top of that, others are conspiring to keep them apart, and Jamie is left holding the baby—or twenty-plus babies—when their fur children have no trouble making a connection. Will a YouTube ukulele serenade convince Liam that Jamie's love for him—and their unborn rat children—is for real?

# www.dreamspinnerpress.com

www.ingramcontent.com/pod-product-compliance
Lightning Source LLC
Chambersburg PA
CBHW070116260626
47160CB00004B/1486